The Best Wrong Move

LILY PARKER

Lily Parker

Choc Lit
A JOFFE BOOKS COMPANY

Choc Lit
A Joffe Books company
www.choc-lit.com

First published in Great Britain in 2025

© Lily Parker

Cover art by Rachel Lawston at Lawston Design

ISBN: 978-1781898178

For anyone who's ever been in a complicated relationship with fate.

PROLOGUE

The Good Day Show
February 14

Why aren't we going to commercial?

I tilt my head, scanning each face behind the frozen teleprompter.

The spotlights.

The cameras.

Everyone looks as shocked as I feel.

Rex just said no.

His words are all I can focus on.

I won't marry you, Liv.

The light is blinking green. We're still on air.

Someone please tell me what to do.

Anyone?

"Olivia, honey?" My producer's voice cuts through the sound of my heartbeat, directly into my ear. I press a finger to my earpiece and swallow hard. "Go ahead and smile, Liv, we've got twelve seconds to commercial."

Rex fucking said no.

I twist my face into what feels like a smile. I think it's a smile. *Oh God, please let it be a smile.*

1

Rex is staring at me, shifting his weight back and forth. He runs a hand through his hair. His Adam's apple bobs up and down each time he swallows.

Pop the question during our Valentine's segment, my producer had said. *Invite him to watch the show at the station. We'll bring him up on stage as a surprise.*

"Thanks for inviting me to watch today, babe," Rex had said back in the green room. Before I went live.

Then he'd kissed me.

He'd kissed me, and, seven minutes later, while standing on the stage together in front of millions of people . . .

He said no.

I twist my face harder. Forcing a smile that just won't come.

"Olivia? No, not like that," my producer is saying in my ear. "Maybe turn your face away from the camera? Can you say something? Make a joke?" She forgets to cut her feed to me before adding, "Someone make sure those confetti cannons don't—"

A huge explosion of crimson and gold confetti comes barreling down from above.

"Who the fuck's in charge of that!" she screams into my ear.

My face quivers. Frozen into whatever crazed expression is taking up the screen right now.

Rex looks pale between the remnants of confetti shimmering around him. Sweat forming at the edge of his hairline. His eyes widen at me, like I'm supposed to know what to do.

My mouth opens to make a joke, but I can't think. A stunted whimper escapes my throat instead.

"Seven seconds!" my producer yells into my ear. "Olivia, say something. Anything. Figure out how to smile."

I turn to camera four. The one closest to me. Green light blinking.

"Olivia, stop doing that with your face!" My producer's voice is high-pitched, bordering on panic.

2

I curl my lips back and feel my brows nearly touch over my eyes, trying to fix it.

"No, not like that! Just smile normally, goddammit!"

I yank my earpiece out. Unable to think.

My voice cuts through the thick silence on stage.

"You heard it here first," I say brightly, picking up some confetti that landed on the counter in front of me. Then I toss them into the air toward Rex. One lands on his eyebrow. "If you're single this Valentine's Day, take a good look at this face." I turn to Rex, who looks like he's having an out-of-body experience. "This guy is officially up for grabs now, ladies! Single as a fucking pringle."

The green light cuts to red.

And I'm free.

CHAPTER 1

Four weeks later

Wiping a bead of sweat from my forehead, I turn the knob again and push hard against the front door with everything left in me, but it still won't budge. My extended stay at this ocean-front townhouse is off to a rocky start if I can't even get inside.

I look both ways, glad nobody is here to witness this battle with the door, now that my face is a viral TikTok following my failed proposal on *The Good Day Show*. This Airbnb rental is supposed to be my home base during the next eight weeks while I wait for things to settle down at the station back in New York.

Since stepping off the plane in Honolulu two hours ago, there's been a thick layer of sweat plastered across my entire body from the humidity. My Uber driver's AC was broken on the ride across the island to the North Shore, so I was practically hanging out the window, wondering if I should just strip my sweater off right there in the car. And now that I've been wrestling with this front door for the last ten minutes, I feel like I might pass out from what is quickly becoming a cardio workout.

I should have traded my jeans for a pair of shorts before I left the airport. I'm sweating through the outfit I left New York in.

I look around for someone to help me, carefully weighing the pros and cons of changing right here on the front porch so I don't pass out. This townhouse is on a fairly busy street, but it backs up to a popular beach. So if a random person does pass by while I'm changing, they'll probably think my bra and underwear is just a bikini — at least until I can shimmy into a pair of shorts and a T-shirt.

I give the door one last try, turning the knob and bumping it with my hip as hard as I can. Frustrated and exhausted, I pound both hands against the thick wood a few times for good measure. My suitcase immediately falls to the ground. I shove it away with one foot, then start bumping the door with my hip over and over while holding down the handle, hitting it with my free hand. I let out an exasperated growl at the end that sounds more like a wildcat in the jungle than a woman in distress. It won't budge.

"Screw this," I mumble to myself. I need to get out of these clothes before I pass out. Then I'll call the owner. I unbutton my jeans and pull them down to my ankles, stepping out as quickly as I can, when I hear someone clear their throat behind me.

I spin around.

A half-naked guy is standing a few feet down the walkway with a surfboard tucked under his arm. He's dripping wet, like he just walked out of the ocean. A pair of red board shorts is hanging off his hips, right below two rows of washboard abs. He's a caricature of masculinity. Broad and ripply in all the right places, with an inch-long scar above one of his thick brows. When our eyes meet, he breaks into a perfectly white grin. Then he looks away quickly, like he's embarrassed that he just stumbled upon me changing out here in broad daylight.

I fight the urge to reach for my jeans.

For all he knows you're in a swimsuit, Liv. Own it.

"Uh, sorry." He shifts his eyes up toward the sky. His attempt at giving me privacy, I think. His voice is deep and smooth, like it's been heated by the sun. "I heard a lot of banging on my way back to my car, and I was just checking out what the commotion was. Are you . . . are you okay?"

"Oh gosh, yeah, that was me. The door's stuck." I point behind me with a sheepish grin, wishing I could stop the blush I can feel rushing across my face. I have sunglasses on so he shouldn't be able to recognize me.

"This door?" He points toward the door behind me, still looking away.

What a gentleman.

"Yes. Could you maybe . . ." I hope the chiseled biceps he's sporting are for more than just looks.

"Oh, you want me to . . ." He breaks into another grin without finishing his thought. It makes my insides do a little flip. "Yeah, sure. I can try."

He sets his board down and starts walking toward me, my heart picking up the pace with every step. A pesky voice in the back of my mind is reminding me that I have no idea who this guy is, and there's a chance he could shove me inside with him the second he gets the door open.

He has a good vibe to him though.

So did Ted Bundy! my subconscious screams. Definitely should have laid off the true crime podcasts before traveling alone for two months.

But it's too late. Within four strides, he's beside me. I try to take a step back to give him more space, but my suitcase is sprawled across the porch, blocking me in. I'm wedged between my door, the biggest suitcase money can buy, and a guy that makes my legs turn to mush when he smiles. He'd probably have to duck down a little to get through this doorway — his shoulders nearly take up the whole door frame.

I press my back against the wall to give him more space. Trying not to stare at the little drops of saltwater trickling off his precision-cut sideburns, slowly dripping their way down the sharp edge of his jaw, to the smooth skin of his neck, and finally picking up speed as they race down his chest. Faintly smelling like the ocean mixed with a subtle hint of cologne he likely put on earlier this morning. Spicy and raw. Almost primal.

He twists the knob, pausing to look down at me.

"Ready?" he asks, as if he needs my consent before pushing inside. His full lips part into a wicked grin, showing a row of smooth white teeth, practically glowing against his deep brown tan. And his eyes are green. Not just green, but the color of thick moss after a rainstorm. Vibrant and playful.

"Ready." I return his grin, vaguely aware that I'm still standing here in my panties, with a very out-of-place sweater on top. But, at this point, I could be naked and not really care. Let's be honest, I may actually prefer it.

He furls his brow and throws his shoulder into the door.

I swallow hard when the door instantly swings open, almost wishing it had taken a few more tries.

"That was a lot more stuck a minute ago." I rock back on my heels. Then I add with more sarcasm, "I guess I really must have loosened it up for you."

I bite my top lip to stop myself from giving him another goofy grin, but I'm not sure the look on my face is any better.

"Then I'm glad I could help you un-stick it." He breaks into another toe-curling smirk.

I glance down at my enormous suitcase still sprawled across the porch. His eyes follow mine.

"Do you want me to set that inside?" he asks. Another drop of water falls off his chin and I force myself not to watch where it goes next.

"Um, no, I can manage." My jeans are still wadded up on the ground next to our feet. Suddenly feeling the need to explain, I add, "I just flew in. It's a lot colder in New York right now and, um, I just didn't have anywhere to change. I was roasting."

Blood pounds all the way down to my toes when he finally allows himself to glance lower — grazing my red lace panties and legs just for one split second — before snapping his eyes back up to meet mine again.

"Oh." His laugh is smooth and contagious, making me feel even more at ease. "I just thought you were wearing a swimsuit."

I can tell he's lying to spare me any more embarrassment, but I appreciate the gesture.

We grin shyly at each other for another beat, but my phone starts ringing, snapping us out of a moment that was starting to feel heated.

"I, uh, that's probably my friend. I should let her know I've made it. She's a worrier."

I grab my phone from my purse and glance at the screen. Abby's picture pops up under her name.

"Okay then." He takes a few steps backward toward the road and his surfboard. "Glad I could help."

"Thank you." I pull my suitcase back up. I position it right in front of my body, blocking his view from my waist down.

He grins at me one more time over his shoulder before picking up his board and giving me a little wave.

"Maybe I'll see you around here again." His eyes dance as if he's going to make sure that happens somehow. Then he disappears around the corner of the townhouse.

I let out a long breath, like I'd been hoarding all the oxygen around me, then press the green circle to answer my best friend's call.

"Abby," I say, panting into the phone, "drop everything you're doing and come join me."

CHAPTER 2

Abby laughs on the other end of the line while I attempt to drag my suitcase inside, but one of the wheels is broken from the airline crew tossing it around like a ball. I packed fairly light for an eight-week trip, but there's still enough swimsuits and sundresses in here to clothe a small army.

"You know I'd rather be with you on a Hawaiian island instead of eating this stale sandwich from the deli downstairs." Abby chews. "I'm living vicariously through you right now. I don't care how boring the details are, tell me everything."

I glance behind me to make sure the guy is truly gone.

"Well, for one, I just had the hottest guy I've ever seen help me get the door open."

"The owner was there?"

"No, just a guy walking by. He looked like he was coming off the beach. The front door was stuck."

"You had a stranger help you into your rental?" Her voice rises an octave.

I clamp the phone between my shoulder and ear so I can use both hands to lift my suitcase over the threshold with an *umph*.

9

"Not *just* a stranger. You should have seen him—" As I look up, the view knocks me back like a bolt of lightning, forcing a gasp to escape my lips.

Two white leather couches drenched in sunbeams, and a little dinette, sit between me and a wall of floor-to-ceiling windows. On the other side of the glass, turquoise waves roll in like melted butter. The sand is just two or three steps down from the deck, and there's a sliding glass door in the middle to take me straight out to the beach.

The blasting AC vent just inside the door instantly dissolves the slick layer of sweat plastered across my body. I pause in the airstream to breathe a sigh of relief, lifting my long, chestnut hair off the back of my neck, while twisting down toward the cool air. It's just what I needed to come back to life.

"Oh my God." I breathe the words into the phone while I shove my overstuffed suitcase past the door frame. It immediately tips to the floor with a thud. I reach out to stand it upright again, but my phone slips off my shoulder and clatters across the tile. I bend down for the phone, knocking over the enormous roller bag again with a bang.

"Ugh!" The phone slips again as I stand the suitcase back up, eyeing the broken wheel. The case falls to the floor for a third time with another *thwack*. I decide to just leave it there, but when I lift my phone back to my ear, it's too late. Abby is already panicking after that collection of muffled thumps, like I was battling an intruder instead of my suitcase.

"Kick him in the crotch!" she shrieks.

"I'm fine!" I yelp back at her.

Then I scowl at the shared wall to my right. It's the only thing standing between me and whoever might be listening on the other side of it in the unit next door. I didn't realize I'd booked a shared townhouse until I pulled up out front, and by then it was too late to change the reservation.

"You scared me! I thought that guy must have come back all Ted Bundy style," Abby says, sounding relieved.

I laugh, knowing how much Abby enjoys true crime podcasts too, then lower my voice. "Sorry. No, I'm fine. I just dropped my suitcase like eight times. I told you about the airline busting the wheel, right?" I nudge the broken wheel with my toe for good measure, like it's a dead snake that might spring back to life. "But I'm totally fine. More than fine. Not thrilled that this place turned out to be an attached townhome. You know I'm going for as much privacy as humanly possible right now. Looks like the back deck might be shared too." I eyeball the long patio out the sliding back door, sitting just beyond the wall of windows. "I don't even think there's a privacy wall between our units out there."

"Maybe the guy who helped you get that door open is staying next door?"

"One can hope." Imagine the luck I'd need to win that lottery.

I picture the meme and matching GIF with my horrified face that's been making its way around the world for the last month, hoping that whoever my neighbor is isn't very tuned in to social media. I wish I'd taken more time to examine the Airbnb listing before spontaneously reserving eight full weeks here.

"Did he recognize you?" Abby asks.

"I don't think so. I had sunglasses on."

"Good. Maybe you can finally catch a break now, even if you had to cross an ocean to get it. I'm so glad you're finally away from it all."

I'm flooded with memories from back home in New York. The onslaught of judgy stares from strangers everywhere I went, the thousands of cruel comments from internet trolls on the station's website.

Her face looks like a deer in the headlights, right before it gets run over!

Idiot! Dudes propose, but only when they're ready!

He's way hotter than her. No wonder he said no.

11

LOL! Look at her face when he finally spits out an answer!
Sexy Rexy, call me for an upgrade!!!

I'd be pissed if my girlfriend ever tried this. Poor guy.

Before everything blew up in my face like a poorly timed confetti cannon, my life was a carefully curated sequence of *correct* choices. But now that I've left everything behind, doing something that could further change the trajectory of my hard-earned career, I can't ignore the taste of imperfection that I've been getting lately.

My entire life, I've strived to be perfect. I went to the *right* college. Dated the *right* kind of guy. And when my producer told me that doing something as bold as proposing to my boyfriend on national television would secure my spot as one of their top morning news anchors? I did that too.

However, what I didn't see coming — what was written all over my face in that viral clip — is that I never once expected Rex to say *no*.

But since that clip started circulating, it feels like everyone in the world knows he said no.

The next *right* step would have been sticking it out at the station. Letting myself be the butt of everyone's jokes until people got bored and moved on. Continue showing up, while everyone laughed behind my back, showing them I was strong enough to handle being rejected on national television.

That would have made sense, even been on-brand for me.

But something in me snapped and I ran.

I ran from everything — my career, my hometown.

I did the one thing that made zero sense in my perfect world. I chose to hide.

And, now, I'm using this eight-week sabbatical from the station to finish something I started three years ago. Something that I hope might get me out of broadcast journalism for good. I plan to go back to New York with a finished full-length film script, so I can start shopping it around to production houses. It'll be my ticket to do what I've always wanted to do. Write films. Produce them. Be the person *behind* the screen instead of *on* it.

It all feels so surreal now. Standing in this townhouse in the middle of the Pacific, knowing what I came here to accomplish — it's suddenly staring me in the face. I'm wondering, with every ounce of my soul, whether or not I have what it takes to succeed in doing something so different from what I've always done. I can already sense that whatever is going to unfold on this trip is going to change me. Potentially more than I might have bargained for.

But now that I'm here, giving myself permission to run from the problems back home without having to fix them? It feels unbelievably good. Downright addictive, even. Like this taste of imperfection spreading across my tongue is more exhilarating than I could have possibly imagined. A drug I didn't know I needed until it was coursing through my veins.

I hardly recognize myself, standing here in someone else's kitchen, a few thousand miles from anyone I know.

And it's day one.

This trip has only just begun.

CHAPTER 3

Pulling a few more sweaty strands of hair off my neck, I slip on a white sundress from my suitcase and walk into the kitchen, unable to tear my eyes away from that view out back.

"Here, let me put you on FaceTime so you can see this place, Abby. The view off the back deck might make that shared wall worth it after all." I hold the phone out in front of me and hit the FaceTime button. "This is it! My home for the next eight weeks."

Abby's face appears on my phone screen. She's sitting in her office chair, even though it's Saturday. Probably with the shades drawn and the door locked, so she can sneak in a personal phone call during work. The biggest law firms in New York take your life in exchange for the legendary paychecks and bonuses they hand out to their associates on day one. Even though Abby's probably loaded by now, she's never actually out of the office long enough to enjoy the money she's traded some of the best years of her life for. Always promising she'll relax after *partner* follows her name on the firm's stuffy website.

Just seeing her face makes me feel a tinge of homesickness. My best friend is gorgeous, even with her thick-rimmed glasses and jet-black hair tied up in a messy bun. The tip of a ballpoint pen is sticking out the top of her thick mass of hair, making her look like a sexy librarian, though she's probably on the tail end of a six-day work bender.

The window shades look dark behind her.

"Oh God, Abby, I forgot about the time change. How late are you working tonight?"

"Is it dark out?" She turns, then rolls her eyes as she spins the chair back around. "I don't even notice anymore. Brett's been riding my ass on this new Chatterton case. I might die of old age by the time I finish the discovery phase."

I fight the urge to tell her to get out of there — to go home to sleep in her own bed, and not that horrible in-office futon that I know is tucked just out of sight. It's the weekend. She deserves a break. But we've had that conversation before. Many times, actually. She's married to that job.

"But" — she perks up — "it's not dark where you are! Show me! I can practically smell the ocean wafting through this phone screen."

I press another button to flip the camera view around, then start walking through the main room first. I hold the phone out in front of me so I can see what she sees along with her reaction. It's the next best thing to having her here.

Abby begins narrating out loud, like she's on HGTV's *House Hunters*.

"Nice kitchen. Oh, I like the countertops. Live-edge butcher block is so *Hawaii*, right? What do you think of that plant though?"

I crinkle my nose at the spidery vines growing along the wall from the kitchen into the living room.

"That might have to go if you're not a fan," she continues. "Unless you end up killing it first."

I scoff playfully. She knows me well.

Keeping the phone held out in front of me, I walk along the edge of the couch toward the windows that lead out to the deck.

"That sofa looks comfy," she points out. "I may need to sleep on it once I murder Brett and flee New York."

I laugh. "You're welcome to join me anytime."

We make it to the wall of windows, and I hold her out in front of me as we both fall silent.

Panoramic views of the sea always make me tear up a little. It's like seeing an old friend after being away for a long time. Too long this time. Even before my failed proposal to Rex, he had to beg me to take any vacation time. I was always too focused on working my way up at the station, never feeling like there was enough time to get away. But standing here, I'm reminded of just how big the world is — whether I'm there to witness the outer edges of it or not.

Abby looks happily transported as she takes in the swaying palms and lazy waves. I watch her shoulders uncurl from up around her ears, and her eyes slowly soften. Two months alone without her is going to be the longest I've ever been away from my friends or family.

"I like the yellow patio set," Abby finally says, breaking her trance. I almost like watching her reaction more than the view. "Oh, and that umbrella with the little fringe thingy across the bottom. So vintage."

"Let's go down to the beach." I swing her to the right so I can grab the handle of the sliding glass door.

"Olivia! Wait!" She suddenly sounds panicked.

I jump back instinctively before opening it, my head on a swivel. "What? What's wrong?"

"You didn't see?"

I flip the camera view around so we're face-to-face again. Her mouth is open, eyes wide, like she's just seen a ghost.

CHAPTER 4

My heart pounds in my chest.

"What do you mean *don't go out there?*" I dart my eyes around the room, then out to the patio where she'd been looking.

"Okay. Don't . . . panic."

"Little late for that, Abby! What're you talking about?" I slide head first behind the white leather couch that stands between me and the wall of windows. Of course there aren't any curtains I could yank to block whoever is out there from seeing me. I'm completely vulnerable in here. "What'd you see?"

"Not one hundred percent sure." It's like she's trying to remain calm, but her whole demeanor is making me want to hyperventilate. "I swear I just saw Rex out on your balcony."

She purses her lips like she's just made a crazed confession.

"No, you didn't," I pant into the phone. "Are you shitting me?"

"I'm not shitting you. It could have been my eyes playing tricks. I haven't slept in twenty-four hours, and he was shirtless, which is not something I saw Rex do very often back in New York, but I swear it was him."

I want to poke my head above the couch to see for myself, but the windows across the whole back half of the townhouse aren't tinted, as far as I can tell. No window coverings and no tinted glass. Who owns this voyeuristic piece of shit townhouse?

And why would Rex fucking Thompson be out on my deck?

I'm sitting on an island, in the middle of an ocean, nearly five thousand miles from home. Abby has to be wrong.

The last time I saw Rex, he was at our old apartment asking if he could keep Toby, our cat, after humiliating me on national television. I'd thrown a handful of cat food at him on his way out. Then sat with my back pressed against the door while Toby purred at my ankles and ate the kibble scattered across the floor. I didn't get up for an hour, praying I'd hear Rex's knuckles tap quietly against the door, so he could tell me he wanted me back. While, at the same time, hating him so hard that I imagined him getting hit by a taxi on his way out.

"That would be completely impossible. Absolutely not. No way. The odds of Rex being here are just . . . I mean, he can't be. Right?"

"Well." Her voice rises, going from trying-to-calm-me-down mode to flipping-the-fuck-out mode. "You did say it's a townhome, right? Shares a wall? And a deck?"

I maneuver onto my knees while staying in a crouched position. Then start rising up as slowly as I can, without attracting the attention of whoever is on the other side of that window.

The top of my head clears the back of the couch while I quickly scan the lanai.

And, sure enough, to the far-right side of the deck, I spot him.

CHAPTER 5

The universe is punishing me. I close my eyes and sink back down to the floor.

"No fucking way," I murmur.

On the far-right side of the shared patio, nearly out of sight, is my almost-fiancé, Rex. He's shirtless, tan as hell, and sweeping sand off what must be *his* side of the deck.

Just this once, I wish Abby was wrong.

Still hunched behind the couch, I roll onto my back and start taking deep breaths, remembering how my most recent counselor said air is nature's cure for anxiety.

"What the hell?" I wail quietly into the phone. "You've got to be kidding me!"

Abby stares at me through the screen.

"Unbelievable." She can't seem to fathom it either. "I can't imagine you having to face all that again."

"I believe I've faced it a few million times already." The last time I checked, the YouTube upload of us on *The Good Day Show* had over eighty-nine million views. "And don't look at me like that. It's fine. This is fine. I'll just cancel my reservation and find another Airbnb."

19

"Okay," she says in a measured tone. "But wasn't this place the only rental within your price range? Most of the other places were, like, two or three times the cost. And it's not like there's going to be a lot of eight-week options at this point."

"Do you think he followed me here?" I know it's a stupid question. No one besides Abby and my parents know the exact location of this Airbnb.

"Not if he knows what's good for him," Abby mumbles.

When my producer suggested the proposal, I wasn't even sure if we were ready for marriage, but I knew I loved him. I could see a life with him. At least I thought I could.

She'd told me not to warn Rex before we started filming the Valentine's Day segment. She'd said it might make the whole moment seem contrived or rehearsed. And boy was she right — nothing about that segment looked rehearsed by the time we cut to commercial. If I could turn back time, I would've never taken that risk. By that night, my relationship with Rex — as well as my reputation as a serious journalist — had both gone up in smoke.

"I can't come home yet."

"I know."

"I subleased my apartment." My apartment lease was due to be renewed soon after the failed proposal. Since he moved out, I subleased it to a nice couple until the lease runs itself out, thinking I'd just find a new apartment to have ready for me to move into by the time I came back. Everything I own is sitting in a storage unit, except Toby, who's having his own mini vacation with Abby while I'm gone.

"You didn't want to live there anymore," she reminds me. "You couldn't stand to sleep in the same room you two shared."

"You're right." My voice cracks. "I didn't want to live in our old apartment anymore. *This*, though . . ." I try to laugh, but the words choke out of me like an ugly, sobbing snort. "This is all so much better."

The phone feels as heavy as a brick, and that look of pity I've grown to hate is creeping back onto Abby's face. I switch FaceTime to a voice-only call and bring the cell up to my ear.

If I'm this sick of hearing myself cry, I can only imagine how exhausted my best friend is by now. She's been my rock since I went viral a month ago, but even rocks can crumble if you put enough weight on them.

"Just because I can't see you right now, doesn't mean I don't know that you're crying," Abby says softly into the phone. "But you have every reason to. Rex is a dick. Of all the people to rent the townhouse on the other side of your wall! You're sure it's him?"

I nod, even though she can't see me, and wipe a stray tear off my cheek. My voice will break if I respond. I stay hunched on the floor behind the couch.

The last person in the whole world I want to see right now is standing on that deck.

Of all the decks.

"Alright, Liv. Here's what you're going to do." Abby turns on her attorney voice. I sit up straighter, grateful she's about to solve this for me. Abby's a genius. I just have to follow her advice. Easy-peasy.

"Okay, I'm listening." I shove my hair back from my face, forcing my lips into a smile. We'll be laughing about the irony of this whole thing over martinis someday soon.

"First, close the curtains," she instructs me.

"There are no curtains." I start to panic all over again. If Abby's best solution is to close some nonexistent curtains, I'm screwed.

"What?" She momentarily loses focus, then snaps back to attention. "Okay, cheap ass Airbnb owner," she mutters under her breath. "Then you need to go to the bedroom or something and make a phone call without Rex accidentally seeing or hearing you through that big, curtainless window. Call the owner and tell them you have to cancel your reservation. While you do that, I'm going to see if I can find you another place to stay so you don't end up sleeping on that big ol' beach out back once your reservation's been terminated."

Right.

I sink even lower onto the floor. I already know there won't be another extended reservation that I can afford alone. This place was a steal of a deal, probably because it's a tiny connected townhome compared to the more spendy single-family homes. I dumped most of my savings into this trip. I'd be lucky to get half my money back, if anything at all, since I've officially checked in now.

"Thanks, Abby," I say quietly.

"Don't thank me yet," she replies. "Let's see if this works first."

"Do you think this is fate? Do you think we were put here together to, you know, give things another shot?" Even saying the words out loud, I'm pretty sure that a second chance with Rex is not what I want. The way he left for good so suddenly, the same day I proposed to him, made me question whether or not he'd already been planning to leave me.

"No." The word shoots out of Abby's mouth with a level of confidence that catches me by surprise. "Just go make that call before he sees you. It's best to let this chapter of your life stay closed for good."

CHAPTER 6

I run to the bathroom and lock the door, even though I know I'm alone in here. Then I open my Airbnb reservation to find my host's phone number, who, according to the app, is named Dom.

I call him four times. He finally answers just as I'm about to give up and send him a message in the app.

"Hello?" His voice sounds crisp, like I woke him up or something, but it's too late in the day for that.

"Oh, Dom, thank God, you answered." I need to chill. I sound desperate. "It's Dom, right? Does everyone call you that or—"

"Who's asking?" He sounds distracted.

"I'm renting your Airbnb. My name's Olivia. Olivia Hillcrest."

"How'd you get this number?"

Okay, now he sounds just plain annoyed.

"Uh, your number was on the Airbnb listing. Where else would I get it?"

"It shouldn't be. That's a mistake. Let me get you the number for my property manager. His name is Phil. Hang on."

"Oh, okay." I sigh, annoyed that I'm getting the runaround to another person.

After getting Phil's information, I reluctantly hang up and call the number Dom gave me. After four unanswered attempts, I call Dom back. Twice. He answers on the third attempt.

"Hello?" He sounds even more aggravated this time.

"Hello again!" I force bravado into my voice, trying to charm him into staying on the line with me. "It's Olivia. Listen, Phil isn't answering his phone, so I thought I'd chat with you instead."

"That wasn't really what I said. You'll need to wait until Phil gets back to you."

"But I haven't even told you what I'm calling for. You do own this place, right?"

"Which place?"

"The left one?"

I hear him snort. "Yeah, that doesn't really narrow it down."

"Oh. How many Airbnbs do you own?"

"I'd really appreciate if you'd work with the property manager on this. Like I said, his name is Phil and—"

He sounds rushed, but there's no way I'm letting this guy off the phone. For all I know, Phil is on a two-week vacation to Shanghai and Dom is my only hope. I start speed-talking with the goal of getting it all out before he hangs up.

"Listen, I have a big request. I need to cancel my reservation, even though I just checked in. I'm here for eight weeks so I know you're probably dead set on having me stick it out until the end of those eight weeks, but I think if you hear my story, you'll understand and let me cancel—"

"Excuse me," he interrupts. "What's your name again?"

I jump up from the closed toilet seat, pumping my fist into the air triumphantly. He's not saying no.

"Olivia." I try to hide my excitement that he sounds ready to listen. If he just hears me out, there's no way he'll turn me down.

"So, Olivia, this is really a question for Phil."

I start pacing the tiny bathroom, not ready to give up. Over a decade in investigative journalism has led me to this moment. It's like a hostage negotiation. If I can just keep him talking . . .

"But I'm speaking to *you*, Dom, and I'm already so thankful you decided to answer my call again. How's your day going, by the way?" I make my voice sweet and inquisitive, like I'm holding out a can of bear bait, luring him in. Like I'd actually want to get to know this random asshole, but whatever it takes to win him over.

"Where are you staying? I need more details than *the left one*," he says. I detect a ray of sarcasm, but at least he's starting to sound amused instead of annoyed.

I nod my head to no one in particular, breaking into a grin. This is progress. "Your townhouse."

Silence.

"On a busy road?" I wish I could remember the street name. I should have looked it up before calling.

"In . . ."

"Hawaii."

"Okay. Wonderful. Listen, I'm not very familiar with my rentals, to be honest. But what's the problem? If it's a maintenance issue, we — I mean, *Phil* — can just fix it."

"My ex-fiancé, well not *quite* fiancé, but the guy I *tried* to marry, he's staying on the other side of the townhouse."

He stifles a laugh.

Nice.

"That's really unfortunate, Olivia. But I don't think that's a good enough reason to break a reservation. Especially an eight-week reservation."

"You don't understand. I can't stay next to him. The last time I saw him, I threw cat food at him."

He's full-on laughing now. A deep, sexy kind of laugh that sounds vaguely familiar, if not a little muffled. But at least he's not hanging up.

"I'm so glad you find this amusing, Dom," I deadpan.

"Why don't you just kiss and make up with him then? Hawaii is all about that island romance. Second chances and all that."

"You're kidding me, right?"

"Listen, I feel for you, I do. But this is a personal inconvenience, not really an issue worth leaving my place empty for two months. Most of the rentals have a thirty-day minimum and I believe the policy states—"

"You know, you don't even have curtains put up here? You have these big, voyeuristic windows leading out to the beach, in the living room *and* the bedroom, but not everyone wants to get dressed each morning in front of a big, open window!"

"That's something else you can let Phil know."

"But it took me six tries to get to *you*. I'd rather just deal — I mean *talk* — with you. You're going to be making the decision on the reservation cancellation, right?"

"Not really, I just let Phil handle everything."

"You don't put curtains up in your properties, *and* you can't handle this for me? Phil's not answering and—"

"I'm very busy."

"Too busy to deal with a woman in crisis?"

And this is the moment I start crying.

CHAPTER 7

After staying on the phone with Dom for far too long, I finally figured out which street I was on, and that I was standing in Unit A. At that point, he got surprisingly jovial, promising to come install window shades himself while talking about shortening the reservation.

Without another place to stay tonight, and no food in the kitchen, I'm also running out of daylight, but I have no idea when Dom will be stopping by. It could be tonight, tomorrow. His whole demeanor was pretty vague.

To avoid starving, I take a little walk to the nearby strip of stores and restaurants to grab takeout. Then I prop Abby up on FaceTime down at the beach while I watch the beginnings of a fiery sunset. If I can figure out a way to ignore the presence of that asshat on the other side of my wall, I'd really like to stay. This island is paradise, so it all boils down to avoiding my past.

If Rex walks by while I'm sitting here, he shouldn't be able to recognize me. I'm wearing a hideous Hawaiian print bucket hat and the biggest pair of cheap, plastic sunglasses I could find at the ABC Store down the road. They're bright red and look straight out of 1982.

The cashier said they didn't sell anything big enough to tack up over the huge windows either, so this ugly disguise was the next best thing I could find. I'm still looking over my shoulder while I eat, but at least I feel less frantic than I did back in the townhome, knowing Rex could peek in the window and see me at any moment without warning. The bedroom has another wall of floor-to-ceiling, curtain-free windows, with a second sliding door that leads out to the same shared deck. There's nowhere to hide from Rex, except behind the couch, or in the small bathroom across the hall. But I didn't feel like eating my dinner on the floor next to the toilet.

"What time is the Airbnb guy coming with your shades?" Abby asks. We're both eating takeout from Styrofoam containers — including an entire bottle of pink prosecco for me — while discussing my contingency plan.

She takes another bite of her pad Thai. By the look of it, she's still sitting at her desk, even though it's eleven o'clock at night in New York. I imagine her curling up on the futon near her desk once we get off our call, only to start the onslaught of legal work bright and early again tomorrow morning. We were both workaholics back in New York, something we bonded over when we met as undergrads.

"No idea," I tell her. "Tonight? Tomorrow? But, even if he does get window blinds or curtains installed, I think Rex will notice me at some point. Even if I keep this ridiculous disguise on."

Dom rents out both sides of the townhouse, which, I reminded him, would have been a great detail to add to his Airbnb listing. Or have Phil add to the listing, I guess, since Dom appears to be annoyingly hands-off with his rentals. The pictures online made the place look like a stand-alone unit.

"I can't believe that guy had the gall to suggest that I forgive my ex," I tell her, still irked from my phone call. "I'd rather eat sand than kiss and make up with Rex right now. Best-case scenario is that I get out of that rental and into another one before he sees me, and I can focus on getting my script done. In peace."

"They really didn't have anything cuter than that hat and shades?" Abby squints at me through the phone screen. "You look like a campy tourist from the eighties."

I shake my head. "I don't know who Dom thinks he's impressing with this scandalous no-window-shade situation," I mutter into my fried rice.

During my call with him, I also learned that this Airbnb listing is brand new — hence the lack of reviews and heavily discounted monthly price to try and drum up business while certain upgrades — like curtains and a front door that opens on demand — are still MIA. This is the last time I'm booking a review-free Airbnb, no matter how cheap it is.

"Okay, I think you're looking at this all wrong," she insists.

"Enlighten me." I take another sip of prosecco, then sit up straighter, bracing myself for the type of wisdom that only a true best friend can dish out.

"If you have to spend the next two months next door to your ex, you may as well enjoy some revenge sex with other people while you're there. He'll see hot dudes leaving your place every morning. Right? It'll drive him crazy."

My mind flashes to the guy who helped me earlier with the door.

"I mean, I wouldn't mind seeing that surfer again, obviously. But *every* morning?" I snort in response. Definitely not the mind-blowing insight I was expecting, but still on-brand for her. "I'm not a sex machine." I root my fork around my nearly empty container of orange chicken until I spear a chunk of meat. "I have a voracious appetite, yes, but not for sex." I chuckle at my own joke, then pop the chicken in my mouth, chewing thoughtfully while I let her latest suggestion roll through my mental haze. The prosecco is definitely starting to kick in.

I guess it's been a minute since I had any sex at all. Leading up to the proposal, Rex was getting more distant.

More distracted. Coming home later in the evenings, working out almost every single day, which was new for him. After the proposal, when we'd fled back to my dressing room, he'd simply told me that he wasn't ready to settle down. I'd clearly been mistaken thinking we were on a path together toward marriage. Rex insisted he was still young and not ready for a lifelong commitment, which would have been great to know before I promptly humiliated us both.

"The more you have it, the more you'll want it," Abby promises. "Sex, not chicken. Or, at least, that's what I remember from back when I had a sex life. Before this place drained my will to live." She waves her chopsticks around the fluorescent room behind her. "I haven't gone out with anyone in nearly fourteen months."

"What about Roy? From accounting?"

"Roy the Toy?" She narrows her eyes into a devilish smirk.

I laugh. "The one and only."

"I'd hardly call meeting Roy in the mail closet every Friday for a quickie the same thing as *going out*." Her chuckle grows into a full belly laugh as the memory of *Roy the Toy* surfaces more clearly. "Remember that time I told you he pulled out an ancient pager from the nineties? And wanted to use it as a vibrator?"

I clamp a hand over my mouth to keep the chicken contained. Picturing Abby's face when poor five-foot-four Roy pulled out a grubby, old pager from his pocket nearly has me rolling. She'd told me there were some pros to having sex with a guy who was a good four inches shorter than her. Eight when she wore heels to work. *Closer proximity to what really mattered,* she'd say.

"Ah, that was the day *Roy the Toy* sealed his place in the Worst Sex Hall of Fame," I remind her.

"I mean, it wasn't all that bad." She's laughing so hard now I can barely understand her, which makes me join in until I'm bent in half too. Abby's high-pitched cackle is as contagious as it gets. "That little thing still had some life left in it. He must have found the old charger too, because that baby powered right up!"

Tears are squeezing out the corners of our eyes. We both swipe them away like seasoned pros, not smearing our mascara.

"I'm just picturing him digging around his desk drawers, trying to find the cord to charge that thing, after being out of service for nearly two decades," I howl. "He had to be so excited when he found it!" I hold my fork up, pretending that I'm Roy holding up the pager. "It lives!"

"That's when you know something's gotta give. When you'd rather fuck a guy with an old beeper than spend one more minute at your desk!" She rubs her forehead and leans on her elbows, still laughing at the memory.

When we finally settle, I wipe away the last tear with my knuckle and smile at her. Then I lean back and sigh, taking in the view of fuchsia sunbeams shooting across the horizon. Remembering once again where I am — and who's on the other side of my wall back at the rental.

"I need to get out of this mess." I sigh. "I feel a little unhinged lately, which is so unlike me. And I'm starting to feel really stupid for running away from everything."

"Following your dream is never stupid." Abby points at the screen, suddenly serious. "Don't second-guess this, Liv. That shorter script you sold to the theater was a sign. You have what it takes. Don't let yourself be thrown off by your ex turning up."

"But that was just a little play. This script is supposed to be a whole movie. It's way more intimidating."

"The contacts you've made at *The Good Day Show* will help get your script where it needs to go. Getting this two-month sabbatical was fate pushing you in the direction you've always wanted to go. Rex has nothing to do with your next move."

"I definitely feel like fate is doing something right now. Though I'm not sure what."

I fish a fortune cookie out of the takeout bag, then crack it open and smile when I read it. Then I read it out loud to

Abby. "Fate makes no mistakes. Just detours on the path to your final destiny." I nod and tuck the fortune into my palm to save it. "That is one smart cookie," I mumble. "What does yours say?"

While Abby starts digging through her own takeout bag, I spear another chunk of chicken, but miss my mouth and drop it onto my lap. I quickly flick the saucy meat onto the sand, but it's too late. There's already an orangey-brown stain right where my crotch is. *Wonderful.*

Abby breaks her cookie in half and pulls the thin white strip of paper out.

"A journey of a thousand miles begins with a single step," she reads aloud.

We smile at each other, letting both fortunes sink in.

"It seems the universe is certainly trying to tell you something." She grins. "I think that's fortune-cookie language for *Keep going, honey. You're on the right track.*"

CHAPTER 8

As the final rays of daylight fizzle out over the horizon, like a laser show of pinks and golds, I say goodbye to Abby and slowly walk back up to the townhouse. Straining my eyes and ears for anyone else who may be approaching, I wipe sand off my feet and push the sliding door open on the back deck, not taking any more chances of getting stuck out front.

When I get inside, I turn on the light and shove the take-out containers into a trash bin under the kitchen sink. Then I turn on the faucet and search for a napkin or dish towel, hoping to wipe more of that orange chicken stain off my dress. But, before I can find either, a knock on the front door startles me.

I freeze.

"Holy shit," I whisper to myself.

I look at the clock on the microwave. It's only seven fifteen. The sun must go down early here, which means that could still be the Airbnb guy with the shades.

I start saying a silent prayer that either Phil or Dom is standing on the other side of that door with a stack of window shades. There's no peephole, so I pull the bucket hat down as low as it'll go and push the enormous red sunglasses up the bridge of my nose. Then I slide the chain lock securely on the door and attempt to open it. It takes me three yanks, but it suddenly jerks back about three inches before the chain catches in place.

It's Rex.

My stomach slingshots to the floor.

I immediately tilt my chin down so my makeshift disguise is covering most of my face, fighting the urge to slam the door in his. It's mostly dark out and I'm only lit from behind by the kitchen light. I hope it's not enough to blow my cover.

"Oh, so someone *is* here!" Rex stammers. "I wasn't sure if this place was still empty or not. I saw a light on."

That voice. I haven't heard it in a month. It hits me like a hundred pins pricking my skin.

My heart beats frantically in my ears, breaking the silence that hangs between us.

I don't know how to answer him.

He'll recognize my voice right away.

I consider just slamming the door again, but out of sheer panic I add a horrible British accent to my voice before responding.

"Checked in today!"

Oh my God, I sound like Eliza Doolittle.

When he doesn't say anything right away, I dip my chin down even lower and squeeze my eyes shut, hoping he doesn't recognize me.

"Right." He pauses. "This place has been empty since — um, well, anyway, that doesn't matter. I'm just having a little get-together tonight out back. I didn't realize someone would be here when I planned it. Sorry. We'll keep it down."

He has friends here? Already? How?

Cologne wafts through the crack in the door. His signature scent. The one that clung to everything he touched in our apartment after he left. Spicy juniper and sandalwood.

If he already has friends on the island, what if he has a date coming tonight, too?

34

My mouth goes dry when I think of him having another woman here. I don't think I'm mentally strong enough to listen to Rex fucking someone else through that shared wall.

These walls better not be as thin as my patience.

"Okay," I squeak out. "Thanks."

He starts to go, but turns back just as I'm about to close the door.

"You're welcome to join too, if it's going to be a bother." He adds a softer tone to his voice. "This shared deck thing is kind of weird. I didn't realize it had that when I booked this place. I don't want to monopolize the whole thing. We can also just head down to the beach, if that's better for you?"

I swallow hard and nod.

"Okay. Won't be too late. Sorry again." He gives a little wave, scrunching his face into a concerned smile. I'm sure he thinks whoever moved in is acting absurd, hiding behind a hat and sunglasses when the sun has already gone down.

After he disappears into his unit, I close the door, resting my forehead against it until I feel the latch click shut.

This is exactly why I didn't want a shared rental. I can't focus on doing anything — especially writing — while my neighbor, aka my ex, is holding a party on *my* deck. Just the sound of his voice a few feet away has already pulled apart that deep-rooted feeling in my gut. The one that hasn't gone away in a month.

I slide to the floor with my back against the door. Feeling just like I did after Rex left me back in New York.

Alone.

And deeply annoyed.

I wistfully stare at my prosecco bottle sitting on the counter, mostly empty. I wish I had a long straw so I could just suck down the rest of my prosecco without getting up.

I drum my fingers against the floor as jet lag hits me like a ton of bricks. I'd like to just pass out right here, then wake up tomorrow to find out everything about today was just a bad dream.

But before I can launch myself into a full-blown pity party, the light on Rex's side of the deck switches on.

I stay slumped on the floor while he appears.

Fluffing up patio pillows and wiping bits of sand off the seat cushions. Prepping for his ridiculous party. Looking downright cheerful about it.

As quietly as I can, I start tiptoeing my way around the townhouse, turning off all the lights until the entire unit is pitch black. Then I grab what's left of the prosecco bottle before settling back on the couch, my bucket hat still pulled down over my face, just in case.

If I have to listen to my ex throw a party right outside my very expensive vacation rental, then I'm at least going to get my money's worth and spy on the bastard.

CHAPTER 9

I wake up the next morning with a fresh headache from hell.

I spent the rest of the evening sitting in the dark, watching Rex have a grand old time on the beach just beyond our shared patio with a small group of friends, like I was a skeezeball stalker.

I'm not proud of it.

Far from it, actually, but the investigative journalist in me reared her ugly head and I couldn't look away. I had to study what he's doing here, and who he's doing it with.

One woman in the group seemed particularly interested in Rex. And by *interested*, I mean all over him. And he was all too happy to return the favor.

She was stunning. The only thing worse than sharing a wall with my ex is sharing a wall with my ex while he promptly moves on — with a woman who rivals Barbie herself.

I stumble to the coffee maker, wishing my own version of Ken with the thick biceps from yesterday would come back, so I could promptly move on too.

Without a Starbucks on every block, like there is back home, I need to figure out this new machine. It looks much fancier than the one we had in New York. I pour a heap of coffee grounds into the spot that looks like grounds should go, then fill up the water tank, and pray for the best when I push the *Brew* button. While the pot bubbles to life, I can't help but think back to everything I saw last night.

Miss Interested-In-Rex was sporting thick platinum hair, wavy in all the right places, with naturally sun-bleached highlights framing her cute little heart-shaped face. She also inherited her eye size from Bambi, apparently. Athletic, yet curvy in all the best places, she reminds me of one of those sporty surfer girls I've seen in competitions on television, complete with a deep tan and toned arms.

In short, she's everything I'm not. Part of what made me so recognizable from the proposal clip, besides my hundreds of hours of airtime on *The Good Day Show*, is my face. I have a dark collection of freckles across the bridge of my nose, surrounding a pair of cobalt-blue eyes and dark chestnut hair.

I'm cute, sure, but I look nothing like her. Cute and stunning are two very different things.

Waiting for the pot to work its magic, I close my eyes as each minute of last night shoots through my brain like a machine gun. Playing like a movie in my head — one I never should have watched in the first place.

The way Rex's eyes lingered on her wherever she moved.

His hand grazing and grabbing at her hip while she smiled up at his face, drawn to each other like magnets. Pulling her body closer to his.

A smile tugging at his lips each time she laughed.

The same smile that used to tug at his lips for me.

And finally, the cherry on top of the whole awful night — the moment they kissed. Dark waves lapping up behind them, a raging bonfire illuminating their silhouettes as they came together. A nearly full moon above, accentuating the outline of their bodies pressed into one thick shadow, in what must have been a quiet moment away from the rest of the group. When their lips touched for the first time, I couldn't pull my eyes away. Wrapped under a blanket of stars, a perfectly cloudless night.

I had gone to bed after that. Feeling the full defeat of what I was watching wash right over me. It's not like I want him back, but I don't want to witness him moving on to someone new either. I should have just gone to bed without spying, but curiosity got the best of me.

I rummage through a nearby cupboard, looking for a mug. My hand finally lands on one, just as my headache takes another sharp turn and I'm reminded of the bottle of sweet, sparkling prosecco I consumed last night. I pull the carafe of coffee off its base and pour thick black liquid into my cup.

A few specks of coffee grounds spring to the surface.

Naturally. Because of course they would.

Is Rex here to escape the same cynicism from strangers that I'm trying to escape too? He said he wasn't ready to get married. Wasn't ready for me to pop the question. But, somehow, he was ready to jump into what looks like it could be a serious relationship with this new woman?

I rub the pulsing spot over my forehead.

No.

There is no way I can stay on the other side of the wall from him.

"Just take the financial hit," I say aloud to myself. "Just take the financial hit and go."

Heartbreak should not be this expensive.

I grab my phone.

I need to call my old New York apartment manager to see if any apartment is available and I can move back into my building. Just for another month or so, while I figure something else out.

I stare at the clock, doing the math in my head. If it's six in the morning here in Hawaii, it's already noon in New York. Which means Sonya should be at the apartment management desk to take my call. But after the tenth ring, I realize that it's Sunday. The leasing office is closed on Sundays. She won't be available until tomorrow.

Whether I like it or not, I'm going to be here for at least one more day until I can figure it out. I pray to God the

Airbnb guy shows up with the blinds soon, so I can start writing in peace. But first I need to clear my head.

I walk to the bedroom and snatch the dress I wore yesterday off the floor, before remembering the glob of chicken still smeared across the crotch. I toss it aside, making a mental note to find a laundromat later today, then pull on a pair of green camo bike shorts and a matching sports bra.

Hopefully I can slip out for a quick walk down the beach without being seen. I need the fresh air to ease my hangover. I grab my bucket hat and sunglasses to disguise myself again — just in case — then slide out the back door, making the quietest exit I can.

CHAPTER 10

After a breathtaking walk down the beach, I'm trying to sneak inside my back door quickly, completely undetected, when I hear Rex's door slide open a few feet away. I quickly jerk the door handle on my side of the lanai, but it doesn't budge.

"What the—" I yank at it two more times without luck.

Why is every door in this place so finicky?

The thick, glass door bucks up instead of sliding easily across its track like it did when I first stepped out. I'm about to duck and run for the front door when Rex's voice cuts through the air between us. My heart nearly cracks in two at the sound of it. I was so close to getting inside without being seen.

"Hey there, neighbor!" He's too cheerful for this early in the day. He was always better at mornings than me.

I turn my body away, tilting my head down, hoping the wide brim of this ridiculous hat is enough to hide my profile. I attempt to shimmy my door open again but it's definitely stuck. I awkwardly twist my face down so it stays hidden, contemplating a quick sprint to the front door.

"Sand gets dragged up here from the beach and jams these sliders pretty easily. But there's a trick to it," Rex says casually.

I can feel his body heat sweep past me when he reaches for the handle, but he's focused on getting the door open, not on me. While I nearly pass out from lack of oxygen, I vaguely wonder if he can hear my heart beating as loud as it is. It's like a drum circle inside my chest.

"Here, let me show you."

Leave it to Rex to mansplain how to open a door.

I allow myself to exhale, followed by a deep inhale. Immediately wishing I hadn't. He smells just like he always does first thing in the morning after rolling out of bed, right before he takes a shower. Sandalwood and clean linens. This time with a bit of musky bonfire mixed in from last night's party. I try not to focus on his familiar scent but it's impossible. Memories of a thousand mornings spent cuddled up in bed spring back to life. My face buried in his neck, his chest, his lips. A slideshow of sweet moments I don't want to remember right now. Not after what he did to me.

I step aside to put more distance between us.

Rex lifts the door up an inch off its track, then jerks it back. Of course, it slides open for him right away. He steps aside triumphantly, holding out his arm for me to enter, as if I'm a guest walking into *his* place, not mine. I shrink an inch and curse under my breath.

Stupid bastard.

He turns to face me fully for the first time.

There's nothing to hide behind. No dark shadows to lean into.

I nod at him from under the rim of my hat, saying a silent thank you.

He takes a step closer, studying me up and down. Too close for comfort, and definitely closer than you'd stand to someone you don't know.

But instead of running into my side of the townhouse before it finally sinks into Rex's thick skull that his ex is standing right in front of him, I pause for one more millisecond. Horrified that my feet won't move.

Maybe I want him to know it's me.

Blood pounds sharply against my eardrums.

Just one more heartbeat before I go.

One more breath, before I figure out how to have this conversation with him.

Hello, it's me. I'm here.

I wring my hands behind my back, unsure of what to say.

The irony of this whole scenario is too much, too perfectly aligned for there not to be some alternate reason why we both ended up here. Maybe, if I hadn't proposed to him, we'd still be back home, watching Toby stalk birds on the fire escape while we drank coffee.

I take another shaky breath, lifting my face half an inch.

"Listen, I—"

"Wait . . ." Rex takes a step back from me. "What the hell?"

My stomach churns as he recoils, pushing his chin into his neck like he can't back away fast enough. Shock visibly washes over him. The fact that it's been me all along, with this terrible disguise. Hiding behind the door. Pretending to be British. Watching him last night while he fawned all over another girl.

A satisfying sense of joy seeps through me when I realize that he's experiencing what I felt only yesterday, the moment Abby and I saw that he was my neighbor.

I squint up at him from under the rim of my hat and say the only word that comes to mind.

"Surprise?"

CHAPTER 11

The ruse is up.

"Olivia?" Rex spits my name out like he just ate something rancid. Then he has the audacity to add, "Did you follow me here?"

"What? No! I know you're probably totally weirded out by this. I get it." I slide my sunglasses down my nose, ready to face him head-on, to explain what unbelievable luck we've had, when I hear another set of feet hit the deck.

The woman from last night steps out from his side of the townhouse.

She's just spent the night with Rex.

There's no time to process. I shove the glasses back up my nose to hide.

"Oh, babe! The new neighbor! Introduce me!" The woman's voice is way too perky for this early in the morning, and, of course, she has an adorable Australian accent.

She's even more stunning close-up, in a silky navy-blue robe covered in pink peonies. This gorgeous creature is walking out of my ex's place at eight o'clock in the morning while I'm standing out here — hungover as hell, in an ugly twelve-dollar bucket hat from the ABC Store.

Rex's mouth hangs open, but he somehow collects himself enough to stumble through a quick introduction. I've had all of last night to get used to the idea of Rex being my neighbor, but he's just learned that I'm here within the last twenty seconds, right when his new side piece is making her debut as well. Poor guy looks like a deer stuck in the headlights of his ex-*almost*-fiancée's car. I almost feel bad for him. But not quite.

"Her door was stuck so I was helping her with it." Rex reddens. "Um, Juju, this is — ah — well, this is Olivia." He gestures toward me. "Our new neighbor."

Your neighbor? I shoot him a death glare, about to correct him, but he continues on before I can get a word out.

"Olivia, this — this is," he stutters, then collects himself. "Well, this is Juju."

Juju? What kind of name is Juju?

"Oh, it's so nice to meet you, girl, I'm Juju!" she nearly shouts, or at least it feels that way with my pounding headache. Then she does the cutest, most nauseating little shimmy across the deck to give me a hug like we're long-lost besties. She even pauses at the end to sway me back and forth against her sizable bosom, like my great-aunt used to do at family reunions. She's soft and warm, and, against my better judgment, I find myself not wanting to let go. I need a good hug, apparently, even if it's from my ex-*almost*-fiancé's gorgeous new whatever-she-is.

"Juju." I force a smile as she presses her enormous chest into my flatter one in a second embrace. Then she pulls me back by the shoulders and leans in to give me air kisses on both cheeks. The whole thing gives me vertigo.

Rex looks like a fish that's been gutted, making me feel a teensy tiny bit better.

"Cute hat." Juju lifts a hand up to finger the brim of my very-not-cute hat. "I think I saw that at the ABC Store, yeah?" She's smiling so brightly I can't tell if she's being serious or not.

"ABC Store," I repeat, sounding like a parrot, mimicking the tail end of whatever she says, but I can't stop myself.

This whole situation is too much for my brain to compute so quickly.

She stops fingering my hat and smiles confidently again. I've always wondered how people get their teeth that white. No matter how many Crest Whitestrips I try, my teeth have always looked less glowy than advertised.

"These rentals are all a minimum thirty-day stay, so you'll be here a while, right?" she asks happily.

"A while. Right." I repeat her last words again. I'm about to start squawking next if I don't pull it together. I'm grateful that she has no idea who I am from social media. *Yet.* To her, I'm just a new friend she gets to entertain as long as I'm staying next door.

"Did you come with anyone?" She glances into my side of the townhouse. "Boyfriend? Girlfriend? Husband? Fiancé?" She looks subtly back at Rex, then down at my empty ring finger. The irony of her question twists the knife already sticking in my gut.

I quickly shake my head. I just want her to stop.

"Nope, just me." I look pointedly at Rex — who's still glaring at me coldly — then back at Juju. "I'm single, actually. Single as can be. Single, single, single as a pri—" *Oh my God. I might actually cry. What am I saying?* I should have stuck to repeating the tail end of her words instead of trying to form my own sentences. "Well, yeah." I clear my throat, reeling myself in. "You, uh, well, you get the idea."

"We should go back inside." Rex looks pointedly at Juju. "Our friends are waiting for us at Pipeline."

She ignores him and giggles, bending at the waist, then flips her long mane of blonde hair back up as she nudges me on the arm.

"You're a hoot, Liv," she says. "Do your friends call you Liv? I like you."

I'm officially dying inside.

She strolls across the deck to Rex's side. Even her walk is sexy. More of a curvaceous saunter than a walk. She rises up on her toes to kiss Rex on the lips, her back to me.

He keeps his eyes wide open, pointed right at mine, silently begging me not to blow this moment by revealing our history.

I lift my sunglasses and mouth, *What the fuck?* at him angrily before she ends the kiss and turns back to me.

I drop the glasses back onto the bridge of my nose, holding my breath.

"She's going to be a fun neighbor, babe." She laughs happily, like we're all about to have sleepovers and braid each other's hair. Then she shoots me a grin. "Listen, why don't you come do happy hour cocktails with us tonight? Just right out here on the lanai. You can't beat the view at sunset." She gestures to the ocean behind us like a model at a car show. "Five o'clock, right, babe?" She turns to Rex, failing to notice how pale he looks. The tan has magically drained from his cheeks.

"Right. We'll probably be gone tonight though," he manages to say. "We have that, um, thing. And we don't need to bother our new neighbor on her first day."

He starts dragging her toward their open door.

"Of course we'll be here." Juju smacks him on the shoulder, planting her feet. "We're here almost every night, babe. Come join us, Liv!"

We're already nickname buddies.

Almost. Every. Damn. Night. Babe.

Fucking hell.

Rex locks his jaw, looking pained.

My stomach dives toward the deck so intensely that my hangover threatens to spill out last night's prosecco all over them both. I can't handle any more of this right now.

"Actually, I believe I'm checking out later today—" I start to say, but stop when a huge man comes hulking through my side of the townhouse, ducking through *my* sliding glass door to join the three of us on the lanai. He shrinks all of us with his height, even Rex.

"What the fuck?" I stammer up at him.

47

CHAPTER 12

It's the guy. *The* guy. The one who opened the door for me yesterday.

He must have come back to murder me. Why else would he be walking through my place unannounced?

Hot or not, I'm about to karate chop him in half and run, but Juju steps in front of me before I get the chance.

"Oh, hello, there!" she squeals, giving him a big hug, not even bothering with air kisses since there's no way to reach up past his shoulders. She turns back to me. "I thought you said you were traveling alone!"

I blink frantically in the new guy's direction, still ready to take a swing if need be.

He grins back at me.

"What are you doing back?" I manage to spit out, taking a step sideways. "And I didn't say you could open my door again! Just that one time."

Juju jumps up and down, grinning between this new man and me.

"Sooo" — she draws the word out like a mother coaxing a confession out of her toddler — "who's this?"

"Yeah, who's this?" Rex echoes, glaring at me.

Like you have any right to be mad?

"I have no idea." I still feel alarmed. If worse comes to worse, I'll shove Rex into him while I sprint away down the beach.

"Dominick," the new guy says, his voice deep and familiar. "But pretty much everyone calls me Dom." He reaches out to shake Rex's hand, sizing him up like a little bug, and it hits me like a ton of bricks.

"Wait. You're *Dom*?" I drop my hands from their defensive position, no longer ready to deck him. He holds out his hand to shake, and I let him. His hand swallows mine right up before he releases me with a little smirk.

"Nice to officially meet you," he says.

I take a step back, staring at his face while my veins turn to ice.

"But you opened my door yesterday. And then . . . How did you not know it was me on the phone?"

"I think I mentioned that I'm not really involved with my rentals. Phil handles all my acquisitions and listings. I'm too busy with my other businesses. I didn't even know I owned this place when I helped you yesterday."

I hear Rex scoff, trying to sound unimpressed.

"You must own Rex's side of the rental too then?" Juju pipes up.

"Turns out, I own both sides," he confirms, studying Rex.

I watch the puzzle pieces all move into place for him. Then he looks back and forth between Rex and me, like he's at a movie theater. If he had a tub of popcorn, I'd smack it out of his hands right now. Incredibly attractive or not, he shouldn't be here watching this mess unfold.

Between the four of us, Juju is the only one who has no idea what's going on. A small part of me feels bad for her.

"Did you at least knock before you came in?" I'm somewhat horrified that this Airbnb owner thinks he can just waltz

49

into my rental at any moment. Although I *did* tell him that he was welcome to come install the blinds at his first availability.

He holds up a stack of long, skinny boxes.

"I knocked, rang the bell, and texted you three times."

Oh.

"Those are the new window shades?" I ask, already knowing the answer. *Too little, too late*, I want to add. *The gig is up.* I'm praying he doesn't make this moment any more awkward than it already is, by saying something about our very recent public breakup in front of Juju. As far as I can tell, she's completely oblivious to who I am. For now, at least. As much as I'd love to blurt it out, I'm not Rex's girlfriend anymore. He owes her the story about our history, not me. I'm here to remain anonymous.

"They are," Dom replies with a smirk, holding up the stack of boxes. I always found Rex to be attractive, with his shaggy blond hair and big hazel eyes. But Dom's stature and mature charm make Rex look like a little boy in comparison. "You've given me the perfect reason to come over here and install them."

Rex shifts his focus to me, looking nauseous, then back to Dom. "So, you're just the Airbnb owner?"

We both ignore him.

I fold my arms, staring only at Dom. "I thought you said you were *busy*."

"Your phone call about the blinds seemed, ah, rather *urgent*, and, since you're here for the next two months, I figured why wait a minute longer?"

Rex chokes. "Two *months*?" He spits the last two words out like *I* had the audacity to show up at *his* townhouse.

"Oh, how fun!" Juju starts jumping around like she just won the lottery.

I manage to smile weakly at Juju, then kick a stray rock off the deck.

"Well, she's signed up for eight weeks," Dom pipes up, sounding far too pleased about it. "If she's not enjoying herself within the next thirty days or so, we'll discuss the second half of her reservation."

Rex runs one very tan hand through his sun-streaked hair. His telltale sign of annoyance.

"And where is home?" Juju asks me sweetly. She's still grinning at me like we're all in one big get-along gang. The innocent puppy in all this, just trying to make a new friend.

"New York." I shift my eyes to Rex.

"No kidding!" she squeals. "That's where Rex is from too!"

"No shit," I mutter, unamused. "Small world."

"I guess a lot of people are from New York." She beams, nudging me. "But still, what are the odds?"

Rex looks like he wants this conversation to end right here, like I just let the cat out of the bag. He's clearly not ready to tell Juju about us.

Rex's profile was the only thing visible about him in the shortened clip of us that went viral, making him far less recognizable than me. So either she hasn't seen the clip, and has no idea that he's the guy from the meme, or she still can't recognize me with this idiotic disguise on.

I'm curious how long he waited before moving on from me, since it's barely been a month. "How long have you and Rex—"

"We better get going," Rex suddenly interjects, pushing Juju back toward their side of the rental. "You still need to get ready to go, right?"

"We're heading out to watch our friends at Pipeline," Juju calls over her shoulder. I have no idea what Pipeline is. "Maybe we'll see you later tonight!"

"Unless . . . you mentioned something about possibly checking out later today?" A glimmer of hope pools in Rex's eyes as he turns around. I hate him for it.

How did we get here? I want to ask. *How did we go from laughing at* Ted Lasso *late at night and love notes stuck on our bathroom mirror to* this?

Instead, I murder him with my eyes from under my seven-dollar sunglasses. I open my mouth to reply, but nothing comes out. So I close it again, feeling fresh tears rushing behind my lids.

Dom answers for me.

"She's going to figure it out," he says stiffly to Rex, giving him the evil eye. Or at least I think it's the evil eye, from way down here with my blurry tunnel vision. I'm probably a foot and a half shorter than him.

Dom turns back to me, flashing me a pained look. "Come on, I'm going to install these right now, if that works for you? Then we'll talk about what you want to do with your time here." He starts nudging me inside with the corner of one of those long boxes.

I swat at the box and start to say something about his stupid reservation rules again, but stop mid-sentence when I see Rex and Juju shut themselves inside their half of the townhouse. One hand pressed against the lowest part of her back before closing the door.

My back tingles at the memory of what that used to feel like. Rex's hand against my spine, leading me wherever we were going together.

I snap out of it when Dom uses a box corner to push me all the way inside my half of the rental before sliding the door shut.

I immediately slump down onto the couch, feeling exhausted from the weight of it all.

"Let's get you some privacy." Dom sets his pile of boxes down on the floor.

Without a word, he grabs a tissue from the Kleenex box on the coffee table and hands it over to me. Then he settles on the floor to start ripping into the boxes.

CHAPTER 13

Dom tosses sheets of plastic aside. Then he roots through a giant soft-sided tool bag he must have dropped on the living room floor before joining us outside.

"That was kind of brutal," he says through a faint smile. Then he pulls out a long window shade from one of the boxes, and starts to examine the instruction manual. "I can come back later if you want, but I'm guessing you'll want these installed ASAP. The last thing you need is that asshat walking around where you can see him. And he can see you."

He shoots me a side-eye. I respond by blowing my nose into a tissue and grabbing another from the box. Then I toss my bucket hat and ugly glasses onto the coffee table. No point in keeping them on now. I blow my nose more forcefully for good measure.

Dom does a double-take in my direction, then sets the blinds down, like he can't focus on anything but my face.

"What, you've never seen a girl passionately blow her nose before?" I ask, giving him a weak smile. I can feel myself turning red, but it's like the dam has burst. All the pent-up feelings I've kept buried over the last month are now spilling out — at the most unfortunate time.

I toss the second tissue onto the coffee table and lean back, crossing my arms at him.

He continues studying my face like he's not sure what to say.

"What?" I ask. I wish he'd speak up, not just stare.

"It's you."

I look away and sink deeper into the couch, not saying a word. Bracing myself for whatever quip is about to come next.

"You're that news anchor from the proposal video. And all the memes. That . . . GIF, too?"

My anonymity on this island has lasted less than twenty-four hours. First Rex. Now this.

"In the flesh." I splay out my arms, then grab another tissue.

"Shit." He sits back on the floor, pulling his legs up toward his chest. "You didn't mention *that* detail on the phone."

I cross my ankles and push my big toe against the coffee table between us. "I'm not here to be recognized." My voice sounds bitter, which I don't love, but I can't seem to rein it in.

"Is that why you're here? To get away from all that viral stuff?"

I nod.

"I'm so sorry you're going through that." There's genuine kindness in his voice, softening my reserve a little. Usually people laugh, or tell me I shouldn't have tried to propose at all. A little show of compassion is rare.

"And you had no idea that he was here, too?" He points a thumb to the shared wall beside us.

"Of course not." I sigh.

"I'll install these, but, if I were you, I'd keep these windows wide open and let him see me walk around here like I own the place. After what he did to you? Shit. He doesn't get to steal this view too, or your vacation."

"It's not really a vacation," I clarify, scrunching my nose. "I'm here to work. I'm writing a film script." If I start

54

thinking of this like a vacation, I'm never going to finish it. Then everything really will be a waste. "My story is based in Hawaii, so I figured immersing myself in this place would help me make the script more realistic. You know, get me in the *mood*."

"You write film scripts?" He sets his tools down to give me his full attention, looking instantly focused, and a bit sharp, though I'm not sure why. "Since when did UBN get into film scripts? I thought you were a news anchor for the network?"

It's amazing what complete strangers know about me from working a job in the public spotlight.

"I am now, yes, but I have plans to be a scriptwriter. Movies, if I can swing it. I have an eight-week break from work while things cool off at the station. I want to get my script finished while I'm here. It can take a while to get one picked up by a production house, so the sooner I can finish it, the better." I lie back across the couch, throwing both arms over my eyes.

"Why did you pick *this* rental?" His voice has turned to gravel, and his jaw's locked in place, like I hit a nerve, or something worse.

"Because it was cheap. And available. And I thought it was a single-family unit, not a shared townhouse."

"Is that all?" He leans in, studying my face as if he's a human lie detector. His green eyes narrow into slits.

"Is there another reason besides that to pick this place?" I tilt my face and study him back, confused about why this conversation seems to have taken a sudden turn.

CHAPTER 14

Where did this tension come from? I've about had it with men for today. First, Rex acts like I shouldn't be here, because I'm infringing on his brand-new fling, and now the Airbnb guy, who's apparently the same guy I've been fantasizing about for the last twelve hours, seems to be confused about why I chose his rental. The rental he didn't even know that he owned until now.

"This place was less than half the cost of other Airbnbs and sits directly on the beach. I booked it on a whim after my boss gave me a two-month sabbatical while I took a break from the show."

He sits back cautiously, still watching me closely.

"I checked in with Phil right after we talked," he admits, slowly. "He's at his niece's wedding in Alberta."

I sit up, feeling vindicated. I knew it was a good move to speak straight to Dom yesterday.

"Phil let me know that his new assistant added my name and number to this rental listing accidentally. That's why you got me on the phone and not him."

"Oh, well, it was nice of you to speak with me for, um, for so long yesterday—"

"I've already had him fired for making that mistake," he continues coolly.

"What? You didn't have to fire Phil!" I feel responsible, even though I did nothing wrong. "And you did it while he's at his niece's wedding? That's awful."

"No, I didn't fire Phil," he clarifies. "I fired Phil's new assistant, the one who made the mistake."

"Oh." I still feel racked with guilt.

"He let me know that this building is a new acquisition of mine, priced well to drum up business and keep it filled while he gets some of these little odds and ends fixed up. So, I'm sorry, there's a few maintenance items to be done."

"Like adding window blinds?" I ask, smiling lightly.

"That, and some other things. Like the front door sticking." He gives me the same mischievous grin that made my toes curl yesterday. I bite my lip as he goes on. "The listing mentioned the cheaper price was due to some improvements needing to be made."

I chide myself for not reading the fine print before booking. I picked it so fast that I didn't even notice it was a shared townhouse, *and* in need of minor repairs. This whole situation keeps getting worse, but at least it's led me to sitting here with this Greek God in my living room.

"I didn't see that in the description." I flop back against the couch cushions again. "I've been trying to stay off my phone as much as possible. The internet in general. It's not really my *thing* lately."

His face softens.

"I get that." He reaches out to pat my knee. It's innocent enough, but it sends a jolt of electricity through me just the same. Even sitting, his limbs take up about a third of the tiny room. "If you're really desperate, I suppose I could let you go."

A pathetic bubble of hope pools up inside me.

"Thank you," I say quietly, before looking away. I should be happy to hear that, but my mind immediately spins with the idea of going back to New York.

As much as I'd fought to get out of this, I'm suddenly feeling stubborn about riding it out. There's no way Rex wins here, especially now that I see he's already moved on to someone new. I came here with a purpose. I just need to think about how to make this work without bringing myself down.

"I already checked to see if I could place you elsewhere, but all my other rentals are booked solid for the next eight weeks. I could refund your fees though, if you decide to stay."

My eyes shoot to his.

A free stay? That sounds far too generous.

"That's too much. I can't stay for eight weeks for free."

"Consider it my ploy to get a better review, considering there's still some work to be done."

Can I really turn down a free two-month stay? Even with Rex next door? I don't think I can. Sure, it's ridiculously generous, but it would also be an amazing gift, while allowing me the time to get the script done and let everything simmer down back at the station.

"Either way, I'm happy to install these as fast as I can to give you some privacy from . . . *that* while you decide." He pauses, throwing a thumb toward the shared wall. "Did you know he was already in a new relationship?"

"Nope." My voice wavers. "And definitely not with a woman like that."

"Nah, you're way cuter than her," he says absent-mindedly, as he examines an ancient-looking hammer before exchanging it out for a drill. They could pass for children's toys in his enormous hands.

I crack a half-smile, though I don't necessarily believe him. Juju is the very definition of attractive.

"I can't believe we talked on the phone right after you helped me get the front door open. When did you figure out that it was me calling you?"

The corners of his lips turn up slightly, like he's been caught. I watch him lick his lips before continuing.

"Toward the end of our call," he admits. "When you finally read me the address of your reservation." He gives me a cocky grin. "Why else do you think I ran over here with a stack of window blinds first thing this morning?"

I feel myself redden. "Well, I'm glad you did."

"Do you have any plans for later?" Dom lifts another long shade out of its box. The question catches me off guard. "You need to get out of here if you're going to enjoy yourself." He pulls out a tape measure and gets to work again. I'm definitely enjoying this whole hot handyman thing he's got going on. I sit back to watch him manhandling his tools.

"Other than shutting off all the lights so no one can see me sit on this couch while I spy on my ex and his hot new girlfriend?" I grin at him, knowing full well how ridiculously serious I am about my plan for later.

Dom sets the tools down, not bothering to hide his amusement. His eyes crinkle at the edges, but he doesn't break into a full-blown smile just yet. "You're *not* spending your evening sitting here alone in the dark, watching your ex outside with that woman. *Juju*." He whispers her name like it's a cuss word and we both stifle a laugh.

"Wanna join me?" I ask, half-sarcastically, and half meaning it.

"Not a chance," he shoots back, not skipping a beat.

Ouch.

When I don't say anything else, he adds, "You should have fun while you're here. Not sit in the dark pining after some guy like that. The best revenge is living well, right? You deserve better. Which is why you should come to Cliff's with me tonight."

"I should probably stay a good distance away from any cliffs for the time being, thank you."

"Cliff's is a *bar*." He laughs, then leans across the floor and pats my knee with his free hand again. The same jolt of energy rushes through me — I wish he'd just leave it there. "It's just up the road. Some of my friends like to go after the surf lets up. Right around sunset."

"Oh." I picture a tiki hut full of shirtless surfers, their boards all piled high by the door. It could be a good research spot for my script, and a balm for my wounded heart. "Maybe."

"Maybe?" he repeats in disbelief. He picks up a long box and points it at me, then jabs me on the arm with it. "I'm making a command decision. You're coming. No way I'm leaving you here alone to spy on your ex in the dark."

"It's not just that," I admit. "I don't want to be recognized." He frowns. "People have been pretty harsh since that clip went viral. Most guys that recognize me in public take it as an opportunity to either hit on me, or insult me. It's made me into a bit of a hermit."

His eyes darken, and his smile disappears. "You'll have me with you."

I let out a soft, nervous chuckle, but he doesn't join in. He studies me more intensely.

"Trust me, no one is going to hassle you. Not while I'm there. You'll have my friends there with you too. They'll bring their wives. It'll be fun, I promise."

I squeeze my eyes shut. His words mean more to me than he knows. I've been facing this whole mess alone for the last four weeks. I'd have given anything to have Rex or someone else by my side to stop every asshole who took my presence as a cue to say their most jarring one-liners to me.

He frowns. "Unless . . . you want him back?"

"Do I want Rex back?" I repeat, considering the question. Imagining us returning to New York together, like none of this ever happened. It should feel right, considering I proposed to him a month ago. But for some reason it doesn't. Not anymore. "I don't think so. No."

"Do you at least want to make him sorry that he left?"

I laugh. "Of course. Who wouldn't want that?"

"And what's the fastest way to do that?"

"Move into the townhouse next door to him for eight weeks?" I laugh sadly at my own ironic joke.

"That part is inevitable at this point, but he's not going to think twice about you if you're sitting here like a bump on a log while he's making out with Juju right outside your door. Why would he?"

I roll my eyes at him. "I don't have any plans to sit like a bump on a log. Just spy on him a little."

His eyes roam over mine.

"Guys want what they can't have," he goes on. "Every one of us loves a good chase. But, more importantly, we always, *always* want one thing."

If by *one thing* he means . . .

"Oh my God, I'm *not* sleeping with Rex just to get him back." I chuck a throw pillow at him, but he catches it with one hand and tosses it aside. I find it oddly attractive. Still, I'm about done with this conversation, if this is the only wisdom Dom is serving up.

"I'm not talking about sex."

Something stirs in me, just watching the word *sex* come out of his mouth.

"Then what else does every guy want?"

His eyes start dancing, as if suddenly lit on fire.

"To win," he tells me. "We all want to *win*."

CHAPTER 15

I admit, the whole idea is almost too delicious to pass up.

I could go out with Dom while also making Rex jealous?

"You want me to make Rex feel like shit by going out with you?"

His grin tells me that's exactly what he has in mind. Just the thought of it makes me turn pink again.

"And what do you get out of this little arrangement, sir?" I raise one eyebrow at him.

"I want a renter who stays put in my Airbnb for the next eight weeks and leaves me a good review."

I shrink into the couch a little. I was hoping for a different answer.

"Got it. I can leave you a decent review." I straighten up my spine. "That seems fair. You don't even have to go through the trouble of taking me out on a fake date."

He laughs, then his face curls into the same wicked grin he gave me yesterday. "I also want to get to know the girl who proposed to a guy on national television, then dropped everything she had to run across an ocean to finish a film script . . . You kind of fascinate me."

"Oh." I blink at him a few times.

"Is that a good enough reason?"

I shrug, wobbling my head back and forth, giving it some thought. I'm all for a real date, but a fake one? What if Rex found out it was all just an act?

"Take your time considering it," he says. "I'm in no rush here."

He then hops to his feet and starts measuring the window frames. The shirt he's wearing slides up above his board shorts, revealing a little sliver of smooth, tan skin. Knowing the row of abs lying just underneath that fabric makes my pulse quicken, then settle right between my legs.

I swear he did that just to entice me.

Admittedly, it's working.

"What would this fake-dating situation entail?" I'm curious, though the whole idea feels ridiculous to entertain, especially since I'm here to escape from drama, not get involved in any more of it. "And how can I know for certain that Rex won't find out it's all just for show?"

He stops what he's doing at the window and turns to face me.

"Well, I've never faked it with anyone, but I imagine that I'd just treat you like any other woman I'm taking out on a real date. Especially when Rex is watching. Or any other boneheads."

My stomach slingshots toward the floor, imagining how Dom treats a woman he's interested in. Even if it's all just pretend.

"So, you'd open car doors for me and act like the perfect gentleman, I imagine?"

"I didn't say anything about being the perfect gentleman." He cracks a smile that breaks the mounting tension between us — just a hair.

The pink in my cheeks pounds into something a bit more red.

"Kidding. But I'd make my intentions clear in front of Rex, if that's what you're asking. We'd have to agree on some boundaries."

I tuck my lips into my mouth, biting the lower half, trying to stop a shit-eating grin from taking over my face. I want to say that he doesn't have to be kidding about not being the perfect gentleman, but I don't. It's been ages since I allowed myself to flirt like this with another man, and it feels delicious — similar to taking a bite from the most decadent chocolate cake after a painfully long diet.

Small bites, I tell myself. *Make it last.*

"Give me an example," I prod. "I need to know what I'm buying here, before I sign on the dotted line."

Dom sets his tools down next to the boxes, putting his hands on his hips, sizing me up. My pulse quickens while he takes me in, but I force myself not to look away. Whatever this guy has going on is magnetic.

"Well" — he takes a step closer — "usually when I take a woman out, I make sure she knows that she's the only woman in the room to me. And that goes for all rooms. This one or any other."

His voice is gravelly. His eyes burn into mine while he takes another slow step in my direction. I bite my lip again and shift my weight on the couch.

Okay, Airbnb guy. You've got some game.

"Technically, there are no other women in the room right now, so that's an easy one." My tone is challenging but nonchalant, like I'm egging him on, whether I mean to or not.

"Oh, I'm not done yet." He twists his face into a suggestive grin before straightening his features out again. Then he rubs his jawline and takes another step toward me, getting back into character. The whole effect of his steps drawing closer — tightening the gap between us — while he's staring at me with that look on his face — it's all making my heart beat out of control.

"I'd also make sure that there's no doubt about who you're with while we're out."

"Mmm, that seems like it might be a bit trickier to do." I frown slightly.

"Not when you're with me." He sounds arrogant, if not a little cocky. "Trust me, no one will question who you're with when we're together. I don't really like to share when I'm out with a beautiful woman."

"Rex would hate seeing that kind of thing."

"That's the idea." He smiles. "But you'd have to be okay with me taking up space."

"Taking up space?"

"Beside you. Existing in the same bubble. It has to look natural."

"Natural," I repeat, cocking my head to the side. "It's been so long since I went out with anyone else, I've practically forgotten what a first date looks like."

"Stand up."

"I don't think I need—"

"Stand up," he repeats more forcefully, though a playful smile tugs at his lips.

"You can just—" But I stop talking when I see the look on his face. He's definitely serious about me standing. "Okay, fine." I get to my feet, then cross my arms over my chest, feeling a bit goofy for going along with the charade, even if I'm thoroughly enjoying it. It's like we're actors in a play and Dom is the director.

"The attraction has to look mutual, not like you're repulsed." He circles one finger toward my arms, which are laced protectively over my chest.

I huff and bring my arms back down to my sides, shifting on my feet.

"This is all a bit silly," I protest, but he's already closing the space between us.

"Liv." He says my name gently, his tone suddenly warm and buttery smooth. "Can I call you Liv?"

Call me anything you want, I want to say. Especially when you say it like that. "Sure. Most of my friends call me Liv."

"Liv. You look absolutely gorgeous tonight."

Then he takes another step toward me as his eyes pour down my body, like melted bronze against my skin.

"It's morning still—"

"Shh."

I stifle a laugh as he takes the last step between us, but my breath hitches in the back of my throat when he slides one hand around my waist, bringing me into him. He keeps the one hand drawn around my spine, but squeezes his palm against my skin, pressing my body into his. I instinctively place a hand on his chest to pace us.

I swallow hard. Dom smells spicy and raw, like his cologne has been mixed with the fresh waves he probably surfed this morning.

He releases me to step back, but, as he does, he bends down to brush his lips against my cheekbone, right where my cheek meets my ear, kissing me so lightly that it sends another round of shivers down my limbs. I have to fight my knees not to buckle.

"Ready to go, sweetheart? My car's waiting out front," he says softly, right into my ear, sending goosebumps down each arm.

Fuck me.

I open my mouth to reply, but nothing comes out. I inhale deeply, collecting myself when he pulls back, his eyes still staring intensely into mine, making everything else in the room fade away.

My heart pounds and, without thinking, I wet my lips like I'm about to be kissed.

This is all a show, Liv, I remind myself. He's just that good.

I scold myself for believing that any of this is real, forcing my heart rate to slow back down to normal.

"That was decent." I sigh, looking up at him from beneath my lashes.

He finally clears his throat, removes his hand from my back, and scratches the back of his neck with it, like he's not sure what to do with himself again.

The spell is over, all heat dissipating back into the air like a puff of steam rising between two pots of boiling water.

"Decent?" He laughs, looking bewildered. "That was some of my best work."

Okay, that makes me laugh.

"Alright, it was perfect." I roll my eyes a little, trying to act like I didn't just nearly hyperventilate from that mini masterclass in seduction.

"Will Rex buy it?" He grins wickedly.

"I think everyone within a twenty-mile radius will buy it." I fight the urge to fan myself.

"Good." He looks pleased with himself before turning back to his stack of boxes. "Then leave that silly disguise here. You won't need it tonight."

I redden and grab my ugly hat off the table.

"Honestly, it might be best if I just leave it on whenever I leave the townhouse. I don't want to cause any extra trouble for you and your friends tonight. You'd be pretty horrified at the things total strangers have said to me when they recognize me."

"You won't need it because this little act is coming with us to the bar, too. You deserve to relax while you're here, and you can't do that if people are going to be all over you. You're stuck here for the next two months. It's the least I can do."

There's nothing in me that wouldn't love this added protection and sense of security, without having to worry about people recognizing me. I can already feel my social anxiety go down a notch.

"My sister had a guy friend in college who switched into fake-boyfriend mode anytime someone was giving her unwanted attention. Worked like a charm. I won't do anything that'll make you feel uncomfortable, but I'm happy to stick with you, even after we leave Rex in the dust. Stay close by."

Men have been unnaturally aggressive since that clip, like it put out a bat signal to every creep in New York that I'm single now, each of them ready to fill Rex's shoes, or tell me how weird I was for trying to propose.

"Thank you." I scrunch my nose, not sure how to respond. I'm still trying to get my heart to slow its pace from those fake moves.

"It would be my pleasure." His deep voice sounds thick and easy, like nothing about this offer bothers him. Meanwhile, my insides are still screaming for another faux embrace. "I'll finish this up, get a little work done, then swing by to pick you up around five fifteen. At your back door."

"Back door?"

"Didn't Juju mention they start their happy hour out back around five o'clock? You can walk by Rex and Juju looking hot as hell in whatever you decide to wear, while he slurps down his drink and tries not to drool over you."

I laugh, appreciating where his head is at.

"Brilliant." I stand up. "This all feels like it'll work. Mutually beneficial. Seemingly believable."

I stick my hand out to him for a handshake, like we've reached the fever pitch of our absurd little negotiation and it's time to make it official.

His face transforms into triumph, the mac daddy of all smirks. That little performance of his won this round and he knows it.

"So we're on for tonight?" He holds his hand just out of reach.

You'd be crazy to say no to this, Liv, Abby's voice rings in my head. I can't imagine telling her later that I've turned this man down. She'd probably rush here on the next flight just to assess my sanity in person.

"It's a deal," I agree.

Our hands meet somewhere in the middle, mine disappearing into his once again, and I briefly wonder if he felt a zing of anticipation up his arm like I just did.

I pull my hand back first, then turn toward the door. If I stay here much longer, we might have a hard time staying in neutral — or *mostly* neutral — territory.

"I'm going shopping."

I'm not in the right mindset to work on my script today, and the cutest dress I brought with me is currently crumpled up on my bedroom floor with a big orange blob across the crotch from that rogue chicken.

"Atta girl," he says appreciatively, flashing me another look that makes everything in me flush deeply. "I'll finish up here and be gone before you get back."

He turns back to the window, reaching both arms up over his head again to measure the top of the vaulted window frame. A solid four inches of his bare torso comes out to play. I haven't been in the habit of checking out any other men in recent years, but now I can't look away. And if I'm being honest, I really don't want to.

You're single now, I remind myself. *Look all you want.*

But he turns — catching me in the act of ogling him. I shift my eyes away before he can see me blush.

Too late.

"By the way." He pauses until I meet his eye. "I meant what I said about Juju. She doesn't hold a candle to you." My joints turn to Jell-O, making my limbs suddenly feel heavy and warm. "And in case you're wondering . . ." He waits again to make sure I'm looking right at him. "I could see it written all over Rex's face that he knows it too."

"Whatever." I turn toward the door so he can't see how red I've become. I don't know what else to say. "Thank you, by the way, for getting over here so quickly to hang those up."

"Nah, don't thank me. I should be more involved in these rentals." He grins at me over his enormous shoulder before turning back to his project. "At least with this particular one anyway."

Then Dom's drill screams to life, ramming thick screws into the drywall, his biceps springing to life overhead. I quickly shut the door behind me, fighting the urge to spy on him just a little bit more.

I'm excited. For the first time in weeks, I have plans that don't involve hiding.

CHAPTER 16

Whether it's the humidity of the island, or the heat from my conversation with Dom, I'm suddenly roasting when I make my way down the driveway toward the strip of stores I spotted yesterday. I pull out my phone to shoot Abby a text while I walk.

> *Met Rex's girlfriend. Going to drinks with Dom tonight. The girlfriend and Dom are both hot as hell. What do they put in the water here?*

I fan myself as I wait for the three little dots on her side of the text thread to turn into words.

> *Rex has a girlfriend already? WTF??? And I thought we hate Dom?*

I smile down at the screen.

> *Dom could be Jason Momoa's twin. We definitely don't hate him. And we have a plan to make Rex jealous. Going shopping. Stand by so you can help me decide which outfit is respectably slutty enough* 😋

I immediately send another.

Wish you were here xo

My phone pings again. I hop over a pothole in the side-walk, then pause to read it.

Wish I was too, but that might get awkward when you're shacking up with Dom later 😆 Forget about Rex & do something wild. Just for you xoxo

Once again, Abby is right. About everything, really. Maybe this trip was a good idea after all.

* * *

I crack a bedroom window while getting ready so I can hear Dom when he arrives. I don't want to keep him waiting too long, and if I'm being really honest, I also want to hear Rex stumble through greeting him again when he realizes why the hottest guy I've ever seen is back at the townhouse to pick me up.

Right at five o'clock, Rex and Juju emerge from their side for their little happy hour ritual on the deck. I peek out the blinds just barely to see them leaning up against the rail, looking out at the view, with two mai tais in their hands. A pitcher and extra glass sit on top of the side table beside them. My stomach jolts when I realize Juju must have brought the extra glass out for me, in case I decided to join them after all. She genuinely seems sweet.

I drop the shades back into place, not wanting to be noticed.

A few minutes later, Dom's feet thump up the steps outside.

I fight the urge to run out there, telling myself to just let this unfold naturally.

Don't look too eager.

My heart is beating wildly. I feel like a kid trying to pull a prank on my parents.

I stand behind the drawn shades, straining to hear them.

"Oh, hey man," Rex says in surprise, sounding stiff. I hear their hands slap together in what must be that bro-ey hand-shake thing that all guys seem to know. "Back to fix something else?" There's more than a little hint of disdain in his voice.

Let the games begin.

"Dom!" Juju trills happily. "Please tell me you're here to pick up that hot new neighbor of ours!"

Dom chuckles, then pauses. I wish I could see their faces right now, but I don't want to pull back the blinds and risk being seen quite yet.

"That's exactly why I'm here, actually," he tells them. "To pick up Liv. We're going out to Cliff's tonight." The faint smile in his voice makes the butterflies in my stomach start swarming.

A pair of knuckles taps gently against the back door.

I take a deep breath. This is it. I slide the shades back and pull the door open, beaming up at him.

Dom is grinning at me on the other side, nearly taking up the whole door frame. He's wearing a soft, light green button-up shirt that matches his eyes perfectly, and makes him look even more tan than he did this morning.

He gives me a subtle wink then brings one hand up to his chest like he's just been shot.

"You look . . ." His gaze sweeps down to my toes and back up to meet my eyes, even more slowly than he did in the townhouse earlier today. Like he's taking his sweet time checking out every inch of my body. If all this feels so real to me, I'm almost positive his act will appear real to them too. "You look absolutely beautiful."

CHAPTER 17

The collection of butterflies in my stomach breaks into a synchronized victory dance as I step over the threshold to join Dom, Rex, and Juju outside. The short red romper I'd picked out was the right choice. It's written all over Rex's face.

"The red one," Abby had texted after I sent photos of my four outfit choices from the dressing room. "Rex is going to keel over when you walk out in that."

Sadly, Rex doesn't quite keel over. Instead, he sucks in a breath and rubs his bottom lip with his finger. If Juju isn't aware of it yet, that's Rex's telltale sign for *you look entirely fuckable tonight.*

It takes everything in me not to spin around triumphantly.

"Liv!" Juju says excitedly when she sees me. "You look stunning! Have just one drink with us before you head out?" She's already filling up the extra glass meant for me. "Let me grab another one for you too, Dom. I had no idea you'd be coming over!" She gives me a sneaky grin before shoving the glass into my hands.

"Oh, we're just heading out—" I start to tell her, but she's already sprinting back into their townhouse for an extra glass.

"Just one!" she calls over her shoulder. "Then we'll let you two go!"

She disappears inside.

When it's just the three of us left on the deck, Dom pulls me into a tight bear hug, as if Rex isn't even there. I wrap my arms around his torso and curl into him. He feels as solid as an oak tree.

He grins.

"Red is definitely your color." My mind swims back to when we were standing at my front porch — the last time he saw me in red. The look in his eyes says he's right there with me. "Beautiful," he whispers. His voice is loud enough for Rex to hear, but soft enough to sound seductive.

As quickly as the heat flashes in his eyes, it's gone, and he kisses the top of my head, his cheek lingering against me.

"Thank you." Even though I know this is all just a show, I'm still unable to stop myself from blushing. He squeezes my hip, sending that familiar wave of electricity through me. "That shirt matches your eyes."

Dom smiles down at me and I nearly forget Rex is still standing with us until he takes a loud gulp of his drink.

Juju emerges again with an empty glass for Dom, which she quickly fills from the pitcher.

"So, what was all that about you opening the door for Liv yesterday?" Juju asks. "It seemed like you two knew each other a little bit before this morning?"

I'm guessing this girl has never known a stranger in her life — she's so friendly.

Dom breaks into a hearty laugh, then studies me closely, his eyes dancing playfully. I can't tell if this is all an act for our little audience, or if there's some truth behind that look of admiration he's giving me.

He squeezes my hip. "Do you want to explain that one? Or should I?" His lips twitch into a grin, then he kisses the side of my hair, just above my ear, hinting to our audience that we've grown more comfortable with each other since this little story began.

74

"You can take this one." I bite my lip, challenging him a bit. I just want to watch Rex's face when he explains how we met.

"Well, I was coming back up from a surf yesterday afternoon, when I heard this huge commotion. Lots of banging. It sounded like something — or someone — was getting beaten up, followed by this wild growl at the end."

I burst into laughter. "Okay, I had been trying to get that front door open for like ten minutes at that point. It's still freezing back in New York, and I wasn't smart enough to change my outfit before leaving the airport, so I was still in jeans and a sweater. Sweating my face off."

"Not by the time I saw you," Dom adds, his voice deepening.

Blood rushes to my cheeks.

Rex's mouth drops open.

I smile sheepishly at them both.

"Wait, what? Details!" Juju takes a sip from her mai tai and leans in, like she's binging on her favorite show.

I shrug. "I was roasting. I didn't see anyone around so . . ."

"So, as luck would have it, this incredibly gorgeous woman here was right in the middle of changing on the front porch when I walked around the corner to investigate." Dom eyes Rex as he finishes my sentence.

Rex chokes on something — either his mai tai or the visual Dom just served up.

I smile to myself, watching Rex's eyes dart between Dom and me while he clears his throat four times.

"You were changing on the front porch?" Rex manages to spit out.

Juju is too busy laughing to notice the look of horror spreading across his face.

"Just the bottom half." I smile innocently at Dom like I'm still embarrassed about the whole thing. "It was practically the same thing as bikini bottoms, right?"

"Depends on what you call a bikini." Dom moves his arm up around my shoulders. He pulls me against him, laughing.

"Girl!" Juju exclaims, nudging me in the ribs. "This is the most amazing story I've ever heard about how two people met. Tell me he got that door open for you. Tell me those muscles are for more than just eye candy!"

Rex chokes again, clearing his throat and pounding on his chest with a closed fist, as if something's stuck.

I laugh, then finger one of Dom's biceps appreciatively.

"Oh, they are definitely functional." I lean into him like we've known each other much longer than we have. "And yes, he got the door open on the first try. Almost wish it was a little harder for him so he'd have worked up a sweat or something."

Dom is eating this up, laughing at my recollection of how it happened. The funny thing is, he doesn't know how that last little part is true. But even if this is all an act, his body feels rock solid against me, and I'm happy to have him here steadying me. To make me laugh through what would otherwise be a painfully awkward moment.

"Pretty much took everything in me not to ask her out right then," Dom goes on. "I'd planned to come back to surf in the same spot the next day, hoping to run into her."

My stomach twists in a knot, wishing that were true. "But we'd better go." He sets his glass back on the table. "That mai tai was amazing, by the way, Juju. Homemade?"

Juju beams at him, nodding. "My secret recipe. I've been perfecting it for years. You're welcome back to have one anytime." She takes my glass from me, giving me a little side hug goodbye. "You two are a hoot. We won't keep you any longer, though. Have fun tonight!"

"Not too much fun!" Rex calls after us.

I roll my eyes as we make our way back through the townhouse, then out the front door.

"Thank you," I whisper to him when we're safely out of earshot. "That was perfect."

"It's my pleasure." He places a hand against the small of my back to lead me. "That guy never deserved you anyway."

When we get out front, there's a black Escalade idling by the sidewalk, a driver behind the wheel.

"I didn't realize you had a car waiting!" I nudge his arm gently. "I hope the driver isn't going to be mad it took so long." I shoot him a nervous glance, hoping we're not about to get an earful from his Uber driver.

"Oh, he won't be mad," he tells me. "He's used to this."

He opens the back door for me.

"Hey, Charlie," Dom says to the driver.

"Hello, sir," the driver says, not turning around, but his eyes look calm in the rearview. This doesn't feel like an Uber situation. "Still going to Cliff's?"

"We are. Thanks for waiting," Dom tells him before shutting my door. Then he walks around to the other side and climbs in next to me.

"Is this some type of ride share that's based here in Hawaii?" I ask, looking for a windshield sticker. Seems pretty high-end.

"It's a private service," Dom says. Then he melts me with his eyes before squeezing my knee, topping it off with a sexy side grin. A tidal wave of desire pumps through my body at his touch, but disappears when he shifts his hand off my knee again. My heart sinks when I remember this is all just a show. Every last bit of it. And now that we're in the car, there's no need for any more contact between us. "I figured we'd have some drinks tonight, so I didn't want to have to worry about driving later. Charlie is going to wait and take us back after, too."

"Wish we had a ride-share service like this back in New York," I tell them.

I see the driver's eyes crinkle as he smiles in the rearview mirror at us, but he doesn't say a word.

After a short drive, we pull up to Cliff's. I'd been right about the bar having a classic tiki vibe. We sit down at a long

77

table outside while we wait for Dom's group of friends. The owner is his buddy, Cliff, who switches between chatting with us and bantering happily with other regulars, taking their orders and welcoming them in.

So far, no one has recognized me, and if they have, Dom's proximity is making them keep a safe distance for now. Everyone just seems happy to be here, and swept up in their own conversations.

As I'd hoped, there's a lot of young Chris Hemsworth lookalikes, with surfboards lined up against the wall near the door, but also a lot of relaxed-looking tourists and locals vibing to live music together in the open air. Surrounded by high-top tables, a row of open-flame torches lining the teak wood deck, the rhythm of continuous waves lapping the shore under a glowing moon mingles with the sound of an older musician in the corner strumming away on his guitar. The sky is in full bloom now, showing off its map of bright white stars, while the air is thick with the smell of plumeria and hibiscus flowers, scattered across the sand from a nearby row of trees.

I smile to myself while taking it all in.

I did it.

I'm here.

A blinding sense of appreciation sweeps through me, admittedly for the first time since I arrived.

Maybe it's unfettered access to the ocean, or the fact that I'm more than a stone's throw away from my ex and no one seems to recognize me, thanks to Dom. Whatever the reason, I feel myself starting to relax and unwind. In a good way. In the *best* way. Just the smallest hint at a time.

CHAPTER 18

Soon after we sit down, a group of four rowdy-looking thirty-somethings walk in and start waving at us.

"That's them," Dom announces as they make their way to our table.

I try to calm my nerves while they circle, each finding a seat.

Two guys that look to be around Dom's age introduce themselves and their wives one at a time. Everyone looks fresh-faced and glowy, with deeply tan skin. The two women instantly welcome me with warm hugs, and Cliff arrives to set two big bowls of fresh guacamole and chips on the table. The guys start bantering with Dom while the two girls instantly want to hear how I met him.

"Dom is the last bachelor among them," a girl named Isla tells me. Then she raises a bushy pair of eyebrows at me and nudges my elbow, leaning in like we're about to share a secret. "Though, if you ask me, he's probably the best catch among them. Minus my husband, of course." I laugh and steal a glance at Dom, who's engrossed in a deep-sea fishing story with one of the guys.

I tell them he's the owner of my vacation rental and that's how we met. They both glance sideways at each other.

"Dom owns many, many rentals, and he's never brought any of the renters here to meet us." Isla gives me a sweet smile. "In fact, I don't think he even knows how many he owns at this point. He's totally hands-off when it comes to those things."

I narrow my eyes at Dom, wondering how that's possible, but he's too busy bantering back and forth to notice, with a guy who has two sleeves of tattoos down each arm.

The other girl in the group, Rooney, grabs my arm. "Once you see what he's working with downstairs, you're gonna wish he was more than just your Airbnb owner!" She eyes Dom appreciatively, then bursts out laughing.

Isla stifles a gasp while her forehead falls into her hands, but she bursts into laughter too. They both look sideways at their husbands to make sure neither of them is listening, but the guys are all too involved in their own conversation.

"Rooney kind of dated Dom before she and her husband got together." Isla grins widely — her front teeth are slightly twisted forward, giving her a cat-like appearance. I instantly like her. "But ignore her. Rooney is ridiculously in love with her husband over there, almost to a nauseating degree. And she's a bit drunk." Isla smacks Rooney on the arm playfully. "We already had a drink or two at happy hour down the road before coming here. She's just reliving a memory from her glory days."

"Can you blame me?" Rooney laughs. "Trust me. I'm happily married. But a girl never forgets a package like that."

"A package like what?" Cliff asks, arriving at the table with a pitcher of freshly mixed mai tais, along with a second pitcher of ice water. He eyeballs the food spread across the table. "You ladies need anything else?"

"More chips and guac, please!" Rooney says cheerfully. "These will be gone before you know it. And, if you're too busy with orders, I'm happy to come grab it!"

They must come here a lot together if Rooney is offering to get her own food from the kitchen.

Cliff smiles at her. "On it. I'll grab you guys some extra plates too."

"No rush," Isla says before Cliff heads back behind the counter. Then she turns to me and says more quietly, "Rooney and Dom hooked up at one point back in college. I don't even know if I'd call it *dating*. More like one random hookup a zillion years ago. You have absolutely nothing to worry about."

I smile, then glance at Dom, trying not to imagine his package, though I'm highly curious now why Rooney hasn't forgotten about it in the last ten years.

"You're all college friends then?" I ask.

"More like college family." Isla smiles warmly. "None of us have real family on the island, so we do all the holidays together. Kind of like a chosen family of island misfits. Dom is our daughter's godfather, but more like her non-blood-relation uncle. She's totally obsessed with him. Here, let me show you a picture. Hazel is about to turn three." Isla pulls out her phone to show me a photo of a tiny brunette cherub with long, dark eyelashes framing a pair of stunning blue eyes. She has two piles of brown curls pulled up into tiny pigtails on the top of her head, wrapped with sparkly pink bows.

"Oh my gosh, she's absolutely adorable!" I exclaim, meaning it wholeheartedly. "She looks just like you!" I grab her phone to look more closely. Hazel could be a little model.

"Even more adorable when she's playing with that one." She points to Dom with a smile. "He's going to make a really great dad one day."

My stomach flip-flops — I feel myself turn pink.

"Ignore Isla," Rooney pipes up again. "For all we know, Olivia might be here for Dom's package size and nothing more! I can hardly blame her!" She widens her eyes, then bursts into laughter. We all join in just as Cliff comes back with more snacks and a second big pitcher of ice water. He sets it all down in front of us, then pours Rooney a big glass before handing it to her. Their completely informal indoctrination into the group is making me feel more relaxed and welcome.

"How's Jack enjoying preschool?" Cliff asks Rooney. She lights up and pulls out her phone, showing him a collection of photos. Her son Jack is a handsome little boy, a backpack almost as tall as he is strapped across his tiny shoulders. He's beaming at the camera with big brown eyes.

I sit back and smile, letting myself fade into the background for a moment. This group already feels familiar — almost like we've always been friends, though we only met minutes ago. Welcoming a stranger with a hug and some humor, somehow makes me feel like part of the inside jokes.

"Good to see you here, Olivia," Cliff says, leaning over to squeeze my shoulder. "When Dom texted us that you'd be coming with him tonight, he told us not to mention your viral clip, but let's just get that elephant out of the room." He breaks into a smile, and I can't help but return one of my own. I was wondering when one of them was going to mention the clip of Rex and me.

Isla smacks Cliff on the arm. "Real subtle, Cliff!" she scolds, trying not to giggle, while Rooney rolls her eyes at him.

Dom's ears perk up at Cliff's teasing and he leans over.

"That took you all of two minutes," Dom says to Cliff, his voice dripping with sarcasm. But he claps Cliff on the back and shoots me an apologetic look. "I'm sorry, Liv. These guys are all harmless though. They'll have your back just as much as I will if anyone dares to give you trouble tonight. Anyone that isn't them, apparently."

"If anybody gives you attitude, I'll just show them the door." Cliff smiles at me. "It's my name on the sign outside."

"Thank you," I tell him, and I mean it. Knowing this group of practical strangers is going to stand by me makes me feel so grateful — even a little weepy inside. After facing dozens of strangers' comments back home alone, it means more to me than I can express right now.

"Now, relax." Cliff's smile grows wider. "Nobody's going to bother you here, at least until the microphone comes out. Then all bets are off."

CHAPTER 19

"Microphone?" I ask.

As if on cue, a lanky woman in a short leopard print dress hops up on stage, setting up a microphone and a little glowing screen. I'm not sure when the musician left the stage. I must have been too busy chatting with Dom's friends to notice.

I study the screen until it dawns on me what's happening.

"Don't tell me that's a—" I start to say, but my question is cut off by the woman's voice booming into the microphone.

"Aloha, everyone, and welcome to karaoke night!" She draws the last word out but is quickly drowned out by a loud cheer erupting from everyone in the bar.

Oh my God.

"Let's kick this off right!" she yells into the microphone over the mounting music.

The first few notes sound familiar . . .

I know this song. Everybody knows this song.

I look around as dozens of grinning faces start bobbing to the beat.

"Dom, you didn't mention it was karaoke night!" I yell over the music as "Don't Stop Believin'" by Journey starts blasting through two huge speakers.

Dom settles back into the seat next to me, scooting it closer, and wraps one arm around the back of my chair, pulling me against him. He wasn't kidding about this fake date vibe. I lean into him, enjoying the fact that no one has come up to me with any rude comments yet. It feels good to be out again, without a care in the world. Maybe no one will recognize me after all.

"Benny, you're up!" Isla shouts. She reaches behind me and slaps the heavily tattooed guy on the back.

I can't remember everyone's name yet, but the guy she slapped must be Benny — he suddenly bounds up on stage and grabs the mic, swinging his hips to the beat of the song that everyone in the bar immediately knows by heart, just before the words kick in.

Karaoke night has never been my thing. It's also something Dom skillfully failed to mention on the drive over. Thankfully, Benny — who turns out to be Isla's husband — is pretty decent at singing the song. He knows every word without looking at the lyrics. Clearly a seasoned pro.

Everyone in the group eventually takes a turn at the microphone, including Dom, who is hilariously bad at his very own rendition of Bonnie Tyler's "Total Eclipse of the Heart," but in an absurdly charming way. Midway through the song he drops to his knees, belting the chorus into the mic, before hopping back up and singing the bridge at the top of his lungs. The whole bar is out of their seats, cheering for him by the end — his friends standing on top of their barstools, whistling and shouting his name. The whole thing is bad-karaoke perfection, and, by the end, my cheeks are stretched and sore from laughing.

There's a two-for-one special on mai tais, so I offer to buy the whole table a fresh round before making my own way up to the microphone. It's my turn, and the extra drinks may or may not be my feeble attempt at greasing them all up a bit before I shock them with my terrible voice.

I've chosen "Sweet Caroline" by Neil Diamond, knowing everyone here will sing along and hopefully drown my own voice out. I make my way to the small stage, wishing I had my disguise with me, hoping everyone is just too tipsy to recognize me. But when I step up on stage, a drunk, middle-aged man stands up near the bar.

He's wobbly on his feet.

"Hey, baby!" he shouts at me. "You're that girl from *The Good Day Show*!" Then he pulls out a phone and starts taking a video of me. Before I can hop off the stage, Cliff is at his side. He grabs the phone out of the drunk man's hands. Then Dom bounds across the bar and jumps on stage to block his view of me.

"Time to go," Dom growls at the drunk guy, while Cliff quickly deletes the video from his phone. The drunk man starts to protest, but Cliff points to the door, handing his phone back to him.

"Not tonight, dude. This girl's not here to be hassled or recognized. Especially by you."

"Aw, come on. I was just—"

"Leaving," Dom interrupts, not smiling. "You were just leaving." He points to the door and takes a step forward. "Time to go, bro."

The guy stumbles toward the door. Cliff follows him, making sure it shuts firmly behind him when he finally disappears outside.

My heart is pounding.

I look around at the sea of faces surrounding the stage, mortified by what just happened. If no one recognized me yet, they definitely do now.

Dom turns around, cupping my face between his hands. The whole interaction has made me feel a bit dizzy.

"Are you okay?" he asks gently. "That prick shouldn't have done that."

"Yeah, I'm okay," I tell him quietly. "I'm so sick of hiding from what happened. Thank you for stopping him from taking another video to post online. That's the last thing I need."

He holds my eyes in his gaze, studying me like he's not ready to let go, heat building between us so swiftly that I think he might kiss me. A cheer erupts from the crowd, and somewhere in my haze, I think it might be because we're about to start making out right there on the stage. It's not until the unmistakable first notes of "Sweet Caroline" ring out through the speakers on either side of us that I realize the cheers have nothing to do with us, and everything to do with the popular song that's starting.

"Oh my God." I breathe out, laughing. "There's no way I'm singing now."

He laces his fingers through mine and we turn to walk off the stage, but Isla and Rooney are standing near the edge of it, blocking our path off.

"You chose our favorite song," Isla announces loudly over the music. She's grinning wildly, not budging.

"And that guy is gone now," Rooney adds, raising her brows at me.

"We're singing it with you," they say in unison.

When their feet hit the stage next to mine, the crowd erupts again.

"Come on," Isla shouts in my ear so I can hear her over the music and noise of the crowd. "Don't let that asshole steal your thunder tonight, babe! Let's do this!"

They pull me back to the middle of the stage, arms linked in mine, and the whole audience breaks into the first few lyrics of the song with them. Dom stands at the edge of the stage, an amused look on his face as his best friends take charge. I can tell he's also keeping an eye on the crowd, making sure no one else starts videoing us again without permission. I'm laughing so hard I can barely form the words, but it doesn't matter — everyone is singing so loud that we can't be heard through the microphone anyway. I never once have to hear my own voice come through the speakers, and we manage to finish the whole song together.

I'm sweaty and grinning by the time I rack up the microphone at the end.

Isla and Rooney pull me into a three-way hug while the crowd gives us a standing ovation. Then we jog back over to the table, laughing and hitting high fives from beaming strangers along the way.

"You cheated," Dom says into my ear, handing me an icy glass of water when I finally make it back to the table. I turn around to protest, but he plants a kiss squarely on my lips, evoking another deafening cheer from the bar. He dips me back, egging the crowd on, before slinging me up to my feet again.

"That was hot," he whispers into my ear. Then he pushes his forehead into mine and kisses me again, before we break apart in embarrassed laughter.

I know my rendition of "Sweet Caroline" was anything *but* hot.

"Bonnie Tyler would have been very proud of your performance too." I peck him one more time on the lips before sitting down beside him. He wraps one arm around my shoulders and pulls me into him from behind, kissing me on the cheek, like he can't keep his hands off me. I lean into him, knowing I couldn't smile any wider if I tried. This might be a fake-boyfriend act to keep any guys from harassing me, but I love it just the same.

"Oh, get a room, you two!" Benny shouts, before slapping Dom on the back with a grin.

Rooney winks at me across the table and holds her palms out about a foot apart, nodding her head like she's just shared a naughty secret. Then she erupts into laughter when Isla reaches over and smacks her hand away. They tumble off the barstools together, chiding each other for being so ridiculous.

I absolutely love them all.

CHAPTER 20

I wake up to the sound of Rex and Juju out on *my* deck the next morning, squinting my eyes at the sound of their voices, grateful they're hidden behind a wall of curtains now, thanks to Dom.

All that vivacious gusto I felt after my night out with Dom and his friends is fading at the sound of my ex's voice, along with my plummeting blood-alcohol level. I snatch my phone from the nightstand and text Abby from bed.

> *Why does Rex think he gets ownership of our SHARED deck?? He's out there right now drinking coffee with Juju. WTF*

She writes back almost immediately.

> *Start walking around nude. That little hangout spot of theirs will be a thing of the past real quick . . . just sayin'* 😉

She knows what to say to make me crack a smile every time I need it. I type back.

*Or it'll make Rex live out on the deck permanently just to
catch a glimpse of what he'll never have again*

I flop back onto the mattress. If I'm going to spend the
next two months next door to Rex, it better not be spent
listening to them making plans to go snorkeling first thing in
the morning.

My phone rings.

"Good morning, or is it afternoon there?" I ask after hitting the green button.

"Does it even matter anymore?" Abby asks. "I've been
at the office since last Monday. It's Thursday. Or Friday? Or
maybe it's still Tuesday. I don't even know. Thank God I
found that cat walker for Toby. The office owes me a fif-
teen-minute personal call at this point. Are they still out
there?"

I tell her they are, and we get to work, brainstorming
every conceivable plan of getting my deck back. Each plan
involves something outrageous. Nudity — which we've
already considered — a blaring stereo, murder, and — my
personal favorite — setting the deck on fire.

"Dom would kill me," I sigh. "And he's really too wonderful to do that to him."

"I need to hear more about this date you two went on . .
. Hang on." Abby suddenly sounds muffled, but I think I can
hear Brett's voice in the background. I swear her boss gets off
on ordering her around. She sounds deflated when she comes
back on the line. "I need to go."

"Should we come up with your plan of escape next?
Something involving fire and nudity too?"

She laughs. "Probably. I need to get out of here and take
a shower today. Brett just told me that my office has a funk to
it, but that didn't stop him from handing me another stack of
records to comb through."

We hang up after I make her promise to take the longest,
hottest shower of her life in her own bathroom today, and then

get a quick workout in to release a storm of endorphins into her bloodstream before she heads into another work bender. I briefly wonder if Abby and I should both forgo the idea of finding love with actual men, and just grow old together on a tropical fruit compound here in Hawaii.

Absentmindedly, I scroll through local land for sale on Zillow while making coffee, then click on a listing near the North Shore. The photos show a blue, two-story house on a lush green lot, perched on a small hill. The listing says it has views of both the rugged green mountains and the ocean, with two acres of fruit crops, including banana trees, avocados, and papaya. There's even a mango tree near the pineapple patch.

I send Abby a screenshot.

Can you believe people actually live like this? They've made all the right decisions in life. Join me in banana farming, please

She responds immediately.

At this point I'd just settle for a shower and nine uninterrupted hours in my own bed. But, sure, let's be banana farmers

I chuckle, wishing with all my heart that she was serious.

CHAPTER 21

Dom promised he'd check in on me later today, after he gets a mountain of work done. After writing for a while, I start hitting a wall of hunger, so I grab a travel mug of iced coffee and set out on a quick jaunt down to the ABC Store. I need sustenance if I'm going to nail this scriptwriting thing.

While checking out, the cashier at the little store recognizes me from the viral clip.

"You here to forget about that proposal?" she asks, but she's smiling sweetly like she genuinely wants to know.

I sigh, forcing back a smile. "And to get more snacks." I set a bag of yogurt-covered pretzels and a box of Raisinets on the counter. Her name tag has *GINNY* written in blocky letters.

"Did you move here or just visiting?"

I guess Ginny likes to keep tabs on her customers.

"Just renting a little place up the road for a few weeks. The snacks are a distraction from my writer's block. Hoping the salty sweetness will perform a small miracle and I'll accomplish what I came here to do." Then I grab a chilled bottle of prosecco out of the nearby fridge and hold it up. "And this is if the snacks don't work."

She drags the bottle's barcode across the scanner. "Ah, you're a writer now?"

I'm not used to the slow, friendly pace here on the island. A grocery clerk would never dream of opening up a casual conversation back home. Everyone is always in too much of a hurry.

"Trying to be."

"Then be one." She smiles, like it's that simple. "And I'll be here when you need more salty-sweet miracles."

She tosses a small pack of Swedish Fish at me, which I somehow catch with one hand.

"You got these last time you came in yesterday, right?" she asks, smiling. "Hopefully they help more today than they did yesterday."

"Thank you, Ginny," I say, feeling touched by her thoughtfulness. Most people like to gape at me, but she seems genuinely sweet. "Even with these, there's still a good chance that I'll see you later."

"I think today is going to be your day," she adds. "But, if not, come see me again. I'll be here."

As I'm walking home, thinking about how everyone seems so nice here, a shabby brown-and-black cat darts between my legs. It nearly trips me, weaving its lean body around my ankles with each step.

I catch my balance, careful not to trip on it, but the cat falls into a trot beside me, dodging over and under my feet until I finally come to a stop. Her coat has a unique coloring, like a bowl of mashed-up prunes.

When I stoop down to pet her, she immediately flops to her side, ribs poking up through the thin skin on her belly. She starts purring loudly, like a heavy rollerball is lolling back and forth inside her chest. I lean against someone's fence and sink down onto the sidewalk, rubbing her soft fur through my fingers.

I might open the prosecco bottle right here while the cat and I have a good chat about writer's block, stupid ex-boyfriends, and sexy Airbnb guys. But after about ten minutes, the owner of the house behind the fence comes out and crosses her arms, watching me like I may be a random drunk leaning against her property line at nine thirty in the morning.

"Aloha!" I say, grabbing my bag. Then I rise to my feet and shuffle down the road again.

The cat falls in line beside me again, following me all the way back to the townhouse, where I have to slide my body through the door and push her out gently with the side of my foot just to get it shut. I can still hear her meowing outside when I sit down to type again.

"Forget the cat, Olivia. Focus on the script," I say loudly, even though no one else is here except me.

Hovering my hands over the keyboard, I manage to type my next sentence.

But she's too cute to forget.

I immediately erase it.

I sigh and look toward the front door, pausing to listen for another soft mew.

Right on cue, an angry meow rifles through, followed by four more.

Without thinking about it, I walk right over and open the door, hoping against all my better judgment that Pru will run in. Pru, short for Prunella — she looks a bit mangy, like a pile of prunes. I started calling her that earlier when we were bonding together on the sidewalk.

I stand with the door wide open, looking around.

"Oh my God, Liv, what the hell are you doing?" I mutter to myself. I can't have a stray cat in here. I don't even have a litter box. I'm about to give up when she suddenly sprints inside. Just a blackish-brown streak flashing past my feet.

"Pru!" I cheer, clapping my hands, shutting the door with her safely inside.

She jumps onto my laptop, then lies down across the keyboard, just like Toby likes to do back home.

"Thank you for joining me," I whisper to the cat. "Toby sent you here, didn't he?" Maybe cats are telepathic like that.

She flops onto her back and starts purring like she did on the sidewalk an hour ago, inviting me to do more belly rubs.

"I knew it."

However, she's a little less naturally intuitive than Toby. Fifteen minutes later, writing inspiration has struck, and I'm shoving her off the laptop so I can get the words down before I lose them again.

I finally free the laptop from under Pru's purring body, and hold it over my head with both hands, wondering where I'm going to write that she can't reach. Maybe this was a bad idea after all. She hops to her feet on the table and starts pawing at my stomach while the laptop waves overhead.

"Olivia!" I hear Juju's singsong voice at my back door, followed by a gentle knock against the glass.

When I swing around, she's watching me, wide-eyed, with two mugs of coffee clasped in her hands.

I still hate these giant windows whenever anyone is out on that deck.

"Is that a cat?" Her voice sounds thick behind the windowpanes.

I nod, knowing I must look ridiculous with a shabby cat pawing at my abs while I hold my computer over my head.

"Well, I want to meet her!" she calls out.

When I slide open the door, Juju hands me one of the mugs, then walks past me to get inside.

"Thanks for the coffee," I mutter, then survey the deck for Rex.

It's empty.

I spin around, wondering if he told Juju about our history yet. He's an idiot if he thinks she's not going to find out on her own, but it isn't my story to tell. He's her boyfriend — it's his job to tell her.

"You got a cat?" She rushes over to pet Pru. There's no judgment to her voice, which I appreciate, since I'm starting to feel a bit unhinged right now. I'd never let a stray cat in my apartment back home.

"Sort of. More like the cat got a human," I tell her. Pru hops off the table and starts weaving around Juju's ankles. "She followed me home from the store earlier. When I opened the door, she ran in."

"There are so many strays on the island," she says sadly, bending to pet her. "Cats and chickens everywhere. I'm glad this sweet little girl has found a good home. Even if it's only temporary." She rises again, beaming. "Have you told the owner yet?"

I can't imagine Dom wanting a cat in his rental.

"Umm . . . I think Pru might just stay with me for the morning, then be gone again by tomorrow?"

"I doubt she'll be going anywhere."

Juju leans down to pick her up. Pru nuzzles her head into Juju's neck, the rollerball in her chest growing louder.

"Why not?" I ask.

She breaks into a wide grin and nuzzles her right back.

"Because you've already named her."

CHAPTER 22

"How was your date last night with Dom?" Juju drapes Pru over her shoulder, heading toward the lounge chairs out back like we're already best friends. She pats the empty seat next to her, wanting me to sit down.

Are we really doing this right now? Me having coffee on my back deck with Rex's new girlfriend?

She hits the seat next to her again harder, maintaining her grin.

I guess that's a yes.

"Uh, it was good." I sit down slowly. I'm a terrible liar, so I add, "I'm honestly not sure if it was a real date."

The coffee she gave me is delicious. Way better than mine has been since I started learning how to make it, but I'm not surprised. I'm sure most things about her are perfect.

The balmy morning breeze sweeps past us while I squint out at the water. I didn't think to grab my sunglasses, but the heat from the sun feels really nice on my face without them. A bird chirps in the trees nearby, sounding nothing like the nasty red-eyed pigeons back home. A half-dozen surfers are bobbing on the water, and I raise a hand to shield my eyes, wondering if one of them is Rex.

"It sure looked like a date to me!" she says, breaking my focus. "That red romper you were wearing is hot as hell. A solid upgrade from that bucket hat situation you had on earlier."

I'm about to be offended, but when I look at her face, I can't help but laugh. She's not wrong. She pushes my leg playfully after successfully breaking the ice, and leans back in her chair, looking more relaxed. *Dammit.* She's so likable.

"This view can't be beat, right?" She sighs happily and takes a sip of her own coffee, pulling a stray hair back from her face, hugging Pru a little tighter.

"Is that Rex out there?" I ask as one of the surfers gets face-plowed into the water. They hit the surface so hard, it makes me cringe.

I hope it's him.

"Sure is," she says, shaking her head. "That man can do a lot of things right, but surfing is not one of them." She pauses to watch him get smacked with another wave from behind and giggles before continuing. "Sometimes I think he might actually drown out there, so I try to keep an eye on him. Believe it or not, he seems to be improving by the day. You should have seen him when he first arrived."

Rex pops out of the whitecap and then quickly gets hit by another wave coming in from behind. He jumps up out of the water a third time, like a resilient little cockroach.

Life is weird. The last time I was oceanside, Rex and I were waking up to a similar view in the same bed together. We spent a week last summer in the Maldives. Rex's idea. It was a surprise gift to me. All I had to do was pack a bag.

I eye Juju suspiciously, wondering why she hasn't recognized me from the viral clip of our failed proposal yet.

"So, are you here on an extended vacation or something?" she asks.

"Sort of," I say slowly. "I'm finishing up a movie script."

"You're an actress?" She perks up and turns her whole body toward me, studying my face. "I knew there was something familiar about you! What else have you been in?"

"I'm a writer," I clarify quickly. "I'm writing a script. Definitely not acting in it." I feel myself turn pink.

"Oh wow, you're here to write." She looks genuinely impressed.

"That and I wanted to get away from New York for a while. My boss offered me a sabbatical of sorts. I figured I may as well choose a beautiful place to write from, plus the setting of the film is here." I don't feel like adding that I couldn't go outside in New York without someone telling me they felt sorry for me. "It's always been my dream. I figured, since I had the time, it was probably now or never."

"What else have you written?"

"A few theater scripts, and a short film. This would be my first full feature-length film script. What about you? Are you here on vacation with Rex?"

"No, I grew up here." She smiles. "Well, I guess if you count moving here when I was twelve. Hence the Aussie accent I haven't been able to shake."

"You grew up here? *And* Australia?"

She nods, glowing. She sets her mug down and Pru flips over in her arms like a baby.

No wonder she seems so comfortable in her own skin, both in and out of the water. She was probably born in a bathing suit. Her face doesn't have a drop of makeup from what I can tell, and she's still absolutely glowing.

"I can't imagine this being my life every day." I wave my hands around the scenery surrounding us. Green, rugged mountains line the bay, rising up toward the blue sky behind us. "What do you do here?"

She smiles. "I own a coffee shop."

"That explains the delicious coffee," I mumble, taking another sip.

"Actually people come to my shop more for the smoothies and acai bowls than the coffee." She curls her long legs up beneath her. "Also, it's more like a little shack on the side of the road, so not like the coffee shops you'd have back home in

New York. I guess I should start saying I'm a smoothie shack owner." She laughs, and I let myself join her. "But I guess *coffee shop* sounds quite a bit more posh to me than *roadside smoothie shack surrounded by stray cats and chickens*. I grow the fruit on my land, then have my employees blend up whatever is the most fresh that day."

I imagine her roaming down a row of banana trees, barefoot and tan, with her hair pulled up in some colorful scarf, accentuating those precision-cut cheekbones as she turns to offer a fresh-picked mango to Rex with a grin. Sun cascading down her slender arms as she reaches up to kiss him, tasting of tropical fruit and sunbeams. No wonder he fell in love with her.

"Sounds like the perfect life," I say wistfully. "I was just telling my best friend back home that I can't believe people live like this here. It makes my life back in New York look—" I want to say chaotic and soul-crushingly cold "—complicated. And gray. I love it there, but it's not the same brand of magic as this island." I wave my arms up toward the sky, which looks like a mirror image of the ocean beneath it, dotted in foamy white clouds.

She rubs Pru's belly before kissing her upturned nose.

"That's what I hear from Rex. He says he never wants to go back." She smiles at me, and I swallow my shock. I thought Rex loved New York.

The whole world wants to be us, Olivia, he'd say. *We're at the center of the universe here.*

"Anyway, I'm blabbing on while you're here to do something important." She stands up. "I should let you get back to writing."

She looks back out at the water, her crystal blue eyes searching the surf, until she spots Rex falling off his board again.

We both laugh, and she rolls her eyes at me.

"If Rex survives this morning, we'll be back out here at five o'clock doing our happy hour thing again. Join us if you need a break from writing! And bring that hunk of a man with you, if he's free too." She gives me a mischievous grin, raising her brows.

I give her a half-grin, shielding my eyes from the sun, while I watch Rex take another faceful of saltwater.

If he wasn't the man renting the townhome on the other side of my wall, this whole crazy notion of me running away to Hawaii on sabbatical to finish my script would have been working out perfectly.

CHAPTER 23

A few hours later, and I'm still dying to hear from Dom after he's done working. Then I hear the heavy door slide open in the other unit.

I peek over my laptop for a clear view of the lanai, just in time to see Rex and Juju slip out toward the deck railing. She turns to give him a quick peck on the lips, but he pulls her back in, his hand wringing in the length of her hair, wrapping his other arm tightly around her tiny waist. He presses his body into hers, like he can't wait to take her back behind closed doors. To tear her clothing off, to lose himself when he pushes into her again and again.

Woof.

I shake my head, trying to rid myself of that visualization. I shouldn't be watching this. I send Dom a text without thinking.

Rex and Juju are playing tonsil hockey on my balcony. Wanna make them jealous?

I watch and wait for his little text bubbles to appear, hoping he responds right away. Wondering if that was too forward. Maybe the real reason I'm here is for personal growth that stems from pure torture?

I wait another beat, then send him a second text.

Kidding . . . kinda? 😒

It's the best I can muster right now to take the edge off my first text.

Juju is giggling when I hear their door slide shut again with them inside.

I'm about to go jog down the beach, just to get away from whatever noise is about to start up next door, when my phone finally pings with a text. It's from Dom.

Can't really blame them. Hawaii inspires extreme levels of tonsil hockey

I roll my eyes, about to toss the phone on the couch, but it chimes again.

Have you put your feet in the water at all since you got here?

I smile. *Getting warmer.* I respond:

Not yet

Almost immediately, the phone pings again.

That's your mistake.

Before I can ask Dom what he thinks I should do in the ocean, another text comes in, sending a tornado of anticipation rolling straight through me.

Pick you up in 15. Get your suit on.

Before I can think twice, I write back.

I'm all yours

CHAPTER 24

Dom's idea of "picking me up" was to meet me at the back door with two surfboards. We walk down to the water's edge, to the exact spot where I watched Rex nearly drown himself earlier this morning.

I'm bobbing on one of the boards in the water, staring up at the shared lanai connecting our two townhouse units. The units look so much smaller from down here in the water, and I have no interest being anywhere near that deck when Rex and Juju emerge sporting a radiant post-sex glow in an hour or so. Maybe sooner. My mind starts to drift when I imagine walking out of my side of the townhouse with Dom, both of us sporting our own post-sex glow . . .

"Eyes on me, not the house, Liv!" Dom barks in my direction.

Gladly.

He was fully clothed yesterday, but today, out here on the water, he's back to wearing my favorite look on him so far — nothing but a clingy pair of yellow board shorts. I try not to stare, but I'd much rather be balanced on top of *him* right now, instead of this surfboard.

I eye the water around us for shark fins.

"Are you sure there aren't any out here?"

"Nope. Definitely not sure about that."

"What?" I yelp, lifting my knees up off the board.

"It's their ocean, not ours." He shrugs, then breaks into a grin.

I pull my feet up and push my knees into my chest, immediately losing my balance. I should've never watched *Shark Week* before coming here. What was I thinking?

"Whoa, there." Dom reaches out to steady my board. His eyes practically glow with the sun reflecting against them. "You've got to keep your legs on either side of that until you lie on your stomach to paddle out. You'll fall off if you sit like that."

I drop my knees to either side of the board again and let my calves dangle off the sides.

The water is warmer than I thought it would be, and I can see straight down to the white sandy bottom, like the whole ocean is filled to the brim with warm tap water. A few brightly colored fish swim by, all canary yellow with stripes of cobalt blue. I wiggle my fuchsia-painted toenails under the surface, saying a silent prayer that anything with teeth prefers yellow fish to pink toes.

"Just focus on catching your first wave. There's a decent set about to roll in. Eyes up!"

I obey his instructions, riding over the next round of waves while sitting upright on my wobbly board. A bigger set comes in next, and I flip on my stomach for this round, managing to balance my way through each one while they surge beneath me. I'm feeling more comfortable when the last wave disappears on the shore.

Dom floats beside me the whole time, holding onto the edge of my board to keep me within arm's reach, telling me about the first time he tried riding the waves with his dad, when he was only four years old, growing up in California.

I'm actually starting to enjoy myself, especially watching my gorgeous instructor balance easily on his board next to me. If this is surfing, I'm totally here for it. Not to mention he couldn't look more delicious, all dripping wet, with the sun bouncing across his body.

"On this next set, I want you to feel the pull of the water right before one starts rolling in. When it nearly drags your board out, that's when you start paddling in toward the shore," he tells me.

I watch him flip to his stomach and start paddling, right before the next wave gets to him. The surge of water practically picks up his board and starts pushing it toward the shorebreak, gaining momentum beneath him. He's not even paddling anymore, but the water is thrusting him toward the sand as he glides effortlessly on top. Then he hops to his feet in one motion and rides all the way in. Spinning around to grin at me before doing a reverse push-up back down to his stomach, he paddles toward me again. His back muscles strain as both arms work the water beneath him. Sparkling droplets of water roll off his skin, thick hair slicked back, green eyes glowing.

I'm officially turned on.

"Okay!" I shout after him. "I'm gonna catch this next one! Hang on!"

I maneuver onto my stomach and wait until the water starts pulling me back toward the deep. When I feel it grab hold of the board, I start paddling as hard as I can toward shore. The water propels the board forward with a jolt, and I know I've caught it.

"I got it! I got it!" I start yelling at Dom. Then I do exactly what I watched him do. Hold onto the board tight, hopping my feet up in one swift motion, but as soon as my feet hit the surface of the board, I tip sideways, rolling head over foot toward the bottom, swept up in the force of the water.

Saltwater rushes into my face, instantly burning my eyes and nose. I find my footing in the sand beneath me and shoot myself up out of the wave, taking a breath and spitting out water. My throat stings from swallowing it, thick with salt.

"Well, that didn't work," I sputter, trying to grin through the searing pain.

Before I can catch my breath, Dom shouts, "Behind you, Liv!" I turn to face where he's pointing, but it's too late. I'm hit by a wall of water again. This one picks me up with it. Rolling me head over foot toward shore, flown like a beached whale across the sand. My hair flops in front of my face and saltwater pours from my nose like a faucet. The Velcro strap around my ankle tugs gently as my board laps back into the water a few feet away, like it's begging me to take it for another ride.

There's too much saltwater in my eyes to see Dom yet, but I can hear him laughing, coming closer. I rub and squint one stinging eyeball open to glare at him, ignoring the burn, then shut both eyes tight and rub the burning water out again. I'm sure my mascara is smeared all over my face. I don't know why I even put it on this morning, other than out of sheer habit.

I roll over toward the sound of his laughter and sit up.

"Olivia, your swim top. It's . . ." Dom has stopped laughing but there's a definite smile to his voice. "Your top needs to be, ah, moved."

A cool breeze grazes my nipple as I get my eyes open to see what he's talking about. I immediately push both hands to my chest.

One side is definitely bare.

The tiny triangle of fabric must have shifted off my nipple, exposing half my chest while I plummeted head over foot to dry land. I shove the material back over the rosy peak of flesh, then adjust both sides of the swim top to make sure I'm fully covered — my eyes are still squeezed shut. I manage to get one open.

Dom is kneeling beside me with his board tucked under one arm.

I'm mortified. But at least he looks like he's just enjoyed the show.

"That was a solid try," he assures me, then chuckles, wiping the saltwater from his own eyes. He's either caught a quick sunburn, or he's turning red from catching me without a top. Either way, it makes me smile.

"You rode the wave. Next time you just have to stay on top of it."

He grabs my board, which is still lapping gently in the shallow waves, then kneels down in front of me on the sand again.

A big smile spreads across his face, water dripping from his chin.

His pale green eyes look translucent against his skin in the sunlight. So close, I could practically taste the salt on those lips — if he let me.

"Okay, you made that look so much easier than it was." I sniff more saltwater, then pinch my nose to get it to stop running again. The fire in my eyes has subsided enough that I can squint up at him without any pain.

He leans over me, and I'm dwarfed by his physique, blocking the sun from my face, along with the view of the rental units. Browned muscles glisten with a mixture of sweat and saltwater, while tiny specks of golden amber pool in his mossy eyes.

"Next time I'll wear a more sturdy bathing suit," I deadpan.

He erupts into laughter, sending my stomach fluttering at the sound.

"Don't worry about that wardrobe malfunction." He says it like it's no big deal, but it makes me wince. "Everybody does that their first time. I've seen more nipples out here than you would believe."

"Oh, so that's why you suggested it?" I nudge him on the arm, chuckling, but my fist slips off his slick skin. I might suck at surfing, but the proximity of Dom's nearly naked body is making me feel committed to the sport. I could do this every day if I get to look at him, dripping all over and close enough to touch.

"Nah, that was just luck." He grins. "I brought you out here so you could do what you came here to do."

I flinch, remembering all the work I left undone back at the rental. "Write my script?"

"No, live your life. And forget about who's watching."

He reaches up to my face — my heart races in response.

But instead of pulling me in for a kiss, he pulls a long, slimy strand of seaweed off the top of my head.

CHAPTER 25

My lips are so desperate for him after last night that they practically ache when he's bent this close to me. I shoot my eyes up toward the rentals to see if Rex has made it outside yet, which would give us both a reason to amp up the physical chemistry between us right now.

But the deck is still empty. Dammit, Rex. No luck.

"Let's get you on another wave." Dom hops to his feet. He reaches out a hand to help me and I grab it. Then he effortlessly pulls me up, wrapping both arms around me, quickly kissing the top of my head before bounding off toward the water again.

I look up at the townhouses, expecting to see Rex emerging now, but they still haven't come outside, which means that quick kiss wasn't just for show.

Or was it?

His back muscles ripple in and out as he moves, dripping with saltwater, making me want to mount him right here.

But another wave?

"Wait, what? No. I think I got the full experience on that one. My eyes are going to be stinging until next Sunday as it is. I'll just watch you."

There's nothing else I'd rather be watching anyway.

He turns and makes a funny face at me, like he can't believe I'd turn down another wave.

"But you're already wet."

I stifle a laugh. *If he only knew.*

"What does that have to do with surfing?" I squint at him, blinking innocently in the sun.

He laughs out loud, then holds his hand out toward me. "Come on, try another. Don't give up before you get the hang of it."

I stand where I am, weighing the pros and cons of getting another face full of saltwater, or exposing my nipples for a second time. Dom has seen me in my underwear, and now with my chest half-exposed. I eye the knot on his swim trunks, wondering when it's going to be his turn to show me something new.

"Plus, you've gotten a feel for it now." He's somehow hotter when he wants something, with his brows curled together like that. It makes me want to fight him a little bit more.

I don't budge.

"Get in the water!" His voice rises in volume. It's a command, not a suggestion anymore, but he breaks into a loose grin. "Come on, Liv, you know you want to!"

He's standing with his feet in the shallow end of the surf, a washboard of abs accented by the sun dipping lower behind him. "Get in the water, or I'm going to make you get in the water!" He takes a wider stance in the sand, like a bull about to charge a crimson flag.

Then he plants his feet and breaks into another ear-to-ear smile that nearly melts me on the spot. His skin's practically shimmering in the sun. Dom bends at the waist and smacks the surf, sending a spray of water flying toward me.

I dodge it, then grab my board and race back at him, laughing.

I repeat his words in my head — *Live your life, and forget about who's watching.*

He's right. I might have come here in order to get away from everything back home. But now that I'm here, I know that I need to unleash myself from a lot more than that. Do whatever it takes to feel like myself again. Or maybe to feel like myself for the first real time. Free from New York. From strangers' opinions. Free from Rex, even if he could appear behind me at any moment now.

Most of all, I need to free myself *from* myself. *Me.* My biggest critic of all.

It's okay to not get this right.

"Okay, okay." I laugh, not caring anymore if Rex and Juju see me fall when they head out for cocktails on their deck.

I don't want to be afraid anymore.

I want to get messy. I want to make mistakes.

Dom races into the surf, diving head first under the first oncoming wave. Watching his joy while he plays in the water — like he doesn't have a care in the world — it's contagious.

The gravity of anything heavy back on land dissolves in this turquoise slice of paradise. I race after him, suddenly buoyant and unmoored as we paddle out into the ocean together.

CHAPTER 26

We surf until after the sun dips low across the horizon. If you can call what I did surfing. I got a few good rides in, though most of the time I teetered off the board before it hit the shore. I didn't even notice that Rex and Juju came out on the balcony, until I heard Juju cheering for me when I finally managed to ride a long wave in — standing up all the way before gracefully jumping off on the sand. I did a little bow toward the two figures on the deck in the distance, twirling back to the water at the end and running in with my board under my arm to catch another.

The last time I felt this uninhibited and free I was just a kid.

When did that change?

Dom stayed in the shallower water with me, even though he could surf circles around me in the deeper water if he wanted.

When I needed a break, I'd straddle my board on top of the shallow end and watch him. The way the outline of his body turned into a silhouette as the sun sank low enough to cast blinding sunlight across his body. I can't remember the last time I saw anyone this happy. His laughter ringing out each time he rides in, the definition in his hips and arms making my heart vibrate — like it takes everything in me just to stay silent and still.

I, on the other hand, became an expert at popping back out of the foamy sea so I wouldn't get demolished by the next oncoming wave, which I consider to be excellent progress.

Dom was right. The ocean was calling me, and she wasn't going to relent. I needed her today more than I thought I might. Getting out of my head and out of that townhouse was the best thing I could have done for myself.

I should make this a morning ritual.

"I might turn this into a hobby while I'm here." I pick up a handful of dry, hot sand before letting it slowly drain through my fingers. Juju and Rex are still sitting on the balcony behind us, two little figures hunched in the distance. Knowing we have an audience has made us both more brazen, sliding back into the role as two actors who are openly falling for each other.

We're settled back on the sandy shoreline now, our boards resting on dry land beside us. I run my hands across the silky white grains, like pillows of powdered sugar strewn across a hot skillet. I pinch more of it and strain it out between my fingers. It feels like a silk scarf tracing along my skin.

The sun is well on its way to disappearing, casting long shadows across the scattered trees and swaying palms. It sets early here, so we don't have to stay up late to catch the final rays — an epic light show of pinks and golds each evening. The ocean has started to calm down too, barely lapping against the shore now. Like she knows it's almost closing time. Time for everyone to take a moment to enjoy the sunset while being gently lulled to sleep by her song.

Other families and couples, old and young, are settling into the soft, sugary beach as far as I can see in both directions, ready for Mother Nature's final gift of the day.

I'm struck by the notion that we're all inexplicably drawn to this as humans. The water, the sun. Casting our eyes outward across the gentle waves, as we slow down to participate in one of the world's oldest rituals.

Everything about this place is pure magic.

I'm overcome with the same feelings I had last night at Cliff's.

Happiness.

Peace.

Clarity.

Like I'm meant to be here. Like I'd repeat every humiliating thing that happened to me to bring me to this exact moment. I belong, without even trying, which is possibly the best type of belonging I've ever felt.

I don't even care that my scalp feels like it has a thousand grains of sand smashed into it, or that I've wiped away any last shred of mascara I had on this morning. In the golden glow of the sunset, I feel beautiful — raw — and, more than anything else, alive. More alive than I might have ever felt.

"You enjoyed yourself that much?" Dom's eyes look like soft green pools in the molten sunlight cast across his face. I could get lost in them forever if I'm not careful.

"Yeah, I really did. Thanks for getting me out of my head today." I steal a peek at his lips, wondering what it would be like to kiss him right now. Salty and sweet and delicious.

I close my eyes and tilt my head back to the sun, feeling the heat pour through my eyelids as I inhale its warmth. The last rays of the day feel good. Really good. Cleansing.

"I can't tell you how weird it is to watch the sunset while a guy I almost got engaged to watches it behind me with someone else."

Dom turns to catch sight of them, stiffening his spine a bit when he turns back around.

I don't bother looking. I already know Juju and Rex are still back there, sitting on patio chairs, overlooking the same breathtaking view, with our silhouettes pressed up against the hot pink horizon in front of them. I wonder what Rex is thinking after watching me play on the beach with Dom all evening. Or if he was too wrapped up in Juju to notice.

I'm now starting to question if I even care. There were so many moments that I forgot Rex was watching us tonight, and those were the best moments of all. Snippets of time that I could just soak up the happiness I felt without having to focus on showing interest in Dom just to make Rex jealous. Moments I didn't want to remind myself that Dom was just putting on an act for him, too.

Every time his eyes caught mine when I stood up on my board, pure adrenaline bounced back and forth between us as the water rushed me forward.

Or when he pulled me in for a slick hug in the shallow surf, our bodies slid across each other, before breaking apart again to catch another wave.

I kept waiting for him to kiss me, which would have been our first kiss right in front of Rex. But it hadn't come. Not yet.

"I forgot they were even there," he says, quietly. A faint smile tugs the corners of his lips.

I dart my eyes up to his, but he's watching the waves, lost in thought.

"You forgot they were there?" I ask, wondering how that's possible since this whole charade is supposed to be for them.

He runs a hand through his hair, droplets of water flying off, getting lost in the heat of the sun. Then he swallows hard and turns to study my eyes for a moment, taking a deep inhale, almost like he has something important to say. I hold my breath until he lets it drain out of him, tossing a handful of sand at the water's moving edge.

"I guess it's easy to get swept up in the moment," he says, smiling so faintly that it looks like it might be a joke.

"Right," I say, my voice a bit hoarse.

We both stare out at the water, letting the sunset fill our silence.

I wish I was forward enough to ask if all these moments between us are truly just part of the charade, the game we're playing to make Rex jealous, but I'm not sure I want to hear the answer to that question just yet. Not when I still have hope that any of this might mean a bit more to him, like it does for me.

"Can't be easy," Dom says, looking at my lips. "You're pretty brave to stay here, considering what that guy put you through." He pats my hand for a second, then slips it off again. I close my eyes briefly, wishing he'd let it linger there a little bit longer. "I hope this isn't weird to say, but I can't really picture the two of you together."

My eyes pop back open. "Really? Why do you say that?" People seemed as shocked as I was when Rex said no to my proposal. Especially my parents.

"I mean, he just seems kind of . . . bro-ey to me. All bravado and surface-level shit. But you seem . . . I dunno. Different than that."

"Not bro-ey?" I laugh, pushing against his bicep with my elbow. It feels warmer than the sun — I scoot closer to feel his body heat all the way down my bare side. Then I glance behind us where Rex is sitting. Both of us in the company of someone new. Someone who isn't anything like who we were to each other back home. Thousands of miles away from what we were together such a short time ago.

"You seem to be filled with dreams that go much deeper than surface level," Dom continues. His eyes stay on mine when he says it. Then he licks his lips, just a flicker of his tongue coming into view, making it impossible to complete a full thought, much less a sentence.

I look back out toward the water.

"How so?" I'm curious what he's noticed about me in the short time we've known each other.

"You have this script you're chasing the ending of, halfway across the world from home. Scratching a lifelong itch that most people might have given up on by now, and, honestly, I don't know many women who would pack up everything they have and move to an island that they've never been to, completely alone for two months. You have some serious *cojones*."

"I never thought of myself as brave. I only saw this trip as a way to escape my worst moment. My ultimate failure."

"That's not what I see when I look at you."

His eyes burn into mine, like he's seeing the most secret parts of me. The ones I keep hidden from everyone — sometimes even from myself.

This part is real, I realize.

Rex can't hear what Dom is saying from way up there.

Breaking away from his eyes, I stare out at the lazy surf reaching higher and higher across the sand in front of us. The tide must be coming in. The sun is almost gone now. Just a wedding ring of gold radiating out above the horizon, slipping away as quickly as the seconds tick by. The sliver of sunlight burns into my eyes, searing the image behind my lids each time I blink.

He continues, "I think some people have everything they need at home, so they never leave. Other people have to move away from home to find whatever it is that they couldn't get there. You came here to find something. To do something brave and new. I came here to leave."

His confession catches me by surprise and I stare at him, trying to piece him together.

"Leave what?" I ask.

"Who I was back home. What I was connected to. The way people saw me."

"I can't imagine you being anything but who you are. You seem to be completely comfortable in your own skin."

"Here, yes. But, back home, I'm different too. I get it. It's hard to change who you are *now*, when everyone just wants to see you for who you *were*."

"You haven't seen me back home in New York." I pick up a new handful of sand and drain it through my fingers. "Something about this place pulls a new side out of me, I think. I just feel different here."

"Or, maybe, you're just different *there*," he says. "Back in New York."

Dom gently takes my hand in his, flecks of rough sand pressing between our skin. Then he dusts off his palm so it's softer against mine. He squeezes, leaving his hand there, like he's forgotten to pull it away.

I flick my eyes to his, then to the balcony behind us.

He smiles, still not pulling his hand away, while a firm understanding washes over his face. He looks back up at the lanai, then squeezes my hand tighter, so I couldn't let go, even if I wanted to.

"I'm not letting you go, if that's what you're wondering," he adds. "Unless—"

"No, I don't want you to," I interrupt, before his thought can even be completed. I want to add, *and not just because they're watching*, but I can't make the words come out. The sting of Rex's humiliating rejection still hurts to my core. I'm not ready for another blow so soon if Dom is simply brilliant at acting the part.

He inches closer to me on the sand, wrapping an arm around my shoulders. Then I rest my head against his chest. His skin is heated, like the last rays of the sun, and I snuggle in closer, enjoying the feeling of his body against mine, even if it's all for show.

"I don't know what this place does to me," I tell him. "But whatever it is, I like it."

"Maybe you've always had it in you. But all this?" He waves his free hand toward the rose-colored sky. "Maybe all this just helps you remember who you are. Who you've always been. And something along the way — maybe that guy up there — just made you forget."

Then he slowly leans over and plants a gentle kiss right on my lips. It's sweet at first, but grows in urgency, like we're the only two people for miles around.

When he pulls back, his brows are furrowed, like he can't decide if that was the right move or not. Then he whispers into my lips.

"Is this okay?"

Everything in me screams for more, much more than we can do on the beach.

I wrap my arms around his neck and pull him back in, answering with another kiss of my own.

His kisses grow harder, both of us acting like we can't bear to stop, until we're both lying back against the sand, the crook of his elbow cradling my head like a pillow.

All I can hear is the gentle lapping of the waves. They're breaking coolly across our toes as he holds my face in his hand, gently tasting and tugging at my lips with his, each kiss lasting a bit longer than the last.

My body aches for him to touch me in places I know he can't, carry me behind closed doors if he must. He pauses and shoots his eyes up toward the balcony once more. I arch my back to follow his gaze, heart sinking, remembering the only reason we're here.

The sun is nearly gone now, just a pat of butter drizzled on the horizon.

"They're gone," he whispers, still frozen above me. His hand is still wrapped around my hip, his thumb gently grazing the sensitive patch of bare skin just above my waistline.

I stare into his eyes — he hovers over me.

Both of us breathe heavily.

My mind is completely blank other than the feeling of him, hard and strong against me.

The last thing I want to do is stop.

Dom closes his eyes and brushes the tip of his nose against mine, our lips teasing one another, just a fraction of an inch away.

The heat of his breath finds the back of my throat. My heart hammers right beneath his.

Then he squeezes the curve of my hip and groans, like he's trying to decide what to do next.

He kisses me once more on the lips, a feather-light kiss compared to the type we've just shared, and drops his head, pressing his forehead into my sandy shoulder.

"I didn't realize this would be so hard," he says, gripping my hip harder, as if trying to regain control of his next move.

I smile into his hair, biting my lip again while he still can't see me.

"I should have known you'd be a phenomenal actress." He pulls back to look into my eyes, searching for an answer, as if that wasn't a statement, but rather, a question. I close my eyes for another kiss, but his lips stop short, hovering just over the top of mine, waiting.

"I've never been able to act before," I whisper breathlessly into his lips.

Then I keep my eyes closed and force my smile away, hoping he leans in to kiss me one more time.

But, to my surprise, I feel him roll off me instead.

CHAPTER 27

I'm two mai tais in and Dom is starting to look more and more like a blurry combo of Zac Efron and Jason Momoa. At least, when it comes to his stature, and the intensity of his green eyes.

After the sun disappeared on the beach — and he left me thoroughly confused about what's real and what's part of this game — Dom suggested we grab a late dinner at Cliff's again. This time just us, without his friends.

Now, the acoustic musician in the corner is playing a slowed-down version of "Brown Eyed Girl" while I watch the happy faces of everyone around us. With Dom sitting close by, no one has dared come near me or make a smartass comment about that clip. For the first time in weeks, I feel totally relaxed, knowing both he and Cliff would jump to my rescue if I needed them.

I turn to him, grabbing hold of his pie-tin-sized bicep.

"This is why I came here," I announce.

He grins. "You came for the mai tais or the music? Both are pretty good, right?"

He takes my drink and pushes the straw aside, taking a sip. He's been nursing a Kona Cream Ale all evening, but every once in a while, he steals a gulp of my mixed drink. If anyone else was doing that, I'd tell them to get their own. Even Rex. But for some reason, when Dom does it, I kind of like it. In fact, I kind of *love* it.

I laugh. "No. *This.*" I dramatically circle my arms around the room, then hold my hand out toward the soft waves rolling in under the moon, just past the bar's edge. "I've never been to a place that so easily feels like . . ." I try to come up with the right word. "Well, for lack of a better way to say it, this all feels *familiar*. But I've never been to this island before, so I don't know how that is."

The flames from the torches near our table are reflected in Dom's eyes, making them flicker with firelight.

"It sneaks up on you, doesn't it?" He smiles faintly, his eyes drinking me in, and I swallow hard. I don't know if it's the drinks or the ambiance in here, but he looks downright dangerous tonight. His darkened tan from our day of surfing is setting off the gold firelight dancing in his eyes.

"Cliff's mai tais?" I giggle, holding the straw between my teeth. "Yeah. He makes them pretty strong."

"Well, yeah, those too." He laughs, and I memorize the sound so I can play it back in my mind later tonight. "But no, I mean this place. The whole island. There's something about being here that's always felt like home to me. It's why I still call it home. Every time I leave, I just want to come back."

"I was ready to get on a plane and not look back a few days ago," I remind him.

"Why else do you think I asked you out? I had to keep you around, right?"

My stomach twists at the words *asked you out*. His hand grips the bottle, then wipes a drip of condensation swiftly up the side. The humidity in the air makes everything sweat here, even the drinks.

"I'm glad I agreed to come here with you that first night. Even if it was all just an act for Rex."

I hold my breath, hoping he tells me I'm wrong. That he really just asked me because deep down he wanted to.

He leans over to take another sip of my cocktail, pushing the straw — the straw that had just been in my mouth a moment ago — aside with his tongue, while I try not to stare. His fingers are long and strong. I bite my lip and look away.

His mouth hovers over the rim of my glass, lips parting with a grin, as if reliving an inside joke in his head.

"I'm glad you agreed to it too," he says, grinning wider, more mischievously.

I can't drink him in enough, like everything about him is intoxicating after today. Like one kiss, one make-out session, will never be enough.

He finishes the sip, sets my glass down, and grabs a stray pen Cliff left on the counter. He starts twirling it around his fingers. I haven't seen anyone do that with a pen since high school. Back when we all wrote everything by hand and always had a pen within reach. "Believe me when I say that taking you out to my friend's bar that night was the least I could do to help you forget about your ex." Each tendon in his forearm ripples every time he flips the pen over.

"Yeah, you have a lot of sucking up to do for making me stay on this God-awful island." I shove his shoulder playfully, but it doesn't move. The man is like a boulder. He grabs my knee again, like he did in the car, squeezing it just once. But his hand on my bare skin, along with that heart-stopping look he's giving me? It's enough to make my pulse throb between my thighs.

The solo guitar player starts strumming an old Cat Stevens song, adding his own Hawaiian flair to the familiar tune. It's a sweet song I recognize from my childhood — my shoulders instantly uncurl from my ears. As if this scene here tonight could get any more perfect.

We listen to him play. The break in conversation feels strangely comfortable for two people who only met a few days ago, but, in this moment, it feels like I've known him a lot longer.

"This song reminds me of my dad." I lean into him when I say it, then pull away. The musician shifts seamlessly to "Morning Has Broken" without missing a note. It's one of my favorites. "He always sang this one to my mom while flipping pancakes at the stove. Every Sunday morning." I smile, picturing the way my parents openly shared their love for each other. "He still does whenever I visit. They've been together thirty-two years, and counting."

"Is your whole family back in New York?" Dom takes a sip from his beer — I watch his lips curve around the bottle.

I nod, smiling. "My mom and dad supported me coming out here. They've always stood behind me. Everything I've ever done. Even my producer's ridiculous idea for me to propose to Rex live on air." I shudder. The version of me who went along with that whole thing seems so removed from how I feel now.

I take a sip of Dom's beer bottle without asking him first.

He watches me swallow and I lick my lips like I haven't noticed his eyes are still on me.

"Are your siblings back in New York too?"

"It's just the three of us. No siblings."

"Only child, huh? Explains a lot." He smiles wider, taking his beer bottle back out of my hand. "You were not going to give up easily the other day on the phone."

I smack him on the arm, but grab my cocktail glass off the counter, trying not to notice when our hands brush in the exchange. The butterflies storming my stomach make it impossible to ignore.

Before becoming single again, I'd been with one person so long that I'd almost forgotten what it felt like to desire someone for the very first time. It's stirring something up in me that's been lying dormant for years. Though stirring seems too tame of a word. Unleashing might better describe what I'm feeling.

"I like to think I'm just assertive," I say. "New Yorker and all that."

He pushes his shoulder into mine, but this time neither of us shift our bodies away. "So why didn't you just take a break and live with your parents then?" he asks. "Why come all the way out here by yourself?"

"The film script I'm writing is set in Hawaii, so I wanted to immerse myself in the island. The culture. The people. *This*." I wave my arms around the bar. "I love *this*. I've always been fascinated by the idea of this place, but I needed to immerse myself in it if I was going to write realistically about it."

"That's it?" He leans forward, looking at me suspiciously. As if he wants to say more, dig deeper, but for some reason he stops short. "There's really no other reason you wound up here?"

"That's it," I confirm. "What other reason would there be for following through with such a completely harebrained idea?"

He studies my face intensely, like he's looking for something other than the simple reason I've given him.

I turn back to the musician when he starts strumming "Somewhere Over the Rainbow" next. Tears prickle behind my eyes. The last time I heard this song, I was listening to it for inspiration, during the exact second I clicked *Confirm* on my Airbnb reservation to set this whole plan into motion.

"I guess there was one more reason for coming here." I turn to face him again, once I'm confident my eyes have cleared.

"Okay. Lay it on me." His face looks steely, like he's gearing up to hear something bad. I can't figure out why me booking his rental seems to be such a suspicious sticking point for him.

"What is it?" I ask, unable to ignore it any longer. This is the second time he's acted funny about why I came here and booked his townhome. "Every time I talk about my reasons for coming to the island you look like you want to call my bluff. If you don't believe me, just say it."

"No, go on," he says stiffly, not moving. "I want to know."

"My reason might sound ridiculous," I tell him. "Those mai tais are stronger than they taste. I'm not usually so open."

"It won't sound silly. I might even understand. Everyone has their reasons."

I watch him take another sip from my glass, wondering if any part of his kisses or subtle touches have been real, or if every moment, every touch, every lingering look he gives me is all just part of the show he's been putting on as my fake boyfriend. If that's the case, he deserves an Oscar.

"Do you ever feel like your life is going at warp speed?" I ask, not pausing for an answer. "Like you're running as fast as you can, to do everything you're supposed to do, right when you're supposed to do it?"

He continues watching me so intensely that my heart palpitates like it's skipped a beat.

But I go on. "And for what? To get to the finish line faster?"

He flips the pen over his thumb without leaving my eyes — it lands right back in his grip. "More than you know."

"When my entire career went haywire, I realized that I didn't like the path I was on anymore. I hadn't liked it for some time."

"Is that when you decided to try to break into film?"

I nod. "Kind of. I've been working on it for years, but I'm using this sabbatical to give it my first real try. That's not the only reason though."

I pause, watching his face to see if any of this is making sense to him.

"Then why else are you here, Liv? Just tell me."

The way Dom studies me, it's like I'm the most interesting person in the room. His attention makes me feel like I want to cower and explode — both at once — so I don't disappoint him when he realizes that there's truly nothing *fascinating* about me at all.

I take a deep breath before answering.

"To run," I tell him.

He leans in closer, studying me. He wasn't kidding about making the woman he's with feel like she's the only one in existence.

"Run from what?"

"Everything . . ."

"Go on."

It all comes tumbling out.

"Everything I thought I'd love about my life but never did. I've lived my entire existence doing exactly what I was supposed to do, exactly how it should be done. I got my degree in journalism from NYU, then got a job at UBN, and worked my way up to the news desk. I dated the type of guy my parents would adore, and when my producer asked if I wanted to propose to him on the air to further my career and land the perfect marriage, I did it. I never thought in a million years that Rex would say no. It was the *right next step*."

"You didn't actually want to marry that asshat?" He grips the bottle again, running his hand up the slick side.

I smile weakly.

"In hindsight, I don't think I did. But, do you want to know the weirdest part?" I ask.

"The fact that your producer asked you to do that whole thing live on the air and you said yes?" Dom side-eyes me, which makes me laugh a little at my own expense.

He finally cracks a smile, too.

"No. What's weird is that, when Rex said no, of course, I was humiliated. That part was written all over my face, obviously. It was that after the cameras stopped rolling and I was back in my dressing room . . ." I pause. I've never told anyone this. Not even Abby. "I felt kind of *relieved*."

Our corner of the bar fades away as I wait for him to answer.

"Relieved?" Dom leans away from where our shoulders were touching. He massages his sharp jawline like he's figuring out a puzzle scattered across the table. Knowing that I'm the puzzle makes me want to keep talking, but only if he keeps looking at me like that.

"I think proposing to Rex felt like the next '*right*' thing to do. Even though, obviously, it was totally wrong. I loved Rex." Something flashes in Dom's eyes when those words come out of my mouth. "But, if I'm being honest, I don't think I was ready either. My producer asked me to do it to further my career. She knew I'd been with him a long time, and she was curious if I'd be up for it. She was sure the clip would boost our ratings. I'm sure she was thrilled when the ratings skyrocketed — more than either of us would ever have predicted." I sigh. "I've always had my eye on the prize. The next best thing for me. I thought doing what my producer wanted was the ticket to my next promotion."

"And coming here? Was that the next 'right' thing?"

I shake my head. "Absolutely not. Probably the exact opposite. Taking a huge financial risk on something that may never pay off isn't smart. But I think coming here was the only way for me to hit pause on my life."

I take another sip of water and push what's left of my mai tai toward Dom. Whatever's in there feels like it's laced with truth serum, so I don't care if he finishes it for me. In fact, I want him to finish it — maybe then some hard truths can start spilling out of him too.

"I wanted to try something that looks nothing like my life back in New York."

Dom leans his forearms on the table, closing the space between us, sucking all the air out of my lungs.

His brows draw together before he speaks again.

"What would you want your life to look like then? If you could pick it off a shelf, like you're shopping for a new life in a store, which model would you choose?"

I consider his question. I've never thought of it like that before. But, clear as day, a vision of the life I want instantly pops into my head, and starts tumbling from my lips, fueled by the liquid courage I've consumed tonight.

"I want to tell stories that make people laugh. Or cry. Or laugh until they cry."

128

His smile grows wider, urging me to go on.

"I want to sit in an overgrown garden somewhere, wearing some gorgeous granny-chic kaftan that makes me feel beautiful, with a million gold bangles jangling up both my arms while I feverishly type out the next incredible story. The one people want to watch twice. And I want to write hundreds of them. Until my hair is long and gray. Most of all, I want to be in love. Not just with someone I think my parents would approve of. But truly, madly, deeply in love. I want to get off the rat race treadmill too, and fall in love with my entire existence. Live in some quiet corner of the world and just soak up everything that makes life beautiful and worth living."

The corners of his mouth curl up toward the stars.

He sits quietly for a minute, letting everything I've said sink in.

I shift on my chair, feeling like I've just laid myself out naked before him. Unsure of where all that came from. I can't imagine telling any of the guys I've met back in New York something so personal right off the bat. This place has put a spell on me.

"So this trip was meant to be your first 'wrong' move?" he asks. "Toward the life you'd choose off a shelf?"

"Maybe?" I raise my brows at him, then shrug, scrunching up my nose. "Does that sound crazy?"

"Not even a little bit. It sounds kind of perfect, actually."

I slide back in my chair and study the faces around us. A few yards down, Cliff leans against the counter, chatting back and forth with someone he knows before letting out with a hearty laugh. The musician has switched to Bob Marley's "One Love," while a table of college-age kids next to us start to sway and sing every word together. A couple sitting at a nearby table lean in for a quick peck on the lips, cartoon hearts filling their eyes.

Everything about this moment makes me feel more intimately connected to the world than a thousand days of my regularly scheduled life.

I turn back to Dom, drinking in his green eyes while they dance together in the firelight.

"I don't think I've ever done anything in my whole life that could be classified as so wrongfully right."

Then I lean across the table and do exactly what I've been dying to do since he rolled away from me on the beach. I kiss him softly, until the song comes to an end and another one begins.

CHAPTER 28

When my alarm goes off the next morning, I'm already lying awake in bed. I didn't sleep very well last night. I kept tossing around what Dom had said, shifting back and forth from hip to hip, pillow to pillow. Frustrated that I couldn't stop his words from playing through my head over and over, wondering if any of this is real to him.

Maybe you're just different there.

Maybe this place helps you remember who you've always been.

Something along the way just made you forget.

I picture Dom sitting on a New York City subway back home. The grayness of winter reflecting in his eyes, instead of flickering firelight and sunsets.

He would be different there too.

On one hand, I'm amazed that he seems to see me so clearly, and so quickly.

On the other hand, I'm not sure I'm ready to face the woman he sees in me, deep down. There's a painful, tugging feeling emerging in me that, once I let her out, she won't go away again without a fight. And that's not a fight I'm sure I can win.

My entire life is back in New York.

But it seems like my entire soul is emerging here.

I toss the covers back and grab my robe from where I left it — draped across my dresser — and cinch it tightly across my waist. Sand crunches under my feet when I walk into the living room, which is not something I'm sure I'll ever get used to. I've already vacuumed the whole place twice, but I can see another round taking over my plans for the day.

My eyes land on the surfboard leaning against the deck railing outside while I wait for my coffee to brew. I forgot Dom had insisted on leaving it there so I could start my day with another mind-clearing round of waves this morning.

I mean, why the hell not?

Dom was right about getting in the water yesterday. If I simply wanted to hide out and write this script, I could have chosen a cheaper location. I can do both.

"She's calling," I mutter to Pru, staring out at the ocean. It's deep blue today, growing into lighter shades of turquoise as my eyes follow a wave all the way into shore. "Alright, alright. I'm coming."

I grin, knowing the call of the waves won't quiet down until I give in. Might as well go now, before I get in deep with scriptwriting.

* * *

By mid-morning, I'm dripping wet and struggling to walk back up to the rental. The sand is deep and my arms feel like Jell-O after an hour of paddling bigger sets of waves than yesterday. The longboard is like dead weight under my arm so I stop to take a breather, puffing to catch my breath. This was much easier when Dom carried both boards for our adventure yesterday.

He made it look so effortless, I think, falling head first into the memory.

"You want help?" a voice calls out.

Rex is standing at the railing of the townhouse deck, watching me.

"Not really," I answer stiffly.

He starts moving toward me anyway.

"It won't take long," he insists. "We haven't really gotten the chance to be alone yet anyway."

Nervous energy shoots through my veins, filling my body with ice as Rex makes his way down the stairs, jogging across the sand to relieve me of the board's weight. When he reaches me, his eyes crinkle into a genuine smile — the likes of which I haven't seen in well over a month. I wish Dom was here, softening the blow of having Rex's full attention back on me again, this time without anything left between us.

We fall in line together. The familiarity between us is there, but deep down I know we'll never be close again.

"You look really good out on the water." He says it so casually it makes me angry. I stop walking for the briefest second before falling in line again next to him, fighting the urge to trudge ahead.

"Thanks." I match his stride. "Your surfing could really use some work. I keep thinking you're going to drown out there, and I don't know whether to be happy or sad about that."

His laughter rattles me. I used to love that sound. Back when I'd do anything I could just to hear it.

"Juju really likes you," he says, swiftly changing the subject.

"Well, why wouldn't she?" I ask.

His smile widens, then he glances over at me.

"Smart girl," he says.

"Very," I add, smirking.

We take a few more steps before I can't stand it anymore. I have to ask. "Have you told her about us?"

"What's there to tell?" He replies so quickly that I nearly stop dead in my tracks.

"What the fuck, Rex?" I demand, refusing to move forward.

He spins around.

He narrows his eyes. "Did you follow me here?" This is the first time we've been alone, and this is how he's going to start the conversation? "Yes or no? You never answered me the other day."

"Did *I* follow *you*?" I want to smack the question right out of his mouth. My jaw hangs open at the audacity of it. *You self-centered asshole.* "Let's see, Rex, did I toss all my money into a burning dumpster fire just so I could fall asleep to the sound of you fucking your new girlfriend across my wall every night? No."

"Then how did we both end up here?"

"The universe has a shitty sense of humor, I guess."

He softens. "I miss you, you know." He shifts his eyes to the sand, away from my face. "I wouldn't mind finding a quiet time to talk more . . . You know, about what happened."

The knot in my stomach catapults into a full-blown churn. His wavering emotions are giving me whiplash. I want to wring his neck for telling me that he misses me. The nerve of this man. I have no interest in being the other woman to Juju. Not now. Not ever.

"Don't say that. You didn't have to *miss* me." I spit each word out like it's laced with venom. "That's on you. You didn't have to say no on live television."

"And you didn't have to ask," he quickly shoots back. Too quickly. Then he takes two more steps away from me toward the house.

I plant my feet and put my hands on my hips, waiting for him to look me squarely in the eye. When he doesn't, I kick sand at his back so he'll turn around to face me.

"What the hell is that supposed to mean?" I nearly yell.

Rex had insisted that I was too angry to have this conversation the evening after I'd proposed, when he came to our apartment to pick up all his stuff. And I probably was. So we just left it at that. I figured we'd both take some time to cool off and then have this conversation. But then days turned into weeks, and now here we are. Finally saying what we want to say, thousands of miles from home.

"Were we really ready for marriage?" He drops my board into the sand, looking irate.

"I don't know." I can feel rage building in my voice. "Maybe I never should have asked, Rex. Maybe I should have laughed when my producer suggested it. But couldn't you have said *yes* in that moment, when the cameras were rolling, and I was live on air in front of millions of people, and spare me from global humiliation? We could have talked about it afterward, even changed the plan. No one had to see that part. I could have taken it all back, if you'd have let me. You didn't have to completely cut me out of your life that day, leaving me to deal with the fallout alone. What you did left me mortified in front of the world, so no one would ever forget."

He looks like a volcano, molten lava about to simmer over the edge.

I press him harder. "How could you do that to me?" I take a step toward him. "I thought we were—"

"How could *you*?" He interrupts, pointing at me, his eyes burning into mine. Then he takes another step toward me. "You didn't even ask for my permission before putting our relationship out there for the whole world to see."

Hot sand digs into my bare feet — I want to run off it, and get away from him. "Why does that matter? How could you move on so fast?" My voice breaks on the last word. "It's barely even been a month."

"If we could just get a minute alone," he says in an even voice. "I could explain, before—"

"Hey, you two!" Juju calls down from the railing. She's beaming at us from the lanai. A cloud of steam rises off her mug. We both turn and wave, like a puppet master has strings attached to our hands. He smiles broadly at her, pretending we aren't caught in some ex-lovers' squabble.

"Why haven't you told her?" I hiss at him through my teeth, too quiet for her to hear.

"Hey, babe!" Rex calls back to her. I try not to grimace at the word *babe*.

It makes me want to punch him.

"Not yet," he whispers back to me, that frozen smile still stuck on his face. "She doesn't really do social media. She has no idea about us. I'd rather keep it that way for now. Just let me be the one to tell her."

I walk ahead.

"You're an idiot if you think she won't find out," I whisper loudly at him over my shoulder.

Then I storm back into my side of the townhome, leaving Rex to carry the weight of the board and everything else he's fucked up.

CHAPTER 29

I heave the sliding door shut with a bang and grab my phone off the kitchen counter, typing out an SOS text to Dom as soon as I get inside.

Rex needs to hear the message loud & clear. Up for a little fun?

He sends back a reply.

Are you okay? Did something happen?

I groan and punch in my response.

I'm fine. Rex told me he misses me. It's time to squash any last thoughts of a rekindling.

Three little dots appear under Dom's last text, then disappear, then appear again. I wait for his reply, but it doesn't pop up. Just as I'm about to explain more, feeling like maybe Dom isn't having as much fun as he was when we first started this little charade, I hear the ping come in.

Is it time to play out that scene from When Harry Met Sally *through those walls? How nuclear are we talking here?*

I laugh out loud. I love that scene.

Let's save the big guns for when we really need them. I was thinking we could invite them over for dinner at my place.

His response is almost immediate.

You want us to have dinner with your ex?

A warning shot fires in my stomach. Is this taking it too far? I want Rex to get the message that I've moved on, just as much as he has. I don't want to be worried that he's going to come corner me on the beach every time I'm walking back to the townhouse alone.

Another text comes in, just as I'm about to take it all back.

I'm in.

I suck in a breath.

Can you be here by five? I'll make sure they can make it.

Those three little dots play another round of hide and seek, blinking on, then off, then on again before his answer comes in.

Game on. I'll bring a few things to grill.

My nerves get the best of me, and by the time Dom shows up with a big bag full of steaks and veggies to throw on the grill, I'm already shaky. I'm glad I had the good sense to let Pru outside, since I'm not quite ready to explain that one yet.

"Hello!" I exclaim, throwing open the front door. "You ready for this?"

He laughs before stepping inside. Juju and Rex are out back on the patio, Rex's arm looped protectively around her waist. I made sure to extend the invitation to Juju, so Rex couldn't decline on their behalf. I can tell he's nervous that the truth of our recent relationship is going to slip out whenever I'm around. And, by this point, I feel like he's already dug himself into a hole that he can't climb out of once the truth finally does come out.

We make our way out to the deck, and Dom quickly gets to work on the grill. Once the food is sizzling, he slips an arm around my waist and settles in, leaning us both against the rail.

Juju brought over a pitcher of her homemade mai tais, which is already half gone, while the sun is starting its evening light show. This time it's a glowy array of golden and amber tones, sunlight bouncing across the surface of the waves like someone's released ten thousand microscopic diamonds from the sky, each one tiny and alive.

"You look stunning tonight," Dom tells me, leaning in for a kiss.

I let his lips linger against mine, feeling the weight of Rex's eyes on my skin.

When we pull away, Juju is fanning herself.

"You two are making it hotter than it already is out here!" she exclaims, leaning into Rex. She looks up at him as if she wishes he would kiss her like that, but he doesn't. He just leans his elbows against the rail, acting far too invested in the sunset taking place behind us.

"Let's play a round of truth or truth!" Juju calls out after everyone's tumbler has been freshly refilled.

Rex scoffs loudly, like he's heard this request from her before.

I truly don't know what I ever saw in him. He seems like a major killjoy whenever I'm around him now.

"I don't think they want to—" Rex begins, just as Dom agrees to play.

"What is truth or truth?" I ask, eyeing Rex since he looks so adamantly opposed.

"It's just like truth or dare, except it's only truths," Juju explains. "Just a fun way to break the ice while we wait for the food. I used to play it in college all the time."

Dom cocks one eye at me.

"Aren't the dares the best part? Why leave them out?" he asks suggestively, squeezing my hip. Then he plants a kiss on my temple while I lean into him. "Though I guess we don't really need a dare to have fun . . ."

I giggle as his kisses make their way down to my jawline — Rex rolls his eyes before looking away again.

"We haven't been in college for a long time," he mumbles at Juju, taking a stiff gulp of his drink.

"I'll start!" Juju calls out, ignoring him. Then she studies the three of us each individually before digging her eyes into me.

"Liv, tell us the last time something horribly embarrassing happened to you," she says gleefully, totally unaware that the last global embarrassment I experienced stemmed from me proposing to her boyfriend on live TV.

I should just admit it. Get it all over with and out in the open.

Rex glares at me, then swallows, blinking frantically.

I smile at Juju and feel myself turning pink when I remember a much more recent moment of embarrassment. One that still truthfully answers the question without ruining her night.

"Well," I start, tilting my gaze up to Dom. A full-blown smirk filled with appreciation takes over his face when he realizes the story I'm thinking of, forcing a deep blush to stain my cheeks. Nothing about this is acting for me. "My bikini top washed off during my surf lesson with Dom the other day," I confess, looking at Juju.

"Jesus Christ," Rex mutters, snapping his attention away from me.

"What?" Juju shrieks, then breaks into laughter. "Girl, if I had a dollar for every time my nipple popped out while surfing, I'd be filthy rich."

"That's never happened while we've been surfing." Rex shoots her a look as if he's personally hurt that her nipples don't make a surprise appearance around him.

"Honey, it's not like I can plan it," she assures him. "Besides, it usually involves being in stronger waves than what you're comfortable with."

She doesn't say it like a jab, but Dom erupts into laughter, then quiets himself by kissing the top of my head, snuffing out his final chuckles into my hair.

Rex glares at him, but Dom doesn't seem to be bothered, if he's even noticed Rex's reaction at all.

"What about you, Rex?" I ask, baiting him. "When was the last time you were deeply embarrassed in front of a big crowd of people?"

I grin at him innocently. Dom squeezes me in closer to him, knowing that I'm poking the bear.

"I don't think a crowd of people was part of the question." Rex frowns, knitting his brows together like he can't recall a time when he was humiliated.

"Oh, just answer the question, babe!" Juju trills, smiling up at him.

"Uh, it had to be the time I tripped up the sales pitch in front of my boss. I started selling the guys at Pyrex the Dover line instead of the Duel."

I scrunch up my face at him like he doesn't understand the assignment. Then I notice Dom and Juju giving him the same look.

The deck is silent for a beat before Juju pipes up. "No, it had to be that time at Christmas when the waiter got your order wrong. Remember? You were so embarrassed about—"

Christmas?

I narrow my eyes at Rex.

Rex quickly interrupts Juju by planting a kiss on her lips.

141

When he pulls back, he calmly brushes her hair back from her face. "Yes, I remember that, you're right. The time the waiter got my order wrong and the kid at the table next to us came and swiped it off us when he realized it was his. But that wasn't Christmas, sweetheart. Dom, I think you're up, man."

"I could have sworn that was Christmas." She looks confused.

"You don't happen to have any more of that mai tai mix in the fridge, do you, babe?" Rex motions to the nearly empty pitcher.

I silently stare at Rex as Juju busies herself by refilling the pitcher inside.

Rex smiles tightly in my direction, before asking Dom some stupid question about the grill, taking his immediate attention away from me while I silently do the math.

Juju had to have gotten it wrong.

How could she be remembering something that happened at Christmas, if I was busy humiliating myself by proposing to him on Valentine's Day?

CHAPTER 30

By the time the second pitcher of mai tais is gone, along with the food, the game of truth or truth reemerges, and this time no one is holding back.

Juju has let us all in on her dream of circumnavigating the world on a solo sailboat, while Rex has confessed his secret affinity for chef shows, which comes as no surprise to me.

"What's wrong with wanting to be named *Iron Chef*?" he asks, and we all break into laughter.

"Honey, I've never seen you cook a real meal," Juju says, holding back a howl. She's wiping tears from her eyes by the time we all settle down again. "What about you, Liv? What's your secret dream?"

I shoot a look at Rex, knowing he already knows. Then at Dom, fully aware that I already confessed this to him the other night.

"I'm trying to make that happen right now," I tell her. "Ever since I was a little girl, I've always had this vision of writing stories in a beautiful place. Usually a garden. Growing old, while I lose myself in a hundred different stories. Probably wrinkly and eccentric in a delicious sort of way."

"With a kaftan or two," Rex interjects.

I stare at him, the veil broken as he forgets the invisible line between us. "Solid guess." I look down, trying to mask my surprise that he's forgotten the ruse.

Dom shifts uncomfortably next to me, squeezing my knee under the table with a little smile. He knows Rex just fucked up, too.

"Wow, good guess about the kaftan," Juju says sleepily next to Rex. "I wouldn't even think you'd know what one is." She gives Rex a lazy smile, almost like she's ready to fall asleep. It's gotten late, and the sounds of the island at night are drawing in. Buzzing and chirping out-of-sight insects reverberate in our ears, urging us all to go inside before we start getting eaten alive.

Rex shoots me a slightly panicked look, knowing he just got lucky that she didn't catch on.

"Well, you two" — Juju rises with a yawn — "if you can't tell, I'm nearly asleep on my feet. Let's clean all this up in the morning. Dom, I'm assuming we'll see you over coffee?" She gives us both a knowing look, like she assumes he'll be spending the night.

I smile back, unsure of what to say.

"I can just get this cleaned up right now," I tell her, grabbing a handful of plates. "I'm not nearly as tired as you yet. You two go on to bed."

"Okay, but I'll see you both in the morning! Sleep tight, you two!"

Dom plays along, kissing me on the lips one more time before Juju and Rex head back into their side of the townhouse, shutting the door behind them. It strikes me again how odd it is to be sharing a wall.

I turn back to Dom, who already has most of the dishes piled up down his arms.

"You don't have to do that," I tell him quietly. "I'm sure you can slip out the front door without them hearing you go."

"Nah." He walks into my side of the townhouse. "We've already committed this far."

144

He places all the dishes down on the counter. Then he shuts the window shades so they can't see him creating a little makeshift bed on the couch.

I stand off to the side, watching as he pulls a blanket off the back of a chair and spreads it over the cushions.

"You're actually planning to stay here?" My breath is picking up speed.

"It's already late, and they'll definitely be wondering why I took off at one in the morning instead of just staying here with you."

He grabs one of the palm-sized throw pillows to add to the couch-bed — I grab it out of his hands.

"You did me a favor by coming tonight," I tell him. "At the very least, you can have the bed."

He narrows his eyes at me, holding back a silly grin.

"You actually think I'd take the bed from you? What kind of gentleman would I be?"

He grabs the pillow back.

I size up the couch, then look at him. It'd be like expecting an oak tree to sprawl out across a narrow two-by-four.

"I insist you take the bed." I plant myself firmly on the couch. I pull my knees up to my chest and cross my arms, showing him that I'm not budging.

He plants himself on the opposite side of the couch, but stretches his legs out, draping my ankles across his lap, so neither one of us is scrunched up on the opposite side.

"I don't think our little show is actually over yet." He narrows his eyes into a wicked smirk. It's the same look he gave me the first time we discussed this fake-dating situation, which already seems like a lifetime ago.

That pesky swarm of butterflies is summoned, once again, by that dark look in his eye.

"They're going to bed. So are we. I'm pretty sure Rex got the message tonight, so thank you." I narrow my eyes back at him.

"And now we're shut up in here, with them on the opposite side of that wall." He juts his thumb out behind him. "It's too good of an opportunity to miss."

"You want to . . ."

He raises an eyebrow at me.

A challenge.

"So you weren't kidding about reenacting the whole *When Harry Met Sally* scene?" I rub my reddening cheeks between my palms.

The grin that stretches across his face makes me burst into nervous laughter. Partially because I hope he's kidding, and partially because I pray he's not.

I bite my lip. "I'm not very good at faking things," I tell him. "So, as much as I love this idea, pulling it off is another story entirely."

He looks at me, confused. "You could have fooled me."

I suck in a breath, remembering our pact to fake everything between us. As far as he knows, I'm a phenomenal actress.

"I'm good at faking some things," I correct myself. "However, you're practically a pro, Dom. You've all but convinced me this whole time."

"Which parts?"

"Which parts of your act have I believed?" I repeat, my voice going up a notch.

"Need a refresher to pick them out?" he asks. "I can give you a rundown of the bases we've covered so far to jog your memory. Maybe some we haven't."

I lick my lips.

There's no one here. There's no reason for him to give me a refresher of anything he's faked up to this point.

CHAPTER 31

Do I need a refresher? I laugh to myself.

Of course not.

Every touch, each kiss he's given me, since we first started this ridiculous game has already kept me up at night. Replaying each and every time the intensity of his green eyes have poured into mine, understanding more than he ever lets on.

The kisses that have been so good they've made me lose sleep.

I can't even handle thinking back to the evening we made out in the sand without getting completely hot under the collar.

My pulse picks up slightly as his eyes burn into mine.

I want him so bad, I can almost taste it. But no one is here. No reason to put on a show.

"You say you've been fooled. By which parts?" he asks again, dragging his knuckles up my ankle and back down again.

"That." I point to his hand against my leg.

"This?" He drags his knuckles higher, pressing into my skin as they go.

"Yes." I crack into a smile, nodding. "Very convincing."

His knuckles trail up to my knee, squeezing it in his palm, like he's done dozens of times. But this time it's different. Because this time we're all alone.

"And that." I smile. "You have very convincing hands."

He erupts into that deep laugh I've grown to love, and it makes me grin harder. He shifts on the couch, closing the gap between our bodies. "There's one thing I'm not sure we're fooling anyone with."

"Which part?"

My heart begins to race as I wonder which part of our whole charade is coming next.

"In fact, I was thinking that we might need a little more practice with it. For the sake of being believable, of course."

"Of course," I mumble back quietly. "I want to make sure we're on top of our game."

He smirks, placing both hands on my legs, dragging them slowly up toward my lap.

My heart starts pounding so loud that I can hear it between my ears.

He leans in closer. His hands reach my mid-thigh the same time his lips meet mine, beckoning them to open. My eyes close and roll back in my head, giving into his kiss as I take it all in.

The fact that no one is here.

There's no reason to put on a show.

Unless we're really going to do this.

And the show is just for us.

I moan into his kiss and pull back from him, already feeling a bit lightheaded and breathless.

"Dom," I mumble, not wanting to open my eyes yet. Not wanting to break the spell. "Do you think I need practice kissing to be more convincing?"

I crack one eye open, hoping I'm not just imagining what I think is taking place here.

He grabs my face between his hands, the weight and heat of them grounding me back in place.

"Liv . . ." He gently kisses my forehead, my cheek, then my other cheek, moving my face right where he wants his lips to go. Finally, he leans in closer, until his lips are brushing against mine as he speaks again. "Your kisses have fooled me so intensely that I think I might be fooled into falling for you." I can feel him smiling against my lips as he pauses to take a breath. "The only thing here that needs more practice is us trying to figure out what the hell this is."

I open both eyes so I can look into his while he talks. Hoping I'm not the only one imagining that this charade between us has become far more than a game.

"But, if you're so unbelievably good at faking this, whatever this is, that I've somehow misunderstood, then I'll—"

"You haven't." I push him back onto the couch, pressing my lips against his.

He swings me beneath him, enveloping me in his arms. Then he kicks both feet out over the edge, shifting again while he tries to find a position that doesn't leave him hanging half-off the couch. But within seconds we're both laughing. He's too big for us to both lie down.

"The bed." I shift up off the couch.

Without a word, he jumps and sweeps me off my feet, swinging me up into his arms like a rag doll. In under ten paces, we're in the bedroom, where he tosses me down across the bed and climbs on top of me, pressing me down into the mattress.

I pull back.

"Just to be clear," I blurt out breathlessly, "this part isn't just practice. Right? Because if it is, I can just—"

"No," he says firmly. "And you're not . . ." He cocks his head to the side, pausing to study me.

"No." I match his tone.

We both smile into another kiss before he swiftly pulls his shirt over his head, then leans down to cover my mouth in his again, making sure I forget that I even asked.

Every little thing we've done up until this point has felt like foreplay.

Him finding me standing in my red panties at the front door.

149

The way his eyes first rolled down my bare skin, like he was trying so hard to be the perfect gentleman, before he burst into the door.

His voice, that first time he said I looked gorgeous.

And the second time, too.

The crimson that spread over his cheeks after my swimsuit top slipped off.

My back pressed into the hot sand while his lips held me captive in the sunset.

Every single time his hand squeezed that sensitive spot over my hip, sending delicious chills up my spine.

All of it building in my body, demolishing any self-control I had left until this very moment.

When I first became single again, I couldn't imagine how I'd feel, finding myself in the arms of anyone else. But now that I'm here, I can't imagine it any other way.

I want him. *Now.*

And the fact that there's no other person around, no one that he could possibly be trying to fool, makes each touch that much better.

I sit up and pull my sundress over my head, revealing just a pair of silky red panties underneath, no bra on top.

He pushes his forehead into mine with a small groan. Then he leans in to kiss me, but stops just before his lips get to mine. I feel them parting, breathing into my mouth, before he starts confessing to me again.

"I haven't been able to stop thinking about those red lace panties I saw you wearing on the porch that first day," he growls.

Then he wraps one hand around my neck, knotting my hair up in his fist behind my head, tilting my face higher to expose my jaw to his lips. I feel like putty in his arms, here to do with as he pleases. His mouth brushes against my earlobe, then travels down to my collarbone, sending a shiver straight through me. "I almost broke down the door that day, just so I could carry you inside and pull them off with my teeth."

CHAPTER 32

He nips at my neck, sending a tingly shiver straight through me.

"You mean these old things?" I try not to shake in Dom's arms while his lips trickle down my neck.

I take one of his hands from where it's gripping my hip, dragging it slowly down my thigh, then up again. Flattening my hand over his, I push both our hands toward the waistband of the red thong I'm wearing.

"They're not the same ones that you saw me in before." My breath hitches in my throat as his knuckles graze the paper-thin lace. "But I'm sure you won't mind."

He exhales against my mouth, his eyes digging into mine while he yanks back the panties, shifting the delicate fabric away from my torso. Then he slides his fingertips underneath the edges, dragging each knuckle back and forth, across the very top of the waistline, not daring to go an inch lower yet.

"This is all I've wanted to do to you since I saw you knocking against that door."

"I hope not." I pretend to be upset. His eyes narrow at me, looking surprised, but I bite his bottom lip. "Because there's a hell of a lot more that I'm hoping you'll do to me next."

His smoldering eyes are the last thing I see before my eyes slowly roll back in my head. Losing myself to his touch when he slips his thick palm between my thighs, pushing one finger inside me, then two. I'm already slick with anticipation when his mouth finds mine again.

"I've been wanting you," I pant into the side of his hair.

"I can tell," he whispers back, his lips tickling my ear.

He covers my mouth with his, finding my tongue and kissing me deeply, before sliding his hands around the curve of my hips, cupping my ass from behind.

I drag my nails through his hair, down the back of his neck, then back up again. I feel him slide lower, pressing my body down with his own, dragging his tongue along the groove of my stomach. When he hits my navel, he presses a deep kiss into the concave depth, then cups my ass again, lifting my hips up to slip the panties from my body.

"You're entirely overdressed." I gesture for him to slip his off too.

He takes a step off the back of the mattress, then slides his boxers down to the floor. His skin is so taut, each muscle is like a ripple across water. Smooth and elastic, with a small trail of dark hair leading down to his cock, standing stick-straight at attention. He searches through his clothes on the floor briefly, then opens a condom and puts it on.

"Came prepared?" I ask, smiling.

He laughs, then nods.

"I prayed to God you weren't acting," he murmurs, climbing onto the bed again.

I widen my legs so I can feel the full length of him between my thighs.

"I want you ready for me, baby," he growls into my ear before slipping down lower on the bed. Before I can open my eyes to see where he's gone, I feel his hands grip my hips, his elbows pushing my knees apart as he opens me up, kissing between my legs for the first time.

I gasp when his tongue hits my clit, circling it, then groan when his fingers slip inside me, slowly moving in and out, teasing me gently for what's to come.

I'm not going to last.

Not after wanting him for so long already.

I've also been thinking of this exact moment, ever since I first laid eyes on him. And now that it's here, I can't think of anything else but having him inside me.

I lift my hips up to meet his tongue and he pushes it in, finding my clit with his thumb as I start to ride him.

Oh my God. Rex never fucked me like this.

I wrap the bedsheet around my fist, dragging it up to my mouth, biting down on the fabric to stifle my moans.

"You don't have to stay quiet, baby." His words vibrate against the pink of my skin, taking me closer to the edge. "There's no reason to hold back."

"Dom!" I cry out, unable to stay quiet. "I can't wait much longer."

The tightly wound coil inside me grips harder, while his hold on me keeps everything from rolling away.

"I need you." I gasp for air, pulling his shoulders up toward mine. "I need you inside me now."

He shifts himself up, burying his lips into my neck, finally pushing his thick cock inside me. Despite his size, he slides in gently, letting me get accustomed to him for a moment before moving in and out, pushing through me with every shared breath.

I grab on to his hair, writhing beneath him while he plants kiss after kiss in the sensitive nook between my neck and collar bone. My entire body is a pool of waves, shocks, and sensations, shooting through me over and over, pulsing with the beat of my heart. I'm so close to coming — I can't hold back anymore.

His breath quickens in my ear, and I know he's close too.

"Dom," I moan, my breath on his ear.

"Just let go, Liv," he groans back, his breath hitching harshly in his throat. "I want to feel you come while I'm inside you, baby. I don't want to wait one more second."

He thrusts twice more, and the coil inside me explodes, spilling me over the edge. Gripping on to his cock, pulsing around him. I feel him go rigid, breathing heavily in my ear, and I shiver away from his lips, unable to take one more microcosm of touch. Shooting stars cry out like sparklers behind my eyes.

"Liv!" he groans against my neck.

"What the fuck was that?" I moan into the sheet beside me. Happily satisfied. I've never been fucked so well in my life. "I've never . . ." I trail off, hoping he catches my meaning, the sheets sweaty beneath us.

"I don't think we have any reason to practice anything ever again," he mumbles into the bed.

I laugh, feeling myself fall somewhere between a potential second orgasm and wanting to wrap myself up in his body, feeling the weight of him, holding me in place while I glide back down to earth from whatever form of ecstasy we just found in each other.

Making a racket was the last thing on my mind, but I realize we probably did anyway. Though I don't even care about that anymore. Nothing feels further than my past with that man on the other side of the wall. And nothing feels more like my future than the way I feel right now.

CHAPTER 33

A few days later, I'm heading back from a morning surf session, trying to stave off writer's block, when I get back up to the townhouse and notice a little black bag sitting in front of my back door. I bring it inside with me and shut the door, hoping it's from Dom and not my bastard neighbor.

I read the notecard hanging off the side.

> *Hey gorgeous,*
>   *You looked too peaceful to interrupt your surf sesh out there in the waves. These are for you. There's a garden you can write in behind the house, if you'd like a change of scenery.*
>   *Wearing these, of course. Call me for the address.*
>   *Dom*
>   *P.S. If the asshat next door asks where you're going, it's to hang out with me.*

I laugh and peek inside the bag. It's a silky kaftan in cobalt blue, stitched with shimmering gold thread. A heap of the most delicate gold bangles is nestled underneath.

"No way." The silky, embroidered fabric is stunning. I don't think I've ever *seen* anything so beautiful, let alone owned it.

He must have gotten these after I told him my secret dream of wearing kaftans and writing in beautiful gardens. I laugh and hug the kaftan over my denim shorts and tank top, twirling around once, before adding the bangles down each of my wrists. Then I move my arms, so the bangles clink against each other. They sound like the opening notes of a music box melody.

Grinning, I pull up Dom's number on my phone, still listed as *Airbnb guy*, and make a mental note to change that. He answers on the second ring, and I can already hear the smile in his voice when he says my name.

"Liv."

"I love them," I immediately tell him, then shake my wrist near the phone so he can hear the bracelets jangle.

"A little granny chic gets you in the mood to write, huh?"

"This is all too much, though, you really shouldn't have."

"Don't even think about it, just enjoy them." His voice is warm and buttery. "If this is your lifelong dream, you really need to do it right. Starting now."

I run to the mirror in my bedroom and spin around, beaming at my reflection.

"We'll talk about this more after you see me in it." I feel giddy. "I've never owned anything so perfect. It's already making me inspired to write more. You know what else gets me in the mood to write?"

"Snacks?"

I laugh. He's already seen my growing pile of junk food on the kitchen counter. Those are mostly an excuse to stretch my legs and hit the market a few times a day. Except the Swedish Fish. Those are strictly for eating.

"Yes, but that's not what I'm talking about. Where is this garden? What's the address?"

He tells me the address and Wi-Fi password. As I write it down, I'm over the moon that I'm finally getting invited to his house for once.

"There's a little bistro table out back with a nice view. I think you'll love it. I have a few errands to run today for work.

But if you're still around when I get back, I'll bring something for dinner."

"Yes, please!" I say, hopefully not too enthusiastically. I'm a terrible cook, and haven't had a truly homemade meal since I last went home to see my parents.

"I hope you like the garden. It's kind of my hobby, besides relentlessly bugging my favorite Airbnb tenant," he says. "It's my second favorite place to be."

"And your most favorite?"

"The water," he says without hesitation.

"I loved being back out there this morning." I'm unable to hide how proud of myself I am.

"Alone? With all those sharks?" There's a tone of mock surprise in his voice.

"No." I grin. "With the sunrise."

"She's getting under your skin," he says, referring to the ocean. I can hear the smile in his voice, and it makes me blush. "I knew she would." I smile silently, knowing he's right. "Listen, I'll be back in a few hours, if you're still around."

"That'll give me a goal to work toward. If I'm still in the garden when you return, it means I'll have had a successful day of writing."

"I hope the setting works its magic for you, so I get to see you back at my place in a few hours."

157

CHAPTER 34

I sit in the back seat of my Uber for another minute, afraid the real homeowners are going to come out of their mansion to see who's parked in their driveway. I've rechecked Google Maps at least three times to make sure the driver has gotten the right address, but this can't be Dom's place.

There's no way a young, thirty-something-year-old bachelor lives here.

I take a photo of the front of the house and text it to Dom.

Is this it?

He responds right away.

I left the gate to the right of the driveway unlocked for you. Head on back

I feel like I've died and woken up as Julia Roberts in *Pretty Woman*, minus the whole prostitute thing. I expected to see a shabby little bungalow when I pulled up, maybe one or two bedrooms, with a row of surfboards lining the wall of a rugged man cave, just grateful he doesn't have roommates. However, I'm looking at what appears to be a sprawling Italian-inspired villa set against the highly desired North Shore beach. Creamy stucco walls — topped with layers of individually molded terracotta roofing tiles — span a roomy courtyard leading up to the double-wide mahogany doors. The home is nestled into a beautifully manicured tropical paradise, with bold orange and pink blooms lining the driveway. Three ancient banyan trees shade the property, with dozens of roots sprouting out of the ground toward the branches, as if pulling the tree slowly back into the earth.

If I didn't know any better, I'd guess we'd driven right into the state's botanical garden.

Grabbing my laptop and solar charger from the seat beside me, I thank the driver and get out of the car slowly, my head on a swivel.

Lush, leafy ferns and palms with blooms of every size and shape spring up around me, lining the walkway that'll hopefully lead me to Dom's backyard. Birds chirp overhead and the sound of waves hitting the shore beckon me to continue down a meandering path flanked by orange Birds of Paradise flowers fanning out along the walkway, each bloom nearly as tall as my hips.

A stark white note card comes into view, taped to a heavy teak wood gate, lined in black molded iron.

Enjoy, Liv. Make yourself at home

The blocky chicken scratch matches the note that was tucked in with the gift I opened earlier.

Okay, if Dom is this loaded, why was he so insistent that I finish out my reservation at first?

And what is he running from back home in California?

Dozens of bangles clink down my wrist toward my elbow as I reach up to push against the gate. It swings open wide enough to reveal the most beautiful garden I've ever seen. A collection of birds in the palms overhead — all yellow, red, and black — chirp loudly as if to say hello in their own cheerful way when I walk inside.

I think I'm falling in love, and not just with Dom. This garden is incredible.

A flock of koi fish rush to meet me in a wide, bean-shaped pond, speckled with lily pads topped with purple flowers. Tripping over one another in a frenzy of orange and gold flashes under the water. I bet they think I'm here with a snack for them.

"Not unless you like Swedish Fish." I pat my purse full of snacks.

Their bodies rush around each other in a dizzying dance, somersaulting and diving, then boldly breaking the surface of the water, all lips and scales. A waterfall trickles down the side of the pool, then drops into a second lower koi pond with another half-dozen black and gold speckled fish, the largest as wide as my thigh, poking its nose out of the water. The ponds are cushioned on either side by a collection of lush green fronds.

The whole effect feels like a fairytale come to life.

I imagine Dom feeding these fish every day as I make my way around a bend, staying on the gravel pathway, anxious to see what's coming next.

After wrapping around a hand-laid stone wall, the roar of waves against the empty shore greets me. The garden's tree line gives way to an open beach, where turquoise whitecaps roll onto soft white sand.

There she is. The ocean, framed by my view of thick, tropical greens, under a sky filled with puffy white clouds.

A hammock wide enough to fit two or three people is strung between two enormous tree trunks, with a stone bistro table nestled beside a smooth river rock wall. I take off my shoes to feel the cool, wet earth and velvety moss between my toes.

What the hell does Dom do besides rent townhouses? There's no way my nominal rental fee affords him this level of luxury. Even if he owns fifty of them.

My phone pings, startling me out of a trance-like day-dream, bringing me back to reality.

His text is only four words, but it makes me smile.

Find your way in?

I settle myself onto one of the bistro chairs, surrounded by carved rock and moss, then take a selfie to send back as my answer. Before hitting *Send*, I bring the screen up to my face to study it more closely, not surprised by what I see.

I look happy.

Genuinely happy. Lighter than I have in months. No filter needed. Wrapped in my new cobalt-blue kaftan, holding up my wrist to prove that I'm wearing at least six inches of thin, gold bangles down each arm, which make me want to dance when I move. I smile at myself on the screen.

I love it here.

Every awful thing that happened in my life the last few months had to happen in order for me to be here. To experience this exact moment right now.

I add a line of text to my selfie before hitting *Send*.

I think I've dreamed of this place a time or two ♥ *Thank you*

Writing here, in a place that looks plucked from my dreams, is everything I ever hoped it would be. Periodically I look around, feeling like I've stumbled into paradise, knowing my dream man is the owner of everything I see around me.

I sit down and start to write, losing track of time from the words flowing onto the screen.

I have no idea what time it is when the smell of something sizzling on the grill pulls my focus from my computer screen. But it must have been a few hours based on the pages and pages of words filling my laptop screen. It's the most accomplished day of writing I've had yet.

Whatever that smell is makes my mouth instantly water with hunger. Garlicky seafood and some type of grilled meat.

I sit up taller, my stomach rumbling.

Dom must be home.

CHAPTER 35

Closing my laptop, I follow another path to a set of stairs that will take me up to a second-story deck. I take them two at a time until a smoky gas barbeque comes into view. Peeking through the windows, I spot him standing at a wide marble island, squeezing bright yellow lemon slices over a platter of enormous prawns. I gently tap on the window, grinning. He's surrounded by more than enough food to feed two people.

"Come on in!" he calls through the glass.

"This smells like heaven!" I gush, glancing around the shrimp and crab legs strewn out across the counter. He has a dish towel thrown casually over his shoulder, like *Top Chef*, but way more handsome. He looks relaxed and totally in charge of his kitchen.

I love this version of him, I realize. It's sexy as hell.

"Tell me you're game to stay. Everything's fresh from the fish market. Caught today." He holds an enormous prawn out to me by the tail.

I grab it from him, ripping the body off with my teeth and tossing the tail into a nearby bin. I feel ravenous. Then I suck the garlic off the tip of my finger, keeping one eye glued to him while I reach for another.

"You must be hungry." He laughs, leaning in for a kiss.

"Oh my God." I cover my mouth while I chew, fighting the urge to smother him in more kisses. There's nothing sexier than a guy who can hang up window blinds *and* cook like this. "That tasted like it came from a five-star restaurant. When did you get home?" I reach for another. It feels like we're playing house.

Besides the platter of shrimp, there's a plate of buttery spiced corn cobs, and something simmering on the stove, in addition to whatever is under the hood of the grill outside.

"A while, but I didn't want to interrupt you. You looked like you were on a roll down there." He grins at me, and I smile back, wondering what I must've looked like when Dom peered over the edge of the deck to see me typing away so feverishly that I didn't even notice he was there. "That whole kaftan thing must have had the intended effect on your writing. You look gorgeous in that, by the way."

I twirl in a circle with my arms out, giving him a full view. Silky fabric sashays around my hips, swirling gently around my ankles as I come to a full stop. "I love it so much," I admit. "It's the sweetest gift I've ever been given. Even better because it means you appreciated my drunken rambling at Cliff's the other night. You didn't find all that a bit silly?"

"Never." He draws me in for a long hug. "You look as good as I imagined when I picked out that color for you. Compliments your best feature perfectly."

"And which feature is that?" My heart starts pumping harder.

"Your eyes. They're my favorite color. Like the ocean — when she's feeling a bit feisty."

God, I want him all over again. Right here on the counter, if I could.

"I'm glad I've done justice to your vision. There's only one problem."

He raises both eyebrows at me, waiting for me to spill it.

"Now that I've officially gotten a feel of what it would be like to live in that silly dream of mine, writing in your garden all afternoon, I might need to stay forever." I pop another shrimp in my mouth. "I was able to pump out a few thousand words today, bringing the script to a much more manageable place than where it was before. It has me hopeful about finishing it before I have to go back to New York. Maybe even diving into a round of revisions, if there's time."

"I meant what I said about you being able to come here any time. I'm gone most days, so the place would be all yours. But, even when I'm here, I'd love to see you more."

He plants a light kiss on my cheek, making everything in me stir. Wanting more. Then he bends over to open a small wine fridge behind the counter. "White or red?"

"Um, white?" I stare at all the food. *And a real kiss*, I want to add.

He pulls a chilled bottle of something out of the fridge and grabs two tall stem glasses from the shelf behind him. Then he gets to work opening the bottle, pouring just a tiny splash for me to taste. Exactly like in a fine restaurant.

I drain the glass and smile at him, holding it out for more.

"It's delicious. Crisp and refreshing. But you're going to have to order a pizza or something for yourself. I could devour this whole spread solo." I lick my lips while he laughs.

Dom has transformed from a handyman who owns a townhouse with missing blinds into a *Top Chef* cooking fine food and pouring amazing wine in the most beautiful house I've ever seen. I'm not sure what to think of it. While he's been busy putting the pieces of my life back together, I still need to figure him out. So many things are still a mystery to me, but he never wants to talk about his life very much. I'm starting to wonder why.

"Honestly, you are living most people's dream here. If my life could look like this every day — writing film scripts in a garden, while dressing like this." I shake my bangles. "And drinking wine that tastes like it was poured down from heaven, you might never be rid of me." And I totally mean it.

"Then drink up. And cheers to that." He holds up his glass while winking at me. "Here's to making this trip all about new beginnings. And leaving old lives on the shelf."

We clink our glasses together, then both take a sip.

He grabs the towel off his shoulder and uses it to pull a pot of boiling crab legs off the stove, then opens the lid to release a cloud of steam.

I look around the great room. It looks far too beautiful and curated to have been designed without a professional. There're silver photo frames scattered throughout, and a custom white driftwood coffee table nestled between an enormously oversized leather sofa that could easily fit fifteen adults across it. I have so many questions for him, namely what he does all day to afford a lifestyle like this. We'll work our way up to the elephant in this palatially sized room, but I decide to start with an easy question.

"What can I do to help?" I step closer to assist him. Our bodies brush, but I don't move aside when an extra rush of blood pounds through me. I can't remember the last time a man's mere presence threw all my senses into a frenzy. Just the proximity of Dom standing nearby is enough to make me feel reckless, with us all alone in a big empty house like this.

"Just keep me company. Take a seat. Drink some wine." He waves some steam away with the lid of the pot.

"Can I ask you another question then?" I perch myself on a nearby bar stool.

"Anything," he says.

"The other night, you asked me what type of life I would choose off a shelf. I never asked you the same question. But you look like you have everything you could ever want right here."

"I do have an amazing life . . . But the life I'd choose is more complete than the one I'm living." He gives me a sad kind of smile, putting his hands on his hips, as if debating whether or not to tell me. "I used to think I'd be fine all alone. I have my friends, my chosen family, but I'm starting to realize that there may be a few holes that I've never really been able to fill."

"So, if you get to wake up every day surrounded by that ocean you can't get enough of, in a home that you love, *and* you own this little slice of paradise in the midst of it all, what else is missing? You seem genuinely happy. What else could you want?"

"Ah, well, that's an excellent question." He smiles. "Not everything is so black and white though. Plus, I don't actually own this place."

CHAPTER 36

"What?" I sit up on the stool and spin my head toward the front doors, starting to panic. Are the real owners about to walk in? Am I trespassing? "Whose yard have I been in all day?"

I race around the kitchen, looking for a clue of who lives here.

"Okay, let me rephrase that. I do live here, temporarily. But my brother owns it."

"Your brother owns this house?" I start studying old photographs of people playing in the waves, or fishing off the Santa Monica Pier. The photos all look vintage though, like they were taken of a happy family years ago. I barely recognize Dom in one of the pictures when he was just a boy, probably around fifteen years old or so, give or take a year.

"My brother still lives back in California. This is one of his vacation homes. I'm just staying here while my own place gets renovated, it's nearby. He rarely comes out. Busiest guy I know," he says stiffly.

"Oh." It looks like I've hit another nerve. "Is he in the vacation rental industry with you, too?"

Everything in Dom's face flatlines when he studies me. There's that unexplained tension rising up again. I wish I

167

knew what irked him so much when we skirt around anything that's about him, or comes close to touching the inner
circle of his life.

"You swear you don't know who my brother is?" He
looks a bit skeptical, and it feels like an accusation.

I shake my head. "How would I know who your brother is?"

He puts his hands on his hips.

"Seriously, I have no idea, Dom. I'm happy to Google
him though, if you'd like me to know." I pull out my phone
and hold it out in front of me, ready to type *Dominick Bryant's
brother* into the search bar. "But I'd rather that you just told
me. What is he, like, a mob boss or something?"

"Put your phone away. I'll just tell you."

But he doesn't tell me. Instead, he continues staring at
me. Something about this conversation feels like a minefield,
a collection of things I'm supposed to know but don't.

"Okay, if it upsets you this much, you don't have to tell
me. It's fine. Really. As long as your brother is cool with me
hanging out here today, I don't need to know anything more
about him."

Yet. I'll just Google him later, when I get home.

I'm starting to get the sense that whoever lives here has
something to do with the reason Dom felt the need to run
away from whatever haunts him in California.

"No, I'll just tell you."

He slowly pulls the towel off his shoulder and plops down
on the stool across from me.

"My brother is a director. A Hollywood director. Quinton
Rockwell. Ever heard of him?"

My jaw falls to the counter.

Dom's brother is Quinton Rockwell.

Holy shit.

Quinton Rockwell is one of Hollywood's biggest film
directors, often mentioned in professional circles with industry giants like Steven Spielberg and James Cameron. He's
well known for producing some of the biggest blockbusters
to grace the screen in my entire adult life.

"Are you shitting me?" I set my wine glass down a bit lopsided without realizing it, then lunge to catch the stemware before it nearly tips over all the way. I almost broke Quinton Rockwell's wine glass. "But your last name is Bryant!"

"Quinton's industry name is Quinton Rockwell. He grew up Quinton Bryant."

My hands close over my mouth — I sit back down on the stool to steady myself.

Dom studies me before responding, his eyes narrowing. "You really didn't know?"

"Dom, how in the hell would I have known that Quinton and you were related?"

"My name got put on your Airbnb listing by accident. I already fired the assistant who made that mistake, and then when you said you were writing a script, I thought maybe you—"

"You thought that I somehow tracked down Quinton Rockwell's brother, who happens to be renting out a little Airbnb in Hawaii, the exact same time that I'm trying to escape my own viral mess back in New York, just to get a leg up in my budding film career?"

Dom smiles like he's totally used to this type of reaction when disclosing who his brother is. Then he goes back to draining the crab, unfazed. "Stranger things have happened. You'd be surprised at the lengths people go to in order to get close to my family. You really had no idea?" He sets the pot down to watch my face more clearly.

"How would I? You don't exactly advertise that you're related on your Airbnb listing. And, even if you did, I clearly didn't read the fine print before booking it."

My head is spinning as I put all the pieces together.

"Well, I feel like an idiot." I leave my wine glass where it is. I need a clear head for this conversation. "Here I am, writing my first feature film script, dressed in bangles and kaftans, while your brother is legitimate Hollywood royalty." I rest my hands against the countertop, still trying to process the fact that I'm sitting at a kitchen island owned by Quinton Rockwell. I press my palms into the cold marble in front of me. *Has Quinton touched this spot recently?*

"Nah." Dom takes the towel and starts fanning the pillow of steam still rising off the crab legs, now sitting in a strainer. The sink is practically — no definitely — as big as my standing bathtub back home. "I think what you're doing is admirable. Chasing your dream — that's more than most people can claim over their entire lifetime. The majority of people just do the bare minimum to get by before they get buried six feet under."

I blink my eyes a few times.

I spent today writing a movie script in Quinton Rockwell's backyard.

"I don't usually tell people we're related. Especially not this fast. But Quinton and his wife are planning to visit in a few weeks. Selma, that's his wife, hates when he tries to work on vacation, but he's kind of a workaholic. Asking Quinton not to work is like asking the sun not to rise. I doubt he'd mind hearing a film pitch while he's here. Especially if—" He stops short, grabbing the pan of bubbling garlic butter off the stove.

Hear a film pitch?

I wait while he pours it into a shallow dish for dipping the crab into.

Then I can't wait any longer.

"Especially if what?" I try to sound more casual than I had a moment ago, sensing a change in the air.

"Especially if it comes from someone I care about." He doesn't look one hundred percent into his idea about me pitching his brother.

"Excuse me, but are we talking about me pitching my film script to your brother?" I can barely believe what I'm hearing. I only just found out they're related, and now he's casually mentioning that I might actually get a shot at pitching him?

"Normally, I would never suggest it. Especially considering some things that've happened back home. But . . ." He sets the pan down and comes to stand in front of me, pulling me off the barstool. He pushes my hair back from my face, gently grabbing hold of my chin, tilting my eyes up to look at him. "I like you, Liv," he says gently. "And I think you deserve a shot."

Just hearing those words come out of his lips takes my breath away. I wasn't expecting any of this. I rise up on my tiptoes, pulling his face down closer to mine.

"I like you, too." I bite my lip before brushing them gently against his. Not quite a kiss yet, but we're almost there. "And I want you to know that it doesn't matter to me who your brother is. I liked you before I knew about any of this." I wave my hand around the mansion behind us. "You definitely don't have to introduce me to Quinton if that makes you nervous. I could tell there was something you felt suspicious about, ever since I mentioned my reason for being here. But, I swear, I had no idea who you were, or who you were related to. Hell, I'm the one that tried to leave the island right after I landed, and you're the one that stopped me."

I close the gap between us, giving in to one slow, sweet kiss. My pulse picks up speed.

"I'd love to introduce you two. Not just because I want you to meet him, but because I'd also like to give you that connection. I got to where I am in the business world because people I cared about gave me a once-in-a-lifetime chance to prove myself. That's exactly what I want to do for you."

He kisses me again while this new information swims through my mind. The way he sees me. This thing he wants to do for me. I've never met a man like Dom. He's not only selfless, but also thoughtful and kind. He makes me feel like I'm home, even when I'm so far away from anything I've ever known. He doesn't have to do this for me — but knowing that he wants to makes me want to pounce on him right here.

"But I have to warn you," he goes on, "there's a reason Quinton's been so successful. If something doesn't feel exactly right to him, he won't take a chance on it. No matter who's pitching."

"I wouldn't expect anything less from a bona fide genius," I tell him, not surprised. "I've met enough people in the film industry as a *Good Day Show* anchor to know that the most successful people in Hollywood tend to be a special kind of eccentric." I crinkle my nose as he cracks into a grin. "But enough about your brother. I came here for an entirely different purpose."

"The food?" He grips my hips on both sides, sending a shockwave down both legs.

I take a step toward him, fighting the urge to close the gap too quickly. I want to make this moment as slow and delicious as possible.

"You may not know this," I say quietly, biting my lip, "but I've been pretty crazy about you since you first shoved open that front door for me. Before I even knew a thing about you."

He lets out a sigh, like he's been holding his breath until hearing those words come out of my mouth. He kisses me again.

It all clicks into place. My own puzzle about Dom. I cup his face between my hands, willing him to look at me again. Wanting to see if I'm about to nail down the reason for all his hesitation when we talk about anything in his world.

"Wait, is this what you've been running away from back in California?" I ask quietly. "Your family? The fame?"

He nods slowly, his mouth twisting into a half-smile, while his eyes turn a dark, stormy green.

"It's a blessing and a curse," he says. "You'd be surprised by what the mere proximity of extreme success can make people do."

"Dom, your brother could be the King of England, and I still wouldn't give a shit." I grab a fistful of fabric from the waistline of his shorts and pull him closer to me. "He could be handing out orders to peasants in the middle of New York City and I'd still just want to be anywhere *you* are. It doesn't matter to me who you're related to."

172

I have a feeling this isn't the last time we'll talk about it. I want to know everything about Dom, and that means knowing everything he's willing to tell me about his family too. So many people would use this type of information to their advantage, drawing people into them. The fact that Dom has been afraid to even tell me until now makes me want to show him how much he means to me — without any of that glitz and glam he's related to — just to wipe any final concern out of his mind.

I tighten my grip on his waistband. "In fact, your face is the second most common thing I think about these days. Ever since I first looked up and saw you smiling at me."

He pulls me in closer. Seeing him smile like that makes my stomach do a happy flip.

"*Second* most common thing?" He narrows his eyes, looking confused. "And what would be the first?"

"This." I run my palm down the front of his body, slowing when I finally hit the growing bulge between his legs.

CHAPTER 37

With no effort at all, he hoists me up so I'm straddling his body where he stands, crossing my ankles behind his back. Then he spins me around until we land against the wall beside us. He pushes me against it so I'm almost at eye-level with him. His throbbing cock pushes up beneath me, while the wall holds me up from behind. I lean away from his lips and arch my back pulling the kaftan up over my head, letting it drop to the floor, taking off my bra next and tossing it to the floor beside it.

He groans as he works his lips down my bare chest. His tongue flicks over my hard, rose-colored nipple, before any trace of pink disappears into his mouth. I groan and arch my spine off the wall again, pushing myself further into his lips. His teeth gently graze the sensitive peaks of flesh, sending a surge of anticipation pounding between my legs.

"You're overdressed," I whisper, then pull back to look into his eyes, filled with desire, a mere inch from mine.

"No way in hell I'm putting you down to get these off," he growls. He pulls a condom from his pocket and rips it open with his teeth before I adjust my grip around his waist with my legs so he can pull his shorts down and get it on. Then he holds me firmly with one arm against the wall as he slips the thin, lipstick-red panties from my body. They fall to the floor beside us. His skin is smooth like velvet against mine.

"Dom," I whisper into his ear. "I want you. Inside me. Ten minutes ago."

"Then I'm running late," he growls back.

I'm more than ready for him — his cock slides deep inside, filling every slick inch of me.

"Dom," I gasp into his ear as our bodies start to move in sync. "Oh my God, Dom."

He presses my back into the wall, burying his lips into my neck, then trails kisses down to my breasts, taking them into his mouth again, twirling his tongue around my hardened nipples, until I'm nearly screaming out his name.

Every bit of him feels electric against me, like we fit together perfectly. His thick, muscular arms holding me against the wall, while I clench his throbbing cock buried deep inside me.

I wrap myself tighter around him, feeling weightless, nearly screaming his name.

"Dom, Dom," I moan into his ear, running my fingernails across his scalp.

"Fuck, Olivia," he groans into my hair. "You feel so fucking good right now."

His body is everywhere I need it to be, and I feel everything in him start to go rigid, deepening within me while I wrap myself tighter around him. He's still pushing me harder against the wall, thrusting harder inside me, until the pulse of his cock throbbing against my G spot finally sends me over the edge.

"Oh, God, Dom!" The words spill out of me, breathless and raw.

He starts to release, his body pushing against me, around me, finally letting himself go, too. I wrap my arms around his shoulders, unable to focus on finding or tasting his lips anymore. All I can do is dig my face into the warmth of his neck, hearing myself moan as we ride each wave of pleasure together.

CHAPTER 38

After we're both breathless and spinning slowly back down to reality, Dom sets me down with a kiss, then hands me my kaftan and a soft cashmere blanket off the sofa.

He kisses me deeply again before telling me to meet him outside.

"Wrap up in these and go sit at the table out there. I'm going to feed you like a fucking queen."

I laugh and start to protest. "I can help get everything to the table."

But he plants a look on his face that tells me not to argue with him.

"Just let me take care of you." He kisses me again before gently nudging me toward the lanai. "I want to. Now go."

"Okay, okay." I laugh. "But I'm taking these out too."

I grab what's left of the wine bottle and my glass from the counter. Then I pull my silky kaftan back over my head and wrap the blanket around my shoulders, not bothering to put anything on underneath.

When I walk outside, the view hits me again like it's my first time seeing it. The long teak wood table overlooking the garden, the shimmering diamond-filled bay below. I take a seat in one of the dining chairs and lean back, resting my head against the tall backrest, feeling dizzy with happiness. After a full day of writing and another top fuck of my life, I know I've hit the jackpot winding up here. Finding him.

My head is screaming that it's way too early to feel this strongly about him, but my heart is whispering that I must be falling in love. I fit so perfectly in his arms that I can't imagine being anywhere else as long as I live.

This feeling of peace and serenity is going to be hard to find back home, among the sirens and noisy bustle of the city. It's not just the palm trees swaying in the gentle breeze, or the water glittering in the distance. It's Dom. The way I feel perfectly myself with him. Like I have nothing to hide when we're together. Free to be myself. Imperfect, closeted skeletons and all.

"You were ravenous when you arrived." He's suddenly behind me. "I can only imagine how hungry you are after that."

"Me?" I laugh. "You just gave yourself a serious cardio workout in there."

He's holding a tray of seafood, along with his wine glass from earlier. There's a post-sex glow radiating from his skin that makes me want to do it all over again if this is what he looks like afterward. A little flushed, like he just got back from a hard run.

"That was just a warm-up." He narrows his eyes. "Don't tempt me into *really* breaking a sweat before you get the chance to fill up. You're going to need to refuel."

I grin. "I like the sound of that."

He sets the tray down and starts heaping our plates with the most incredible looking seafood I've ever seen.

* * *

By the end, I'm happily sprawled across cloud nine. Shrimp, king crab legs, and Wagyu medallions seared to perfection on the grill. It was just as good as the fanciest meals I've had back in New York. Maybe better since I got to enjoy it with him.

I finally push myself back from the table. "I'm going to kiss whoever gave you cooking lessons."

"My father would probably love that, but my mother, not so much." He pretends to look appalled. "And neither would I."

I lean over and kiss him.

We've already watched another spectacular fuchsia-streaked sunset while we ate, and now we're sitting under a blanket of Edison bulbs mixed with the stars.

"Your dad must have been a Michelin-star chef."

Our first bottle of white wine turned into a second about an hour ago. I am deliciously tipsy, enjoying Dom's company while listening to the sound of the waves crashing ashore in the distance. A faint light from a boat on the surface of the water catches my eye. I watch it bob up and down, unable to imagine what it would be like to float out there right now, surrounded by nothing but dark waves and the creatures swimming below.

Quinton's outdoor patio is heaven on earth. The table is sandwiched between two blazing gas firepits, overlooking a full moon that cascades across the ocean as far as I can see toward the horizon. The palm trees swaying gently below us make everything feel serene. Solar lights line each pathway, highlighting the palm trees' shadows as they sway in the salty breeze. Probably still hovering around seventy-five degrees out. Warm enough to not need a sweater quite yet. I could stay right here forever and it would never grow old.

"No, my father definitely didn't have a Michelin star." He pours himself another splash of wine. My glass doesn't need it quite yet.

"Well, even without one, he must have taught you well," I insist, gently trying to coax out more stories about his life growing up in California. I want to know more, and how it all led him to this moment, an ocean away from it all.

"True." He smiles over at me, like he wants to say more. "We were pretty spoiled growing up, especially in the kitchen."

I laugh. "Don't tell me your dad is Gordon Ramsay." I have no idea who his father is, but nothing is off the table, considering his brother.

"No." He laughs, finally relenting. "Dad owned Paramour Studios."

"What?" I deadpan, trying not to gape. The hits keep coming. I stare at Dom, my heart pounding. He's so humble and down to earth. I never would have guessed that two men in his family are Hollywood royalty.

"My mother is Royce Carsen. Dad fell in love with her on set in the late eighties. That's also how Quinton got his start. He began tagging along with Dad to do films when he was — gosh, around four years old. Old enough to sit still and know when to be quiet while he got to watch the magic of a movie set unfold. He learned the basics of directing when most other kids were learning how to play t-ball. Runs in his blood now."

"And you were never into that?" I study his face for any of the tension he appeared to have earlier.

"I rarely talk about this stuff." He shifts on his chair. "I usually try to keep my personal life separate from all that."

"Why?" I genuinely want to know. I feel like I'm finally peeling back the layers of his life. Which, until tonight, have been mostly a mystery to me. "Don't they count as your personal life too?"

"Money and fame have this weird effect on people. I've been burned so many times when people find out I have some heavy hitters in my family. It's happened my whole life. I was engaged at one point." His eyes shift to mine, looking slightly embarrassed — pained, even.

"You were? What happened?" I try to picture the type of woman someone like Dom would propose to. A tinge of jealousy rolls through me.

He sits back in his chair, taking a deep breath. His face looks stern, like he's practiced closing off whatever hurt he's about to reopen.

"Her name was Taryn. She swore up and down that none of that stuff mattered to her. The fame, the fortune, the red-carpet events, and everything else that comes with your dad owning Paramour Studios."

"And then what?"

"I found out that she tried seducing Quinton for a movie role three weeks before our wedding."

"Oh my God. You must have been devastated."

"To say the least."

"I'm so sorry. I'm sure you loved her, but she sounds like a real asshat."

I smile, hoping he's not offended at the joke.

He erupts in laughter at first, then quiets down to the sad chuckle at the end of a joke that hits a little too close to home.

"Turns out, she was." He smiles weakly, like the wound has reopened. "Quinton told me what happened right after. I was furious. Mom had to call all the guests, which was like eight hundred of their friends and family. I never saw it coming."

"That explains why you didn't tell me much about your family until now."

He nods.

"She wasn't the only one," he says. "Just the first one who was caught so brazenly."

"So, now you try to hide it." I realize what a huge deal this was for him to bring me here and tell me about his brother.

"People treat us differently. All of us. Once they find out." I watch it all pour out of him, like he's letting go of something he's held close to his chest for too long. "It's hard to know who to trust, and who's just looking for a handout."

As much as I would love the opportunity to pitch Quinton Rockwell my script, the look on Dom's face right now tells me that I can't take him up on that offer.

"Dom, I can't pitch your brother," I say quietly.

"What?" His voice is suddenly all gravel and steel, like he can't believe what I'm saying.

"Not after what you've just told me. I don't want to risk you thinking that I'm just using you for the connection with your brother. You deserve a clean slate from all that. And someone who isn't going to take you up on that offer. I'd rather just take my chances with the connections I have back home and not risk muddying the water with you over this."

His eyes shoot to mine, and he leans back in his chair. "But I'm the one that offered, it was my idea. At first, I thought maybe there was some chance that you'd found out who my brother was, and that was why you chose my rental while you were here finishing your script." He takes my hand in his, smiling. "But I'm certain now that you had no idea I was on the other end of that reservation."

"I don't want to put you in the position of feeling taken advantage of. I won't pitch him if it's going to bother you, even if you tell me you don't mind. I have contacts in the broadcast industry. I can make it without you."

He smiles, then laughs before looking at me in disbelief. "Well, this is a first." He leans over to kiss me. "Someone actually trying to turn down a family favor from me. You are full of surprises, Liv."

"Have you dated anyone seriously since Taryn?" I ask quietly.

"No." His voice has turned soft again. "I've never had any interest in getting that close to the flame again. I'd resigned myself to flying solo. I knew I had pretty much everything most people would consider to be the recipe for a perfect life. I told myself that was enough. That I didn't need anyone else. Until I saw you standing there in your underwear that day."

He cracks a smile — I burst out laughing.

Then he leans over the table to give me another long kiss, letting his lips linger against mine for as long as I want.

CHAPTER 39

I can't imagine how awful it must have felt for Dom to find out that his fiancée was willing to trade sleeping with his brother for her future marriage with him.

"Not everyone is like Taryn," I say firmly when he pulls away from our kiss.

"I wouldn't be here tonight sitting across from you if I didn't agree with that." The way his eyes are suddenly burning into mine sends a tingly shiver down my spine. Then he breaks into a boyish grin and squeezes my knee. "But I'm still going to introduce you to Quinton. And I'd really like for you to have the opportunity to pitch him."

I start to protest, but he puts a finger over my lips. I pretend to bite it, before breaking into a smile, touched by his persistence, and the trust he has in me.

"Just think about it." He's studying my eyes. "You don't have to say yes right now. He won't be here for a few more weeks."

"Deal." I kiss him back. "So, even with all that Hollywood blood rolling through your veins, you never got into directing or acting? Not even when you were little?"

"No." He sits back against his chair again. "I tagged along plenty of times, but I was more into the set building and staging I saw in the production houses. Those set builders could

182

create anything you could imagine. Make a whole house full of rooms out of thin air in just a few days. As a kid, it was as good as magic — seeing what they could do with a few sketches and a team of skilled tradesmen. This was before CGI was a thing, when pretend worlds had to be built with their bare hands."

"Is that how you got into the vacation rental industry then? You like the idea of making little homes? Building or fixing them up?"

He chuckles a little, then takes a deep breath, like he's about to let me in on something else I should know. "I own a property development company. Among other ventures. While Dad gave Quinton a shot at directing, he gave me the gift of investing in my first company when I was sixteen."

"Your *first* company at sixteen?" I feel like I'm unwrapping all of Dom's hidden layers tonight, but as carefully and slowly as possible. "How many do you own now?"

"I'm not sure." I study him for any signs of fibbing, but he looks like he's telling the truth.

How many companies would you have to own to lose track?

"Just like you weren't sure how many rentals you have on Airbnb when I first called."

I'm trying not to stare at Dom too intently. What he does for a living — or the fact that he's related to Hollywood legends — would have been boasted about on a first date back in New York. But Dom has been so quiet about all of it. I understand why, but it's like I'm seeing the full picture of his life now, and it's a lot to digest.

"You're a man of many hidden talents," I say, watching him carefully. He grabs my face in his hands and kisses me deeply, until my head feels like it's swimming in a sea of stars.

"There's a few more hidden talents I plan to show you." He pulls back, a suggestive edge deepening his voice. "If you'll let me."

"Yes, please." I bite my lip, hard, keeping myself from mounting him again right here on the table. The air between us feels like it's practically erupting with steam. I'm already panting for another round, and we've barely just finished the last.

His eyes travel down the kaftan, then spring back up to my lips, watching me smile. "You look beautiful tonight. In case I haven't told you enough times."

I smile. "You have. But I don't mind."

"Well, it feels like a sin not to say it enough." He glances at my lips again.

Between the ocean waves, a slight breeze rustling the garden around us, and sweet compliments like that rolling off Dom's tongue, the soundtrack of my life right now sounds like a new song I never want to end.

"Care for a swim?" He stands up suddenly.

The meandering soundtrack in my head screeches to a halt.

"A swim?" I sit up and look around. "Did I miss the part of the garden with a pool?"

"The pool is down the path on the other side of that rock wall." He points past the stone table where I sat working earlier today. "But I prefer the sea."

CHAPTER 40

My eyes dart out to the vast expanse of water. I can hear the waves rolling onto the shore slowly, almost like the ocean is getting sleepy, but it looks nearly black against the sky. Majestic and menacing at the same time.

"That? At night? You're not serious." I grab what's left of the wine bottle and pour it into my glass. I take a sip, narrowing my eyes at him. However, the look on his face appears to be dead serious.

"If you haven't gone night swimming while you're here yet, we need to cross it off your bucket list. Tonight."

He can't actually expect me to get in that. Not with all the creepy night creatures I was just thinking of moments ago.

"I distinctly recall a very wise man telling me that sharks feed at night. And besides, I don't have my swimsuit." I smile, knowing full well my lack of swimsuit will only encourage him even more.

"Who said anything about swimsuits?" Dom grins back at me. A rush of new adrenaline runs through me when I realize what he's suggesting. Then he stands up. His ab muscles practically dance in the firelight, daring me to take the bait.

I lean back and drain my glass, then set it down thoughtfully, enjoying what I'm seeing already.

I laugh. "Don't tempt me with a good time. I'm perfectly content with my current view." I let my eyes wash down his body, suddenly hungry for dessert.

"This isn't a temptation, as much as it's a promise."

Then he takes off, sprinting toward the crashing waves in the distance.

* * *

"I've never been skinny-dipping." I'm standing breathless at the water's edge. The sand beneath my bare feet still feels warm from a day spent baking in the sun.

I have yet to pull my kaftan off, still fairly unconvinced that we're actually going into that dark water.

"How is that possible?"

"No one is exactly stripping down to jump in the Hudson River these days." I giggle nervously. "At least no one that I know."

He's standing just inches away, looking down at me with a stark white grin, all the whiter in the near darkness of the moonlight. Heat from his body pushes through the thin fabric I'm still wearing, making my entire body pulse harder, screaming at me to get in the water if it means having another go with him. I wish he'd sling me over his shoulder and dive under the waves with me, just to get it all over with.

He bends down to kiss me, gently at first, then hungry for more.

Adrenaline courses through my veins. I'm unable to ignore the fresh wave of desire rushing through me, filling me to my core.

"You ready?" he whispers.

I pull the kaftan over my head in one swooshing motion, just as Dom tosses his board shorts aside.

CHAPTER 41

He spins around toward the water's edge, letting out a whoop, before running away from me in a flash.

My feet stay planted as time instantly stands still.

Remember every detail, I tell myself, knowing this moment will be a favorite to look back on long after it's done. A memory I never knew I needed to have until it's unfolding right here in front of me.

Watching the hardened muscles in each of his legs lengthen as he runs, propelling his lithe body toward a horizon of glistening waves. His tight ass disappearing into the dark. Thousands of miles away from anything that makes sense, from anything I ever thought I wanted. *How did I get here?* Running naked into the sea, with this unbelievably sexy, complicated man, under a moonlit sky.

Knowing simply, and with all my heart, that there is nowhere else in the world that I'd rather be. And no one else I'd rather be with.

When he dives head first into an oncoming wave, I take off next. Sprinting down the sand in his wake, my footprints smaller than his. The humidity in the air dampens my skin, making each nipple tighten up toward the stars as my breasts move freely while I run. Sand sinking beneath my feet with every step, arms pumping at my sides. I shriek into the midnight sky, the wildness in my own voice catching me by surprise.

Dom surfaces from under the water before I can make it past the blanket of waves. Spinning around, instantly taking me in. I catch his eyes grazing beneath my belly button, then shoot upward toward my breasts, before finally grinning, eyes locked into mine. Falling backward — like he can't stand another second — into another oncoming wave.

I dive in head first just like I watched him do a moment ago, quieting the butterflies that quickly storm my stomach when the water shocks my skin. It's all I can focus on. I gasp at the surface and shoot out of the wake, both feet sinking into the waterlogged sand beneath me.

Hopping back and forth, feeling weightless in the sea, I draw my knees up to warm my body, suspending my limbs beneath me in the salty water. Then I tilt, floating up on my back, and push my belly button up toward the sky filled with diamonds. Just like I was taught to do as a little girl. Filling my lungs with air, I close my eyes before letting them adjust to the familiar sting of the ocean. I don't even care that I'm exposed, floating above the surface under such a perfectly beautiful sky. It doesn't matter. Nothing matters across the world, this far from home. Splaying my arms out to each side, like a starfish unfurling, I'm home. Untethered and free.

The gurgle of gentle waves rolls beneath me, tickling my ears on the surface of the water. It washes out the air, the sound. Just the muffled sea, and me.

"My God, you're beautiful," Dom says gently, over the sound of the ocean filling my ears.

I hadn't noticed him come closer, but now I peek over at him with just one eye, watching him take me in. Feeling bold, and sexy. Uncharacteristically unmoored.

Dom makes me feel like few people ever have.

Like being beside him is the greatest adrenaline rush in the calmest moment.

It's too soon, and maybe foolish to say, but I already can't imagine another soul giving me that combination as long as I live. Safe yet unhinged, perfectly cradled, yet falling desperately into something new and exciting.

He clasps my hand in his. Then he scoops me up off the surface of the water, kissing me once again. Our bodies press together, his hands pushing back my hair, and I can feel his excitement growing between my legs.

"I'm on the pill, if you want to—" I whisper in his ear.

I part my legs for him, letting him know I'm okay to do this here, and now, if he is.

I feel him push into me, filling me again, like he did back in the kitchen, his body hot against mine. He buries his face in my neck, groaning. I feel weightless in his arms — he's planted in the sand, becoming the anchor I need to push him deeper inside me.

He slowly starts moving, more carefully than he did back at the house with me pressed against the wall. He's watching me in the moonlight this time, my breasts bobbing against the surface, our breath mingling between us. Gasping between kisses, watching each other's eyes as they start to plead for a sweetened release.

"Fuck, you feel so fucking good." He's clenching his teeth. I watch his eyes burning, just an inch or two from mine, filled with the reflection of the moon in the waves. They churn into mine, daring me to come first. But I want to watch him this time. Want to watch a man like him lose his bearings on everything while he's clenched deeply inside me.

"You feel like you were made for me," I groan back. "You fill every part of me."

His breath grows more ragged.

"I want to watch you lose control of everything when I make you come."

His body starts to tense, his fingers digging into my waist. We move together faster as his breath starts to quicken.

"Fuck me harder," I tell him. "Don't stop. Don't ever stop."

I clench myself around him, swallowing his cock with throbbing pulses of my own.

His eyes close as his jaw locks into place, both of us tipping over the edge, stars bursting behind my eyelids, ripples of water fanning out from around us in a harsh rhythm, made from our bodies moving so fast together. Then he holds me in the waves, wrapped gently around me, in me, becoming a part of me, until I remember where I am again.

He kisses my forehead, then my lips.

"Come watch the stars with me," I whisper when his mouth finds my neck, nipping and begging for more. "Float with me. I don't want tonight to end."

He kisses me once more, then lets me go. I tilt up onto my back again, cradled in the sea, watching him join me from the corner of my eye.

Our bodies rise and fall in line with each rolling hill of water gently spinning into shore. The ocean lulls us into a trance, rocking us gently in her sweet, rhythmic song. Black sky stretches above, moonlight shimmering off the water, bouncing light into the white plumeria blooms in the branches back on shore.

Our own little peaceful oasis, too beautiful to miss. I've never seen anything more enchanting.

I close my eyes again and squeeze Dom's hand, lacing my fingers tightly between each one of his. My hair floats around me, tickling my cheeks, while water gurgles in my ears. Unable to recall another time or place I've ever felt so happy — so at peace — in all my life.

CHAPTER 42

The next morning, after Dom drops me off at home, I'm filling Pru's food dish when my phone starts pinging over and over. They're all texts from Abby.

Are you awake?

Wake up and call me.

Call me!! I have to tell you something. What time is it there?

What is she talking about? I hope everything is okay.
She answers the phone on the first half-ring.
"Abby! You're scaring me. What's wrong?"
"Have you Googled Dom yet?" she bursts out.
I lean against the counter, suddenly very awake.
"What? What are you talking about?"
"I Googled him."
"Oh." My stomach lurches, thinking she's found something indescribably awful. Not wanting the memory of last night to be tarnished by whatever it is, I close my eyes, bracing for the blow she's about to deliver.

"He's a fucking billionaire, Liv."

My eyes shoot open.

"What? No, he lives in his brother's house, which might make him look like one, but—"

"Is that what he told you?"

"No." I search my memory for any indication that he's as successful as Abby says. The companies. The fact that he's not sure how many he owns.

"You said he has no idea how many rentals he actually has, right?"

"Oh, God." I swallow hard, searching my memory for any other details that might dispel this little rumor she's calling about. "That doesn't mean he's a billionaire. Someone can have a few rentals and not know the exact number . . ." *And companies*, I want to add.

"Liv, the internet doesn't lie."

I laugh until I realize she isn't joining in. "I love you, dearly, and I mean this so kindly, but you're out of your mind if you think this guy is walking around all casually like a closeted, self-made billionaire. He's too young for that. And hot. He's too young and hot for that."

"You're probably in shock, and I totally get that, but you need to get online and look for yourself."

"You're claiming the guy I've been seeing is a full-blown Mark Zuckerberg?"

"He's not even in the same league as Mark Zuckerberg. He's more like a bazillionaire who looks oddly similar to Jason Momoa. Why didn't you send me a picture, by the way? I had to snoop on this guy online to see him for myself and — damn, Liv . . . I'm surprised you even come up for air if that's who you've been spending time with."

I smile into the phone, remembering the exact moment he sunk into me last night. The first and second time. Then I close my eyes as swirls of lust flow through me again. She's not wrong. I'm not sure why I even left his house, other than to get a fresh change of clothes this morning. Otherwise, I'd be tempted to chain him to a bed for the rest of the day.

"Liv, are you still there? Or have you fainted from the news?"

I snap back to our conversation. "The internet lied to you, Abby." I'm a little annoyed that we're still on this whole kick. Google isn't the most truthful place to research someone, especially if they're tied to a family that tabloids would be interested in selling false headlines about. "Billionaires don't couch surf at their brother's house."

"Are you forgetting what I do for a living?"

"You've added *private investigator* to your résumé now?" I ask, teasing her as I open cupboards, looking for the bag of bagels I was sure I still had in here somewhere. I'm starving after the workout I got last night.

"I don't make mistakes when I'm looking into someone's background. I'm meticulous about this kind of thing."

"I haven't told you about his family yet, which probably just makes him look like he's uber rich too, just like his dad, and his brother, and his mom . . ."

"Right. His dad owned—"

"Paramour Studios. I know."

"And his brother is—"

"Quinton Rockwell. Trust me, I know! I was going to tell you all this when I got home."

Abby clears her throat, then silence. Like she's waiting for me to pick up what she's putting down.

The clock ticking on the wall grows louder as it all starts to sink in.

"Abby? You sure you're not wrong about this?"

Silence.

I frown at my hand, still frozen on the cupboard knob.

"Go make yourself some coffee," she finally says, "so we can have a real conversation about it."

I turn toward the coffee maker. My heart's pumping so fast I'm not sure I need more caffeine, but I follow her instructions anyway.

"I'm walking to the coffee pot now. He's not even living in his own place right now because his house is getting renovated."

"Listen, I know you haven't dated in a hot minute, but these days you have to Google everyone you start seeing. Haven't you watched *Dateline*? Anyway, when you told me you spent the day at his place yesterday, I wanted to make sure he wasn't Hawaii's version of Ted Bundy or something, so I Googled him."

"I don't really think that information would be on Google. I mean, if Google knew, then the police would know, and—"

"Liv, put the coffee grounds in the little spot for coffee grounds. Pour the water . . ."

I do as she says and press *Brew*. The coffee pot bubbles to life while I lean against the counter.

Billionaire? No. Successful? Sure. But billionaire status? Google has to be wrong. It's probably intermixing his net worth with Quinton's.

* * *

"*This* is why you're in that townhouse, Liv! *This* is your shot! None of it has anything to do with Rex."

"Abby, it's not like that. Dom offered for me to pitch Quinton when he comes here in about six weeks. But I'm not sure I can take him up on that. I don't want him to think it's the only reason I'm seeing him."

"Are you shitting me?" She's practically screaming into the phone. "How close are you to being done with that thing?"

"It's getting there. But I can always just call one of my contacts at the station when I'm back home. We've had so many actors and directors on *The Good Day Show* since I've been there. I have other people I can pitch once it's done. I don't need to mix business with pleasure."

I can hear her sighing on the other end of the phone. "Let me just read this from Google for you."

It feels like we're somehow snooping into Dom's private life. I try explaining that to Abby, but she refuses to hear me out.

"Everyone Googles the people they start dating. Especially when they're related to film industry legends. You need to be informed about what you're getting yourself into."

I close my eyes and press my fingertips to my lips, remembering what it felt like to have his mouth hungry against mine. The moon hanging overhead while we held onto each other's hands in the gentle waves, under a sky filled with stars.

"I couldn't care less who his brother is, or how much money he has. That's amazing, yes, but it's just a bonus. If I could spend every single day for the rest of my life coming home to those eyes. And that smile. And the way he makes me feel like I'm the most fascinating person in the room. Any room."

She stops clacking away at the keyboard. I press the FaceTime button so her face pops up on the screen. She's back in her own apartment for once. Toby's white tail is twitching in the corner of the screen, almost out of sight.

"Hi, Toby!" I call out. He doesn't turn, but his tail twitches back and forth like a pendulum.

"He's still mad you got a new cat." Abby is covering his ears, smiling. "Now, spill it."

"Last night was one of the best nights of my life." I can feel a huge shit-eating grin wrapping its way across my face.

"Oh my God, you're really starting to fall for this guy, aren't you?"

I smile and nod. "He's the most incredible guy I've ever met. Even without any of that other stuff added in. I've never met anyone like him."

"Does he have a brother that isn't married to a former supermodel by chance?" She must have already read about Quinton and his wife, Selma. "This is a superior upgrade from Rex. So glad you're finally leaving that dick in the dust."

"I don't know how I'm ever going to come back to New York." Just thinking about it makes my eyes sting.

"Oh, honey." She sets aside her laptop, putting everything she just learned about Dom out of sight. "This is more than a vacation fling. I haven't seen that look in your eyes in way too long."

"It was supposed to just be a fun diversion from living next door to Rex. I'm not sure how it morphed into . . ." I can hear the conviction in my own voice. "My life back in New York already feels so far away, and I still have a few more weeks to go here. I can't imagine where I'll be, mentally, when I have to board that plane to go home."

"Are you sure you don't want to know any more details about him? There's nothing bad to say. But this guy you just happened to stumble upon? He's a ten, Liv. Outlandishly successful, seemingly private, and handsome as fucking hell. This guy might be the reason why everything happened the way it did. The proposal, the public backlash, the sudden sabbatical to Hawaii. Maybe Rex has nothing to do with why you're there. Maybe it was all just the universe's way of lining you up for success, *and* for love."

"It's messier than that. He has a past too. And his is possibly even more complicated than mine. He was engaged once before, and the reason it ended makes everything I'm trying to do here a little more complicated when it comes to him and me."

"What do you mean?"

"How much time do you have?" I sigh.

"I'm calling in sick." She grabs Toby and settles into the couch with him draped across her shoulder.

I'm surprised. "You never call in sick."

"This is worth a few hours off. Besides, I need a break. Badly."

"You sure?" I feel touched that she'd take a few hours off just to catch up with me.

"One hundred percent sure. Now, tell me everything."

CHAPTER 43

When I'm done telling Abby about Dom's failed engagement, and how he's been too nervous to introduce women to his family since then, she finally gets it.

"I need to talk to Dom," I say slowly. "Do you think he's going to be mad that I Googled him?"

"Well, *I* Googled him, not you. And it's all out there online. If he doesn't like that, he needs to talk to the internet gods. These are modern times and Googling your date is part of the package now."

I smile. She's right. If Dom is mad about it, then that says more about him than me. I've Googled Tinder dates for my friends before letting them meet up with someone random. So this is hardly an invasion of privacy from me or Abby. Plus, I don't want to hide that I know more about his personal life than I did the last time I saw him.

A text pings on my phone.

> *Can't stop thinking about you. Or last night. I can be there in 20 min with croissants and Starbucks*

A rumble of anticipation rolls through me. Twenty minutes to shower, tidy this place, and hide Pru.

"Dom is coming over," I tell her. "I've got twenty minutes. He's bringing breakfast."

"Go! Go get ready!" she cheers. "Are you going to bring all this up?"

I consider her question carefully. "I think I have to."

"Good. Start off with no secrets. Now go!"

Speaking of secrets, I stare at Pru.

I race around throwing dirty laundry into the closet, wiping rogue toothpaste from the sink, and finally rinse off in the shower, then throw on a silky, pink pair of shorts and a matching camisole. It's pouring rain outside — I'm just putting Pru in the closet with a bowl of cat food when I hear Dom knock on the door.

"Please, just take a little nap, I'll be back to get you soon," I tell her. Then I close the closet door and run to greet Dom.

I smile as I open the front door. "You know, you don't have to knock at your own place." His hair is still a little disheveled, and he's wearing a soft white T-shirt with a red pair of jersey shorts. God, he looks sexy with his hair still ruffled and messy like that. His biceps strain at the sleeves of his tee, and I can see the outline of his pecs underneath. I pinch myself, remembering why he's here.

He shoves two coffees and a bag of pastries on the counter before lunging at me, wrapping me up in a bear hug, then tipping me backward and kissing my neck. I shriek with a laugh, throwing my head back when he dips me toward the floor, giving him more access to my collarbones. He kicks the door shut with his heel and picks me up in one swoosh, carrying me straight to the bedroom.

"What about breakfast?" I yelp, bouncing down the hall.

"That was just an excuse to get you back in bed," he says gruffly. "It'll still be there later. First, we need to work up an appetite."

Dom tosses me onto the bed, then immediately crawls onto the mattress above me. I wrap my arms around his shoulders — solid, like two oversized softballs — and revel in the weight of him pressing me down.

"I didn't sleep at all last night." He leans down to kiss me before pulling away. "Every time I closed my eyes, I saw you." He pushes my hair back and kisses me again. "Every inch of your body." Dom runs one hand down to my ass and squeezes once, then trails it back up to my hair. "You, floating under that moonlight." He kisses me again. "Tasting your salty lips." Another kiss. "I could still hear your laughter in my dreams when I finally did manage to sleep." The next kiss is longer, and it ends with him nipping my bottom lip. My whole body is on fire. I feel like I could explode, and we haven't even gotten undressed yet.

He tilts my chin up, staring down into my eyes, before devouring my lips again.

"I can't believe I let you leave after all that."

I laugh. "I still can't believe we *did* that."

He cracks into a smile, the intensity in his eyes melting a little. "Which part?"

"The swimming at night part. Naked."

"Afraid of being seen?" He leans back to see my face more clearly.

I look up at him from below my lashes. "Actually, I kind of liked it."

"Skinny-dipping?" He leans onto his elbow, looking amused.

"There was kind of a rush in doing something so . . ."

"Out in the open?" He looks delighted about what I've just said.

"I guess." I grin. "Back in New York, there are so many people everywhere, at all times, there was something kind of delicious in being so open and free in what would usually be such a private moment."

"Maybe you need to come back and try that again. Tonight."

He starts kissing my neck, the sun streaming through the window, across his back. Then he sits up and pulls his shirt up over his head, tossing it aside. Looking like an absolute dream, with tanned muscles everywhere. Then he bends down to kiss me again.

He turns his back to the radiating sunlight and drinks me in. I open my knees another inch, which is all it takes for him to practically levitate back onto the bed.

CHAPTER 44

Dom slips my shorts off when he reaches me, leaving on only my silky cami and a white thong. Then he kisses my neck, trailing kisses to my breasts, and eventually reaches my hips. He pauses to catch my eye before running his tongue along the top rim of my panties, then down the fold of my inner thigh, pulling the fabric back just barely so his tongue can taste my skin, then back up to my hip bone again. He releases the fabric and it springs back to cover me up again.

"The best revenge is living well, right?" I say, reminding him of the words he told me, back when we devised the whole silly plan to make Rex jealous. It seems like a lifetime ago. I scoot my hips to the center of the bed, the most intimate parts of me facing the window, and open my legs again, inviting him to continue down the path of what we both want him to finish.

Dom obeys, kneeling beside the bed, grabbing my ass and pulling me closer to his waiting mouth. Sunlight streams across the bed, across my body. Warm and sensual, heating me in places that have never felt the sun, as Dom pulls back the thin, lacy fabric, revealing every part of me to him in those golden beams of light. I feel him take me in his mouth, French kissing every fold — then, the deepest part of me.

My eyes roll back as Dom picks up the pace, and I splay my knees out wider, begging him to go deeper.

"Don't stop."

He grips my ass tight, then pushes my knees apart with his elbows, circling my clit with his tongue until I'm biting the flesh on the back of my hand, grabbing a pillow to muffle the moans escaping my throat. I throw the pillow aside and sit up halfway, wanting to see what he's doing to me. Wanting to see his mouth pulling and tasting the ridges of my body, while I reach down and feel the wetness between my own fingers. He grabs one of them between his teeth, then pushes it into his mouth. I pull it back slowly from his lips, and start circling my clit with my fingertips. He joins in with his tongue, weaving the slickness of his mouth through my fingers and along my opening, until I can hardly tell where his mouth ends and my fingers begin. I fall back onto the bed as I start to shake and writhe against his lips.

"Oh my God, Dom." I run my other hand through his hair as he digs his tongue into me again. I push myself harder against the bed, throwing my head back toward the ceiling — wanting this feeling to last forever, but nearly screaming at him to take me over the edge.

I meet his eye, pushing myself harder into his tongue, my breath catching, until I can't stand it anymore. And, just as I explode, my entire body convulsing and pulsing from the way his mouth is fucking me, I finally close my eyes and scream.

"Dom!"

A wave of pure ecstasy rolls through me.

CHAPTER 45

Shuddering, I roll my body to the side, then turn and wait for Dom to join me back on the bed again. Needing to feel his body against mine.

"You're unreal." Dom climbs up and lies beside me. I can tell he's ready for his turn.

I climb on top of him, pushing his cock deep inside my body. He groans when I start to ride him, sliding up and down, as slick and slow as I can.

I lean over him and push down against his shoulders, kissing his neck as I ride his cock back and forth, deep inside me.

I bite his earlobe. "Take me in the shower."

Then I hop off the bed. He jumps up to follow me, grabbing my ass as I walk down the hall in front of him. Kissing my neck from behind while we make our way toward the bathroom.

When we get there, I bend over the side of the tub to turn the water on. While I wait for it to heat up, I brace my hand against the side of the tub, arching my back, giving him a full view of my ass bent over. I look over my shoulder, assessing him. He's standing two feet behind me, his cock practically dripping in anticipation, knowing full well what I'm doing to him.

"This is going to take a minute to heat up . . . We could just . . ." I wait for my suggestion to take hold.

He closes the gap between us and, without a word, enters me from behind. I groan when his cock fills me, putting both hands against the wall of the shower to brace myself against him. I instantly start writhing and bouncing my ass against his cock. The full length of him from this angle feels like it's going to take my breath away.

I squeeze my legs in closer, arching my back, so my ass is lifted as high as I can go, giving all of him deeper access, finding my G spot with every sensual thrust. His hand cups me from behind, finding my clit with his fingertips.

"Your ass from this angle," he groans. "And your back, arching up like that. My God, Liv, you're so fucking hot." He wraps his other hand through my hair, pulling it back gently. "I'm not going to last long with you moving like that."

I'm circling my hips around, pushing him deeper into me, both hands splayed on the shower wall. The steam is starting to rise from the tub, filling the bathroom with hot mist. It's making my skin glisten all over as he grabs my ass, picking up the pace. I can hear him starting to groan, but all I can focus on is the feeling of my tight wetness, gripping onto his erection with every thrust.

"I want you so fucking bad." His breath hitches in his throat. Then he releases me and flips me around so we're facing each other again. We both step into the shower, turning the water on to the rainforest shower head above us. It streams over both our bodies while his lips slide across mine, heat from the water mixing with the heat from his lips, as he grazes my neck with his teeth. I'm facing him when he enters me again, wrapping my arms around his shoulders, bracing myself up against his body. He takes both my wrists and holds my arms high above my head, pressing them against the shower wall.

"I never want to stop," he growls.

I cover his mouth with mine again.

He slides in and out of me, hot water sliding between us, pressing his hands against mine. Pushing me harder into the tile, before shuddering around me, throbbing inside me. His lips are frozen against my cheek, giving me all that he has.

My lips curl into a grin, reveling in the way this enormous man becomes lost inside me. How just the feeling of my body is enough to send him over the edge.

He presses his forehead against mine, our hands still intertwined above my head.

"I will never let you leave this island," he says gruffly. He kisses my neck again, then my lips, dragging my bottom lip into his mouth with his teeth, before releasing me again. We're both still panting as the water from overhead runs down our eyelashes, our lips, our chins, our wet bodies pressed together. Then our hands slowly slide their way back down the wall, wrapping around each other, holding tightly to the only thing in the world that I know I can't live without anymore.

CHAPTER 46

After we fog up the entire bathroom with a long, hot shower, I'm toweling off in my bedroom when I see my phone light up.

What the flying fuck was that?

It's the first text I've gotten from Rex since I got here, and since it's following the noise Dom and I were making, it's likely about what he's just overheard. Well, isn't that rich, considering what I've been putting up with through the wall. I angrily punch in my reply and hit *Send* before I lose my nerve.

That was me fucking someone, or did you forget what that sounds like already?

Three dots appear on his side almost immediately, then disappear. I stare at the phone until they reappear again, followed by a message.

I hope you're happy.

I soften, just a smidge.

I'm very happy.

He responds instantly.

I miss you.

And now I'm mad all over again. Why did he have to go there?

Don't. You have an incredible woman who actually wants you. Juju deserves your full attention. Don't reach out to me again, no matter what you hear through these walls. Besides, you're one to talk.

I chuck my phone into the pile of pillows that covers the floor from when we cleared the bed earlier.

I've grown rather fond of Juju, against all odds, and now I just feel bad for her. I hate the fact that she's probably not going to look at me ever again once she finds out the secret I've been harboring about her skeezy boyfriend. I should have blurted it out that very first day. Ripped off the Band-Aid. By this point I feel more like an accomplice than an ally, and I hate that.

Dom walks out of the bathroom with a towel draped loosely around his hips. He's so built that it barely closes over the front of him.

I sit down on the edge of the comforter.

"That was fucking hot." I grin. "But I'm pretty sure Rex heard everything through these walls."

He hops onto the bed next to me and the towel dips even lower. I fight the urge to just take him again — right here, right now.

"I think I might get an abysmal review by your ex on my vacation rental." He sounds amused.

I lean back against the headboard to face him, stretching my legs out in front of me. He kisses the tip of my pinky toe, then grabs my other foot to start rubbing it.

"I think you'll be alright." And now I don't feel like I should wait another second to confess. "Abby Googled you. I think you'll definitely survive one bad review."

I give him a pointed look, hoping he catches on to what I'm saying.

"Ah, the Google search." He sighs, shifting over to his side, propping himself up on one elbow while leaning his head against his hand. His feet hang a good two feet off the edge of the bed. He rubs his jaw and lifts an eyebrow, looking ready for a proper chat. "It's inevitable these days, I guess. Go ahead, lay it on me. What dirt did she find out?"

"No dirt, actually, but a lot of surprises."

He nods, like he knows what's coming.

I squint up at him. "You're not mad?"

"I'd probably be more mad to know you were gallivant-ing around with some new guy that you *didn't* Google. It's just a smart thing to do these days."

I smile and lean down to peck him on the lips, happy to hear he's not upset.

"When you have an entire Wikipedia page dedicated to you, it's kind of inevitable that you're going to get Googled. I'm surprised it took this long."

"Why didn't you tell me you were so successful?" I ask quietly.

"Because none of that success is necessary to fall for some-one." He looks down at the bedsheets, a shade of crimson seeping into his face. I smile back at him, then kiss him on the corner of his lips, relieved he's not upset. And I like hearing him say that.

"You're listed as one of the top richest men in the world. Why would you be here, fixing my window shades yourself?"

"It was an excuse to come back."

I smile at him. "You didn't need an excuse."

"When you called me out of the blue that day, at first I was annoyed that Phil's new assistant had made that stupid mistake. But then it was so refreshing to have an ordinary conversation with someone who had no idea who I was. You were charming, and funny, not to mention you had no problem telling me exactly what you thought about me." He wraps my hair back around my ear, his mouth twitching into a half-smile. "Once you gave me the address, and I knew it was you — the girl I'd already met half-naked on the porch that I couldn't stop thinking about — I was a goner. I had to come back."

CHAPTER 47

I run my hand down Dom's arm until I find his hand, then grab ahold of it. This is all making sense now. Knowing Dom put all his big-wig stuff aside just to come meet me again, based on a pretty absurd phone call, is making me fall even harder for him.

"I haven't seen the inside of any of my vacation rentals in about four years. They're really just a hobby business of mine that I don't give much thought to anymore. I have people who handle almost every aspect of my life, so it gets a little boring sometimes. You gave me a reason to show up, completely anonymous, and after that — well, it got a little addictive." He smiles, unabashedly. "*You* were addictive."

"The second you left, and I walked inside this place for the first time, I was already fantasizing that the guy with the muscles was going to magically find me again after unsticking that door." I grin back at him. "I can tell your friends really adore you too. Isla and her little girl. Even Rooney. Nobody seems to treat you any differently than anyone else, even though you're kind of a big deal."

His eyes drop to the bed, and I notice that he only gets this embarrassed look on his face whenever we talk about something that has to do with him. Like he's happy to discuss me, my life, and everything else in the world, except how wonderful he is.

"I prefer it like that. I just like people to know me for me. Not for anything the internet says about me. None of that means anything if I'm not surrounded by people that I love. Who I know like me too." He drags his eyes back up to mine.

"I don't know *what* to picture anymore." I shake my head. "You're humble, and kind, and full of the most unbelievable talents." I lean in for another kiss.

He smiles and I grab his hand, rubbing circles on the back with my thumb.

"Where do you live then? I was literally picturing you going home to a tiny little bungalow bachelor pad while living in your brother's shadow all your life."

He lies back and looks up at the ceiling fan, laughing at my poor assessment of his life.

"You don't need to picture me going back to a sad little bungalow all alone. My house is actually bigger than his."

"Oh." Bigger than that villa? I can't even imagine it. "Where is it?"

"Here. On the island, but on the northwestern side. It's less crowded over there. I helped design the place. I'll show you sometime, when it's less under construction."

"Do you live there full-time, when it's not being worked on?"

"Most of the year, yeah. I've been everywhere you can imagine, but nowhere feels as much like home as here."

"What's it like?" I plant a kiss on the back of his hand. I'd love to see something Dom designed.

"It's on its own bay. No other houses around it. There's a few groves of pineapple plants and mango trees. Pretty much every type of tropical fruit you can imagine. But the surf right outside the back door has the most incredible waves, hardly any rip. It's this unbelievable slice of paradise all to myself. I want to take you there, but it's completely ripped apart right now. My guys hope to have it finished by the fall."

"I still want to see it." I lean in for a kiss. "Even if it's a heap of rubble right now."

He reaches for his phone and pulls up a few photos of a sprawling estate, nestled into its own emerald bay. Green mountains tower up behind it, and it looks like the grassy grounds are full of tropical plants of every shape and size, similar to Quinton's estate, but somehow wilder. More like Dom.

"You . . . *live* here?" I can feel my face turning pink. It almost doesn't seem real. I thought Quinton's place was extravagant, but Dom's estate looks enormous — streamlined and masculine — just like him. Everything Abby found must have been true.

"Most of the year, yes. I also have a few homes elsewhere, but this one is special. Every room is situated in a way to make the most of the view, whether it's facing the surf in the front, or the mountains in the back. When you're in the rooms at the top, it almost feels like a treehouse, or something you'd see out of *Swiss Family Robinson*. Like some boyhood dream I had as a kid, except I made it real."

I roll onto my back, staring up at the ceiling fan. Dom is still Dom, but he's somehow morphing before my very eyes.

How can someone this successful be so quiet about it?

"I was always planning to reimburse you for the reservation, no matter what happened with us or however long you stayed."

I turn to him. "You really don't have to do that. What if this thing between us doesn't work out? Or you decide that you actually don't like me as much as you do right this second? I made the reservation, and I can still pay for it."

He watches me ramble on, suddenly quite serious, like he's confused.

I stop rambling. "What? What's that look for?"

"People have been trying to get favors out of me my entire life. Yet here you are trying to return a favor that's virtually nothing to me, but *everything* to you."

"It still feels wrong, even if it's nothing to you." I can't imagine a world where thousands of dollars means *nothing* to someone.

"Then think of it this way. I should have let you go back when you asked. I didn't, for my own selfish reasons—"

"But I'm glad you didn't. My soul needed this place, even more than my writing. If I'd gone home, I'd still be pining away over a guy I can't even imagine being with anymore. Being here has put everything into perspective. You encouraging me to stay is probably the best thing that's ever happened to me. And not just because it led me to you."

Dom's laugh rings out in my bedroom, but I just grin slowly, absorbing the joy as it spreads across his face.

"You drive a hard bargain, Miss Hillcrest." He kisses me gently. "Keep your suitcase here or a drawer full of socks or whatever. If you'd like. If that makes you feel better. However, I fully expect you to spend any time you want at Quinton's place with me, at least until my place is done. I don't want us trying to keep quiet, just so you don't hear from Rex out of the blue again."

"You have a deal." I push him gently onto his back. Then I climb on top of his hips, straddling his steadily growing erection. "Now, how about taking me for another ride before we break into those croissants?"

CHAPTER 48

Quinton's garden has become my favorite place to write. I'm suddenly filled with inspiration, and spend the next few weeks writing feverishly from inside the lavish green oasis. Regardless of feeling silly for riding to someone else's house to write, the view and ambiance are unbeatable. Plus, there's something extra special about writing a story from Quinton Rockwell's garden, which Quinton Rockwell himself will see in a few weeks.

Most days, Dom and I share dinner when he comes home. Although he could afford to hire anyone in the world as his private chef, he insists on cooking dinner for me if I'm there when he arrives. He says cooking relaxes him. As someone who does anything *but* relax in the kitchen, I'm pretty impressed with the whole idea of cooking being calming.

So my new favorite hobby involves drinking wine at the enormous kitchen island while watching Dom making some mouthwatering concoction. Squeezing lemon slices over fresh mahimahi, dipping shrimp in his from-scratch cocktail sauce, taking a sip of my martini before he hands it over to me, making sure it's just right. Whenever he looks stressed at the end of a long work day, he's fairly chill by the time he's put a full meal on the table.

It's like I've found a unicorn of a man. One that only existed in my dreams, except the real-life version is better than anything I ever allowed myself to imagine.

Today, though, I'm back at the rental to give Pru some much-needed cuddles. I can't abandon two cats in the same year.

She's sprawled across my keyboard while I try to Google whether or not Oahu has a decent New York-style bagel shop to surprise Dom with my favorite breakfast.

I glance up from my screen to watch Rex and Juju on the deck with coffee mugs in hand. Pru purrs gently at my elbow on the couch, then buries her face into a cushion.

"I still can't believe your Auntie Juju is sleeping with that idiot."

Pru replies by rubbing her chin against my elbow, her special way of asking for belly rubs. I oblige and she flips onto her back, humoring me with her best dead possum impression.

"What am I going to do with you when it's time to go back home?"

Rex and Juju lean into each other at the rail outside. I haven't talked to Rex since that day he heard Dom and I against the wall. He's sent two more texts about missing me, which I haven't had the patience to reply to with anything resembling kindness. I've sent a few that make it clear I'm not interested in being a side piece to him while he's in a relationship with another woman, especially one as wonderful as Juju. And, besides, I'm in a relationship with Dom now. We shouldn't be texting each other at all.

Pru flops across my laptop and starts purring loudly, pushing the screen back with all four feet.

"I'm sorry, Pru, but I'm going to need this laptop today. I *have* to do some research on bagels. I've lived off Dom's cooking skills long enough. Bringing a breakfast that someone else made is the least I can do, at this point."

I plead, but she doesn't budge. Even when I slide her onto the table instead of my keyboard, she stays in the same position.

I give up and grab my phone to research, just as a text comes in.

Would you mind if I bring over a new curtain rod for the shower?

I reply right away.

Dying for a distraction

He responds.

See you in 5

* * *

Dom has billions in the bank and could hire anyone else in the world to do it, but here he is with his craggy old toolbox again. I have a hunch he does it as an excuse to hang out with me, which I'm totally here for. Watching him handle those tools reminds me of the second time we met, the day he installed the window blinds. He says he likes working with his hands, that it reminds him of all his days working backstage with the set builders he idolized as a kid.

He probably doesn't need an audience while he works, but he's telling me something about growing up in California, which means I can get away with standing here watching him even longer before I return to writing. There's something about a man with tree trunks for forearms wielding a big ol' drill that really gets my heart pumping. Writing may have to wait.

". . . so that's when Quinton got into the studio as a director's assistant. Our mom always figured he'd be the one

216

to do something out of the ordinary with his life. Follow in our dad's footsteps."

I sigh dreamily. "I can't even imagine what Thanksgiving is like at your house."

"Yeah, he brought Katarina Lowen one year, before he and Selma got married. Katarina asked my mom if she could bring her own vegan turkey. My mom couldn't wait to see what Katarina Lowen's vegan turkey tasted like." He laughs, pausing the drill overhead.

"Katarina Lowen was at your family's Thanksgiving dinner, eating tofurkey?"

"All six feet of her. Super models are like an entirely different species of human. You don't know it until you see them in real life."

I imagine Dom casually eating tofurkey next to one of the most well-known models in the industry. These little details are so commonplace to him, but absolutely fascinating to me.

Pru chooses this exact moment to start meowing behind the bedroom door. Dom still has no idea that Pru's taken up residency in his rental, since I'm still waiting for the perfect moment to tell him, and I'm not about to let him find out like this. She's been so good at just taking a nap in the closet when he's here, at least until this visit.

"Oh! Hey, I forgot something in the bedroom!" I'm talking louder than normal, trying to mask the meowing behind the door, but her little paws start scratching at the wood. "Be right back!"

Dom starts the drill, buying me some more time to figure this out. I run into the kitchen, grab a can of cat food from the pantry, throw it into a shallow bowl, and run back to the bedroom. After a failed attempt to gently shove her back when I open the door a crack, she pushes out past me and into the hallway. I lunge after her, falling to my stomach, just narrowly missing her slim body before she saunters toward the bathroom where Dom's drill is still whirring loudly. She pauses outside the door and stares at me, challenging me with her eyes.

The angry twitch of her tail says, *"Come any closer, and I'll jump on his back."*

I sigh into the carpet.

So much for keeping Pru a secret any longer.

The drill stops.

I close my eyes and wait for Dom to see her.

Silence.

"Pru!" I hiss loudly, holding the bowl of food out to her, lifting my face up an inch, hoping there's a chance Dom hasn't seen her yet. "Pru, get back here!"

I shake the bowl, hoping the smell of food wafting down the hall will bring her sprinting back — before Dom turns around to see a surprise cat. If he hasn't already.

"Pru!" I whisper louder. "He's not for you! Get back here!"

She startles when the drill starts up again. I lunge at her since she's momentarily distracted. Wrong move. She bolts into the bathroom to inspect the sound — I slide down the hall after her, hoping to catch her before—

The drill halts again.

I hear Dom mutter something, then the sound of metal screws clunking into the tub.

"Olivia?" Dom pops his head out.

I freeze.

CHAPTER 49

He wasn't supposed to find her today. If this doesn't go over well, I'm really not ready to say goodbye. Where will she go? Back to the streets? A shelter?

"Yes?"

I'm ready to plead on her behalf. I put my chin in my hand, trying to look cute so he won't be mad, even though I'm still sprawled across the floor in the narrow hallway.

"Please tell me this cat somehow managed to get in here undetected, right now, and you're not actually harboring a stray."

"Pru is not just a stray." I hop to my feet and walk in the bathroom — she's weaving through Dom's ankles while he's got half a shower curtain held up over his head. She's purring so loudly, there's no way he's not at least a little charmed by her.

"You named it?" He looks horrified.

Okay, he's not a cat person. "Her. I've named *her*."

"No, no, no, no. She's not staying. The island is full of strays. You can't just take one home with you."

"*She's* been helping me get over my writer's block whenever I have it. I've been . . ." How do I begin to explain this to

Dom without sounding completely unhinged? "I was lonely when I first got here."

"When you first got here?" He locks his jaw. "How long has it been here?"

"She's been here a few weeks. I already took her to the vet and the shelter a few weeks ago. No one has tried looking for her, and she's healthy as a horse."

He answers me with a glare.

"I'm a New Yorker! I'm used to having people around everywhere I go. So Pru here has given me someone to talk to when I'm home. Besides myself."

Admitting to Dom in the same breath that I'm not only talking to myself, but that I'm also in the habit of talking to a stray cat I brought in from the street — it sounded better in my head than it does streaming out of my mouth at warp speed.

"Phone a friend if you need someone to chat with. Come out with my friends again. Have dinner with me." He sets the curtain rod down. "I'd like to keep this place cat-free."

He eyes Pru, wearily, then sits on the closed toilet lid, scooping Pru up between his biceps. She looks tiny in his arms. This unexpected sight of him being all cuddly with Pru suddenly makes me want to introduce him to Toby too. I'll make him a cat person.

"She doesn't have fleas?" He looks concerned.

I shake my head. "Please?" I put my hands together in unofficial prayer. "You said you have some renovations you want to do to this place anyway. You could just add anything she might mess up. Plus, she's been here nearly a month and hasn't ruined a thing."

"A month? Where has she been hiding when we've—" His mouth is hanging open.

I smile and shrug. "No need to focus on the past."

That gets a laugh out of him. "Pru, you said? That's her name?"

"I thought she looked like a mashed-up prune."

I walk over to him and stroke her long back, down to the tip of her tail. It ticks back and forth like a metronome, counting down the seconds to his verdict. His eyes crinkle up at the edges when he laughs, and that dimple in his chin I've grown to love deepens.

"The whole place is tile," I say. "She really can't do that much damage. I'll let her outside again before I go anywhere, so she isn't left alone, if it makes you feel better. And I'll keep an eye on her when I'm home."

He mulls this over while she purrs and nuzzles into his neck, like she knows this is her only shot. I have no idea what I'll do with her once I'm back in New York. Toby is the man of the house — I don't think he'd like the idea of a sweet little stray from Hawaii taking over his home turf. But I'm sure I could find another home for her here before I go back. Anything it takes from keeping her out of the local animal shelter or, even worse, the streets.

"Please?" Our hands brush between Pru's fur, and I lean in to kiss him.

"I can't believe I'm going to say this . . ."

I grab her out of his arms. "Pru! You hear that!" I hold her up and dance around the tiny bathroom.

"If she's that important to you, I'll just replace the whole interior of this place if I need to."

I beam at him.

"You wouldn't do anything to hurt Dom's rental, would you, Pru?" I hold her up to my face — she licks my nose. "He's going to let you stay!"

CHAPTER 50

A few weeks later, I'm putting the finishing touches on a scene between my two main characters, waiting for Dom to pick me up. It's Hazel's third birthday party tonight. Isla and Benny invited us both to come celebrate with the rest of their friends at a beachfront barbeque. I'm excited to see Dom's group of friends again. They've started to feel like real friends to me too over the last couple weeks.

Just as I close my laptop, there's a knock at the back window. I glance up to see Rex standing outside.

I shove myself away from the table and slide the door open, already annoyed.

"Dom is picking me up any minute," I tell him. "Where's Juju?"

"Working. I was just hoping we could talk." He looks annoyed at the mention of Dom's name. "Alone."

"Honestly, Rex, there's nothing left to talk about. You're with Juju now, and I'm more than happy with Dom. Unless you're wanting cat custody of Toby back in New York, which you're very much not allowed to have, then we don't have anything left to say."

"You haven't returned any of my texts lately." He has the audacity to look hurt.

"Why would I? And I never pegged you for a cheater, so you better stop whatever this is you're trying to do before you become one." He's sent me three more texts telling me that he misses me. I haven't replied to a single one. "Emotional cheating is still cheating, so knock it off."

"Can we just find a time to talk then?" He sounds a bit desperate.

"No, Rex. I'm not interested in talking anymore. Sorry."

He looks like I've just slapped him across the face.

"Hey there, guys!" We both spin around toward Dom, who's walking into my front door.

"Hey, man," Rex says when he reaches the lanai. Then he gives Dom a firm hand-slap, handshake bro-thing. "I hear you're taking my girl out tonight."

My girl? What the fuck, Rex?

Dom clears his throat, frowning, as an awkward silence follows. "I don't think there's anything about Liv that could be considered *yours* anymore, Rex. No offense." He sounds calmer than I feel.

I laugh louder than I should to break the tension Rex has just created. I want to say, *Oh fuck off, Rex*, but I'm smart enough to keep the tension low. Dom has a long fuse, but it seems to be running out when it comes to my ex.

I punch him on the arm. "I think the whole world knows I'm not your girl anymore. Most specifically this guy here."

I smile at Dom. He rocks back on his heels and pushes his lips together, staring down at the deck. Rex narrows his eyes at me, but I turn to Dom.

"You ready?" I ask him. "I know I am."

"I'm so ready." Dom smiles coolly at Rex. He wraps an arm around my shoulder, leading me away, and shuts the sliding door behind us.

From the look on Dom's face, it occurs to me that he got exactly what he said all guys want at the very beginning. If this was a duel between Rex and him for my affection, Dom has clearly won.

When we get in the car, he turns to me after starting the engine. "You can stay at my place from now on. Or, if you're not ready for that, I'm putting you in one of my hotels. There's no reason for you to be back at this rental with him anymore."

I let this new information sink in. "You own hotels too?" Despite Abby's pleas, I never read more about him on the internet, knowing everything I needed to know would come out naturally, like this. But it doesn't slow the shock I feel knowing this guy also owns the hotel chains on the island too.

"I just didn't think you'd want to be stuck in a hotel room for weeks at a time. But if you're more comfortable with that, instead of staying with me, then I'm happy to—"

I lean over and smother his lips with mine, stopping any more words from coming out.

"I don't mind going back and forth, keeping things at the townhouse, but I'm at your place practically every night anyway, at least until Quinton and Selma get here for their vacation. I'll go back to the rental when they arrive. I don't care if it's only a night or two before I fly back to New York by that point. I can handle myself with Rex. I'm just sick of looking up to see him staring at me through that window every time he's around."

"I should just kick him out of that place right now. Fucking asshole."

Dom looks genuinely pissed for the first time since that drunk guy at Cliff's tried taking a video of me, like he can't stand to think of me around Rex for one more second.

"You really don't need to worry about me with Rex." I hold his hand tighter. "Trust me. Even before you came into the picture, I was so done with him."

He studies my face. "Just let me kick him out so you're rid of him for good."

I imagine Rex getting kicked to the curb, trying to find a last-minute flight back to New York, where he doesn't even have an apartment to go back to, as far as I know.

I purse my lips. "It's fine."

He laughs, finally giving in. "Fine. I get it. Let's just have a good time tonight celebrating my goddaughter."

I point to the almost-life-size pink unicorn stuffy in the backseat. "Is that what you're giving Hazel?" I already know the answer. "I can't wait to watch her face — and Isla's — when you walk into the party with that thing."

"That and a matching pony ride down the beach for the birthday girl. I asked the stable company to dress their cutest pony up to match the stuffed unicorn, with a fake pink horn and everything. Isla and Benny are going to die when they see it. There will be a photographer there to capture it for them." He breaks into a grin.

"I never pegged you for such a softy." I squeeze his hand. Then I kiss him with everything I have left in me. And I'm thrilled to not have to go back to that rental, next to my ex, alone — at least for a while.

CHAPTER 51

By the time we get back to Dom's house from Hazel's party, I feel breathless, like a tiger about to pounce on its prey. Watching him treat Hazel like a little princess tonight was the sweetest thing I might have ever seen, and it's made me absolutely ravenous for him.

"Show me the pool," I demand. It's a gorgeously warm night and I don't want to be stuck inside. As my weeks here have gone on, I'm becoming more and more aware of how little time I have left before I'm back in the concrete jungle that is New York City. I want to spend every moment I can outside. And with Dom.

He looks bewildered. "The pool?"

"Please," I demand, pulling him out the back door.

He hits a switch when we get outside — the collection of firepits throughout the garden erupt into balls of flame, one by one, until their shadows dance across each wall. The effect is stunning, tossing silhouettes of swaying palms against every vertical surface.

"I love this place so much." I breathe out, briefly imagining us making love on the outdoor daybed sprawled across the deck, overlooking the ocean below. "I don't know how Quinton isn't here more often."

He pulls me along the path toward the pool. I haven't actually seen it yet. Too busy writing and admiring the view each time I've been here to find it among the collection of hedges and towering trees. But tonight I want to take another swim, like we did that first night I was here.

If we can control ourselves long enough to get that far.

As we skip along, I think back to that night we went skinny-dipping in the dark ocean together. My pulse picks up and travels down my body, resting firmly between my thighs. I squeeze Dom's hand tighter, not letting him let me go.

The estate is enormous, so it takes us a few minutes of walking through huge red hibiscus blooms and little white plumeria trees, which litter the ground with cream-colored flowers the size of my palm. The air is thick with the scent of tropical blossoms — an intoxicating mix of delicate flower petals, still damp from the misty rain we got earlier today.

I stoop to grab the most perfect white plumeria blossom, each petal streaked down the center with canary yellow stripes, like someone took a paintbrush down each one. I inhale its sweet center, wondering how to get these to grow in my apartment back in New York so I never have to live without this scent. I've become addicted to them since first finding the flowers scattered everywhere across the island.

I reach down to pick up another from just off the path, inhaling the new one before stretching out to snatch just one more.

Dom is watching me when I rise, backlit by the enormous moon sitting heavy on the horizon.

I hold my collection up to his nose. "I can't walk by these without taking at least a few from the ground. They're too beautiful not to touch."

He brushes my hair back from my face, shooting goose-bumps down my arms, followed by a shiver down my spine. He presses his body to mine, and I can feel his cock growing harder by the second. I don't know if we're going to make it all the way to the pool before stripping each other naked.

"I feel the same way about you, you know," he says gently.

I bite my lip, unable to stop myself from smiling, then run my hand along his shaft from the outside of his pants. Up and down, as slowly as I can.

"I can't stand to think of you anywhere but here." He squeezes my hips. "You belong here as much as those flowers do. They'd never blossom back in New York, but they thrive here."

The air between us mingles with our breath as I study his lips, then raise my eyes up to his. I grin as he lets out a throaty laugh, kissing me just once. Then he takes one of the flowers from my palm and tucks it behind my ear, slipping a stray lock of hair behind it too.

"Just think about it," he says.

"I'll think about it," I promise, feeling pulled in two very different directions, split straight down the middle. My job, my friends, and my family are all back in New York. But Dom is here. His heart is here. And the longer I stay, the more I know that leaving him here means leaving my heart behind too.

When he kisses me again it's slower, his lips parting and lingering against mine, finding my tongue with his. Soft and supple, but firm enough to leave me wanting more when we finally break apart. I try leaning in again, but he holds my arms down firmly to my sides, stopping me from taking his lips, or his shaft.

"Not here," he whispers. "Not yet."

"Then we'd better pick up the pace." I grin. "I'm not going to be able to wait another second."

We continue rushing down the dimly lit path, but it takes every ounce of willpower left in me not to run ahead to wherever he's taking me. Just to get there a little faster.

But I let him lead me. Surrendering to the night, and whatever else he has in store.

CHAPTER 52

Dom pulls back a huge palm frond that's a good foot taller than me. "Here's the pool."

I step back in awe, gripping the stems of the last two plumeria blooms I've been carrying. This clearing is like all my wildest fantasies rolled into one.

I turn to Dom and smack him in the stomach.

"You've been hiding this? The whole time?" I step in front of him, not caring that my jaw is hanging open like a fly catcher.

An infinity pool stretches out with a shallow, soft sand entry on one side. There's a two-story waterfall, made of natural red stone boulders, trickling fresh water into the side of the pool. There's a matching smooth stone grotto beside it, housing an enormous hot tub. The hot tub is nearly hidden by tropical shrubbery of every shape and color, clinging to the stone and covered in flowers and moss, acting as a natural camouflage. In the middle of the pool, just above the surface of the glossy water, there's a slick bamboo baja shelf with a pair of creamy white day beds. Matching linen drapery blows gently in the barely there breeze. A collection of matching chaise lounge chairs encircles the deck, each with their own umbrella and side table for holding drinks or snacks from the wide stone bar. Behind the bar, there's an aquarium the size of a small SUV, filled with an army of colorful fish illuminated by a clear blue light.

He laughs, pulling me into him. "You told me your dream was to write in a garden, not on a pool deck. Besides, you know I prefer the ocean."

Beyond the glass edge of the pool is another stunning view of the sea, with a grand flagstone staircase leading down to the sandy beach. The moon casts its light along the water, rippling across it like a puddle of milk pooling on the surface. Millions of stars glitter across the waves, like tiny diamonds encrusted in black velvet. They sparkle in Dom's eyes when he turns to look at me.

I've never seen a sky like this. Or a view like this. It's like something out of a movie.

"Pinch me," I whisper.

He kisses me instead, but I pull away from him so I can get another look at the view.

"This is . . ."

For once in my life, I'm completely speechless. There're no words to describe this kind of heaven. I didn't realize places like this actually existed outside of hotels, or that people actually lived in them. "Why don't you just live right here? In the pool? I've never seen anything like it. I'd never leave."

He smiles and takes my hand. "Quinton has really done well for himself, hasn't he?"

"Why do I feel like yours is better?"

"Because it is." He grins before kissing me again. I love that Dom is humble, about everything, really — but there's something really hot about those sparse moments when he owns his success.

I press my hip gently into the bulge in his pants. "I'm not surprised."

"I can't wait to show you." He grabs me around the waist from behind. We watch the waves reflecting the stars as they roll into shore for a few minutes. Every now and then he kisses my neck, shooting lightning bolts of desire through my hips.

"Your life here is incredible." I finally turn to face him. "I had so much fun with your friends again tonight. They're starting to feel like family to me too." His face melts into surprise. "That probably sounds weird, they were just so warm from the start. So welcoming. People don't act like that back where I'm from. I would have had to run through a wicked gauntlet if my boyfriend introduced me to his gang of friends at a bar."

"The way you describe your life back home — I just don't see that side of you here. It all sounds so stuffy, so contrived, and not like you at all."

"Then what do you see when I'm here?"

"I just see a beautiful woman, sitting in a garden, writing to make her biggest dream come true."

Dom's simple yet beautiful description of me makes my eyes water, just a little.

"I'm going to get that tattooed down my arm." I start laughing. "I can honestly say that this whole harebrained idea of mine has turned into the best wrong move I've ever made."

He kisses me sweetly.

"You've changed my life." I can't hold back any longer. "No matter what happens, I'll never be the same again. But I have to go back to New York. My job is there. You could give me everything I could ever dream of here, I know that, but I'm not entirely ready to leave everything I've worked for without a solid plan for this next stage of my career. It could take a long time for a production house to pick my film script up, especially if Quinton doesn't go for it. And, in the meantime, I need to figure out how to be here *with* you, not *depending* on you. But I fully plan to be bi-coastal." I smile, searching his eyes. "I want us to stay together, but temporarily we're going to need to be apart. I hope you can understand that."

"I know how important your career is to you, Liv. I had a feeling you'd be stubborn about leaving everything behind without a solid plan in place for your next career move." He breaks into a sad smile, before his eyes brighten again. "I already have Phil working on closing a real estate deal on a penthouse in New York for me. So we'll have a place to land there too when you get back. We'll have my place here in Hawaii, and a place in New York. We can be together no matter what city we're visiting."

I jump into his arms and he spins me around, squeezing me to him.

"You have no idea how happy that makes me," I tell him. "One day I'll be ready. I can feel that in my bones. I belong here. *We* belong here. But I have to work out the logistics first. Make a plan. Stand on my own two feet."

"It's something I love about you." He kisses me while dropping one shoulder strap off my dress, so he can continue kissing down my neck uninterrupted. Then I step back, staring into his eyes as I slowly unzip the front of my sundress, stopping only when I reach my navel.

"Tell me something else you love about me," I beg him, my voice dipping provocatively.

He gently brushes the other strap off my shoulder and, just like that, my dress falls to the ground.

"I'd rather show you."

CHAPTER 53

His eyes linger on the pile of fabric around my feet before slowly moving their way up my bare skin. The way he's looking at me makes me feel like a goddess, standing in the moonlight.

"I know I've said it already a hundred times, but you are absolutely stunning." His voice is barely above a whisper. "Like Venus herself, standing right here on earth."

I still have on a sheer, cream-colored bralette with stripes of thin lace across each nipple, paired with a matching set of panties. I kick off my strappy stiletto heels and turn around, posing like I'm ready to dive into the pool.

"You were such a goddamn gentleman that first day we met." I smile, remembering how he kept his eyes pointed at the sky while I stood there in my underwear. But tonight he's drinking me in like a tonic, full of every type of drug he needs. "I was so relieved to find out that you're not always a gentleman."

"I don't intend to be much of one tonight." He unbuttons his shirt before tossing it to the side. My stomach does a tiny little flip. Even though I've seen him shirtless dozens of times, I still enjoy the view as if it's my first time.

233

I pull my bralette over my head.

"I wouldn't want to get this wet." I toss it aside. "The panties are already a goner, though." I grin innocently at him.

He chokes out a stunted breath, then clears his throat, his face curling wickedly.

He takes a step toward me, but I hold up one finger, making him wait just one more moment before I give in — the anticipation almost as delicious as the deed.

"You are a master of suspense," he growls, though I can tell he's enjoying it as much as me.

I smile back. "Some things are worth the wait." I kick my panties off before diving head first into the water.

It feels like a heated bath.

When I reach the surface for air, he's already in the pool beside me, wrapping both arms around my waist. The heat from his body fills the water, and he pushes back my wet hair, holding my face between his hands, bringing me in for a kiss. We dunk under water while our mouths are still intertwined, then emerge again, dripping wet and starved for each other.

He sweeps me toward the wall, completely weightless in the water, so my back is pressed against the smooth stone. His hard cock is already pushing between my legs, putting pressure right where I want it against my clit. I widen my stance so he can press harder. Our tongues fight each other, tasting and exploring, while his hands start to travel down my body. The warmth of his palms slides across my stomach beneath the water. His fingers slip against my hip bones, drawing a line back and forth between my thighs. I reach under the water and push his hands down, giving him permission to go where we both want him to go, and he tucks a finger inside me, his thumb circling just above my opening, until I want more than just his fingers. I grab his cock in my hand, and push it into me.

"Fuck." I push into him, then out again, pulling back from his kiss abruptly when I realize I don't want this feeling to end too fast. "Not in here."

Without waiting for an answer, he lifts me by my waist and sets me down on the edge of the pool ledge. Then he pushes my knees apart and thrusts his mouth between my legs. It's instant electricity.

I lean back, my hands against the bamboo deck, spreading my legs wider as he wraps his tongue through the silky folds of my exposed interior, expertly rimming my clit, my lips, my open walls, deeper and faster, as he pushes me closer and closer to spilling over the edge. I moan, then open my eyes, suddenly self-conscious of who might be within eyeshot of us outside.

I manage to speak between gasps and moans. "Can anyone see us here?"

He kisses my inner thigh. "There are no cameras here, if that's what you're asking. And it's completely private." His eyes take me in, and I feel everything in me tighten as his gaze rolls over the most electrifying parts of me, open and pulsing gently in front of him. "This view right here is all for me."

I start to feel myself throbbing, begging him silently for more of his mouth.

He kisses me once between my legs, then draws his gaze up again. "Tell me what you want me to do."

"Take me." I'm nearly out of breath as I near the edge of sweet release, like everything in me is drawn tight, ready to unfurl. "Just fucking take me, Dom."

He lifts himself out of the pool and scoops me up from the edge, dropping me onto one of the nearby lounge chairs. My body is panting for his, my clit practically pulsing at his slightest touch. His skin is slick and warm when he lowers himself down on top of me, pushing himself inside. I gasp at his size, wrapping my arms around his torso to steady myself while I feel his skin glide across every inch of mine. I immediately start to shudder and shake, clenching myself around him.

"Dom," I moan, "give me every fucking inch of your cock."

I'm begging for a release — I try to hang on as long as I can, pressing my forehead into his chest. I grab his arms, holding his body over mine, using them to push myself against him harder and harder. In and out. He's biting at my neck, sending shivers down my entire body, until everything in me explodes, shooting stars into the blackness behind my lids. I hear my voice scream out his name again and again as pulses of ecstasy roll through me, then him, then both of us together.

Even after we're done, I don't want him to leave my body. I lie beneath him, kissing his neck, reveling in the feeling of his back muscles bulging under my touch. The weight of him feels secure, like I don't want him to leave this spot inside me. Possibly ever.

He kisses me where the curve of my neck meets my collarbone.

"I could stay here forever." I sigh, wrapping my arms around him, breathing in his scent.

"Oh my God." A glowing smile takes over his face. "Money can buy a lot of things, but I'd give everything I have to stay exactly like this, inside you, until the end of time."

I hold his cheek in my palm, staring past him into the sky filled with bright white stars. Without leaving me, he reaches over to pick up a nearby plumeria from the pool deck.

Propped up on one elbow, he slowly drags the flower petals across my cheek, gently up to my hairline, down to my jaw, then brushes it along my chin before pulling my lips into his.

"Olivia, the world is yours here. Everything you've ever wanted would be yours. Me included."

I revel in the feeling of his fingertips when they slide the delicate flower behind my ear, tucking it back in place again, right where it belongs. Then he smooths my hair back and kisses my earlobe beneath the bloom.

I smile, allowing myself to picture what a life here with Dom would look like, knowing that, no matter what happens, wrapped up with him like this is exactly where I'm meant to be.

CHAPTER 54

A few days later, I'm back at the townhouse while Abby is helping me sort through my outfit options on FaceTime. I came back to the rental last night for the last time, just before Quinton and Selma arrived on the island, and I already miss Dom fiercely. Like a piece of me is missing, even though it's only been one night. I don't know how I'm going to board my plane to New York tomorrow.

My dinner with them is tonight, and my bed is now heaped with every outfit I've tried on for Abby, except the one I'm currently wearing. It's a white tank with a deep, square neckline, paired with a silky high-waisted sage green skirt that ties across my hip.

"Be honest," I say to her. "I can't mess this up."

"Put the strappy gold sandals back on and let me see it with those." Her forehead is nearly pressed against the phone screen, as she squints to see me better. I miss her so much, but I get teary at just the thought of leaving tomorrow. If I can get Quinton to agree to produce my film, then I could fully transition my career to film writing right away, leaving my UBN position for good. There's a lot riding on this pitch tonight, including an easier future with Dom here in Hawaii without having to leave him so soon.

"If only you were here to help me in person." I slip off the black strappy heels in favor of the gold gladiator sandals I brought from home. Then I wrap each long golden lace all the way up my foot and ankle, finally standing in front of the camera once they're tied. My phone is propped up on the dresser against a wall, while Pru sleeps in a tiny patch of sun by the bed.

If I think about leaving her too, I might cry.

"Yes!" Abby yells triumphantly, like our favorite team just won the big game. "You're going to look professional, yet a bit saucy and eccentric. Basically unforgettable, which is exactly how you need to look tonight. It's perfect. We'll be celebrating your new contract by Monday!"

I turn in front of the camera. "What do you think his wife is like?"

"Drop dead gorgeous. Savvy. Rich. Basically amazing."

Selma was a top model in her early twenties. No doubt she brought her own small fortune into her marriage to Quinton. They don't have any kids, and just live as two DINKs with a serious income between them. I've since learned they have equally impressive estates in Lake Como, Aspen, and Palm Springs for quick vacations out of LA, along with a modest penthouse in London.

I finished the script yesterday, and already had Abby comb through it for any edits. She returned it to me within twelve hours, even taking the day off to give it her full attention. It came back to me full of funny comments and high praise, telling me she could see a box office premier in my near future.

But I'm not so sure.

Moments like this come once in a lifetime, and I feel like I could have prepared for this for years without ever feeling completely ready. Throwing it together within a few weeks seems like a Hail Mary pass, and my heart rate has been erratic all day as I try to practice what I'm going to say to him.

Dom said he'd mentioned to Quinton that he wanted to introduce him to me. But I have no idea if Quinton knows

I'll be pitching him my script, or if he thinks I'm just joining them as Dom's girlfriend.

"I'm shitting bricks, Abby." I flop down on the bed. A few shoes clatter to the floor, startling Pru. She looks up at me like I've insulted her sleep, then rolls to her back, tilting her chin toward the sunlight.

"If anyone can charm the pants off a Hollywood director tonight, it's you. You need to remember how hard you've worked for this moment. It's too serendipitous to fail."

I'm so in need of a solid pep talk. I drop the shoes I've started picking up to give Abby my full attention.

"Are you sure you weren't just being my best friend when you said my script was decent?" I have a gut feeling that my best friend is trying to build me up since there is literally no more time to work on it. "I was up until three in the morning going over any last-minute changes."

"It's perfect. You look perfect. Everything will be perfect." She beams into the phone. "And if, for some reason, it doesn't all pan out, it'll be a great experience pitching Quinton in person!"

"You think it's not going to work out?" I start to panic. "Why?" My voice rises four octaves in just one word. "You really think it's not going to work out?" I grab my laptop off the nightstand and fling it open. "Was it the scene between Sal and Andrew? I knew it felt too forced. Hold on, let me read you the alternative lines I gave them." I start scrolling down my open Google Doc.

"No, Olivia, stop. Seriously. I was just putting a positive spin on the *what if it fails* notion you keep having, to put your mind at ease. He's going to love it."

I groan impatiently, trying to find the lines I'm looking for. "I just wish I had more time."

"Life comes at you fast, honey," she says. "If I had a dollar for every time I wanted just one more week of prep before walking into a negotiation, I'd be rich."

I close my laptop. "So how do you force yourself to feel ready when you don't know if you are?"

"I tell myself that whatever moment I'm having is as good as it's going to get. And I need to make the most of it."

I groan. "I wish I had your confidence right now."

"You can," she reminds me. "You just need to own it."

A loud banging interrupts us, making everything inside me drop eighteen stories to the floor.

"The driver must be early," I say. "Fuck. Fuck. Fuck."

Abby grins. "Go get 'em, tiger."

"Oh my God, I'll keep you posted." I'm beginning to break out in a cold sweat.

"No matter what happens, this is as good as it's going to get. You've been waiting for this kind of opportunity your whole life. So get in there and own it, Liv."

CHAPTER 55

Instead of seeing a driver outside my front door, it's Rex.

"Not now, Rex," I say quickly. "I'm going somewhere important."

I start to shut the door, but he sticks his foot in the way to block it.

"You look even more pretty than usual. I saw you coming up from surfing this morning, but it's been a few weeks since I've seen you around here."

I don't have time for this. I should have just gotten ready at Dom's. After being away from the rental for so long, I can't exactly say that I miss running into Rex all the time.

"I have dinner with Dom." I pause, just to watch him deflate a little. Then, I can't help but add, "And Quinton Rockwell, along with his wife Selma."

His eyes grow wider — he pushes the door all the way open again, leaning against it with one arm, as if to steady himself.

"Shut . . . up." He breathes each word out one at a time.

I smile like I've already won the Academy Award. "No, seriously."

"Like, *the* Quinton Rockwell? *The* director?" His eyes are nearly falling out of his head. Rex and I may be very much over, but I know he's still going to be proud of me for making this happen. We'd spend hours talking about what I wanted for my future career, planning it all out. It was always going to be part of our long-term future together. It feels good to tell him that I'm finally making it happen.

"Quinton Rockwell is Dom's brother. He and his wife have an estate here on the island."

"So that's where you've been spending all your time, then? With Dom?" He's not hiding the fact that he's upset.

I can feel the seconds ticking by. "Obviously." I really don't have time for this.

The air churns thicker between us. *Not this again.* Rex leans harder against the door frame beside me, still blocking the path to close it. Then he rocks back on his heels and folds both arms over his chest.

"I'd knocked on your door hoping we could finally talk. Before you go back to New York." He smiles, but it doesn't quite reach his eyes. Rex rakes a hand through his hair, then puts the hand on his hip. Taking a step forward, then back, then forward again, like he's not sure how to stand.

"What did you want to talk about?" I'm hoping he'll stop bothering me if he just gets on with it. "But I have to warn you, my driver is arriving any second."

"It can wait," he says. "You have something way more important tonight. Let's not ruin your focus. You've been working a long time to get a shot like this." He gives me a wide smile. "I'm really proud of you, Liv. We'll talk after."

I scrunch my nose, unsure of how to answer.

We stand frozen in place, but he's not moving from the door.

"I'm pretty nervous about tonight." I'm not sure what else to say.

"You're going to be amazing," he tells me quietly.

This exchange has lasted less than a minute, but it's enough to give us both what feels like a moment of warmth toward the other. We share a sad sort of smile — the type of smile that gets more across than a few fumbled words.

I'm sorry it had to end like that.

I'm sorry, too.

"There's a reason we ended up here together," he tells me. "And this is part of it. It's your shot, Liv."

The irony of it all.

Me, finally making a real effort at the dream we dreamed together, smiling at each other — thousands of miles from where it all fell apart. Suspended for one final moment, caught between the two very separate worlds we're both living in now.

The sound of tires rolling into the driveway out front startles us both.

As if the moment snaps shut, we both turn away. I quickly reach for my purse as he takes a step back.

"Good luck." He slips his hands into his pockets while he watches me grab my phone off the table.

I turn back to him, my heart nearly thumping out of my chest when it registers again where I'm heading.

To Quinton. To Dom.

To my future.

I take one last look at my past.

"How do I look?" I ask nervously, holding out my arms, peeking down at my feet. When I look back up at him, an unexpected surge of emotion catches in my throat.

Ten thousand times I've left our apartment asking him how I look.

Ten thousand times he's looked at me just like that.

Ten thousand times he's told me that I look beautiful.

And ten thousand times we've parted ways with a kiss.

I smile sadly at him, knowing this will truly be the last time I walk away like this. I leave tomorrow, and don't plan to be in contact with him once I'm back in New York. This is our very last goodbye.

Deep down, I know that I'm finally getting the type of goodbye that I wanted all along. One that's civil, heartfelt, and kind. One that does justice to our years that were filled with love together. Not angry texts, or revenge sex behind a thin, shared wall. *This* is what my heart wanted all along to fully close this chapter and leave it in the dust.

"You look perfect," he says.

My phone pings. It's the driver, letting me know he's here.

"Of all the things to be late for, tonight isn't it. You've got this, kid. I can't wait to hear what Quinton says."

"Thank you." I smile.

Finally, I walk out the front door with my head held high, knowing Rex is still there, watching me leave.

"Goodbye, Rex," I say over my shoulder.

And this time I mean forever.

CHAPTER 56

Within a few seconds of knocking, I'm faced with the man, the myth, the legend himself — Quinton Rockwell opens the front door.

He's dressed in gray board shorts and a glossy white shirt. Three buttons are undone, exposing a single, thick gold chain with a cross around his neck, peeking out through a mound of curly peppered chest hair. In all my years of interviewing and working with extremely successful people at the news station, I've noticed that most wealthy people have an expensive air about them no matter where they are, or what they're wearing.

Quinton is certainly no exception.

Although, if I had to guess, at first glance I'd say he was already drunk.

"*Ma chérie!*" he exclaims, shooting out an arm and pulling me inside. Then he kisses the air on each side of my face, like he's French. Wealthy west coast LA types tend to do this, I've noticed. "You must be Olivia!"

"And you must be Quinton." I pull out my best mega-watt smile, then hold my hand out to shake his.

"No formalities here, my dear." He pulls me in for a hug, foregoing a handshake. "If Dom is bringing you around here to introduce us, we're family already."

Just then, Dom pops around the corner — looking handsome, if not a bit nervous.

"What about formalities?" he asks before breaking into a wide smile when he sees me, still tucked under one of Quinton's long arms. Quinton is the older of the two, and his lifestyle has certainly aged him more than Dom. The crow's feet beside each eye branch out longer than Dom's when he smiles. The stubble across his jaw is peppery, like his chest.

"Oh, I bet Dom brings all the ladies by." I'm still smiling to put Dom at ease, while hoping to break the ice with Quinton. Though he seems to be doing a fine job of that himself with the pet names and air kisses. And now bear hugs.

"Quite the opposite, actually." He pulls his brother in, so we're both tucked under one arm, with Quinton in the center.

I can smell the familiar scent of whiskey on Quinton's breath, and even that smells expensive.

"Dom hasn't brought a lady around Selma and me since, oh, it had to be that nice little redhead back in college. Tori? Tami? Tara?"

Dom looks faintly annoyed. "Taryn."

Quinton isn't listening anymore. He's studying me closely, mere inches above my face. The whiskey on his breath has a hint of smoky citrus, so I assume his drink of choice must be an Old Fashioned. I vaguely wonder how many he's had.

"I don't remember Taryn being this pretty."

I try not to wince, forcing myself to smile. I never know what to say when men compliment me boldly like that.

"Easy, Quinton." Dom pats him on the back, then rolls his eyes at me. "Ignore this guy. And go easy on her, Quinton." There's an edge to his voice when he addresses Quinton, a slight warning shot I wasn't expecting.

"Oh gosh" — I wriggle out from under Quinton's arm — "you're too kind." I hold up the most expensive bottle of wine I could find at the ABC Store. "I brought wine!"

"Ah, I'm more of a whiskey man," Quinton says.

I fight the urge to reply, *I can tell*.

"Though I appreciate the gesture, love."

"Ah, you've arrived!" Selma — formerly known as Selma Hatfield, the international supermodel — floats around the corner. She's easily the most beautiful woman I've ever laid eyes on in person. At least six feet tall in bare feet, probably weighing in around one hundred and ten pounds, practically gliding on air. When she hands me a glass of white wine, I'm blinded by her diamond ring. It's the size of a ping-pong ball and looks even bigger than that balancing on her chop-stick-sized finger. I peel my eyes off it to study her face as she studies me back. She's absolutely exquisite.

"Selma!" My voice sounds breathy and awkward. I'm grateful for the full glass of wine she's just handed me. "Thank you for the drink. And for having me here tonight."

She holds out her hand to shake mine, then pulls me in for a hug. Her frame feels so thin, as though she might break if I squeezed hard enough. Like a tiny bird with hollow bones.

"A pleasure to have you." She shows me the infamous smile that's made her one of the most recognizable people in the world.

"You're gorgeous," I stutter, knowing she hears that all the time, but it seems like I can't be in her presence without acknowledging it out loud. She practically radiates perfection.

"Aw, Dom told me you were sweet." She presses a hand into Dom's shoulder. "Come help me in the kitchen."

I'm relieved to have a job to do so I'm not just awkwardly standing around, though I'm surprised to hear that Selma is cooking. I figured either Dom would cook or they'd have a private chef for the length of their stay.

She hands me a frilly pink apron when we get to the kitchen, then snatches it out of my hand and tosses me a crisp white one. "Goes better with that outfit." She quickly winks at me. "Don't want you clashing on my account tonight."

I smile, feeling like she and I are going to get along just fine.

"I appreciate that. Your place here is incredible, by the way. Dom's been nice enough to let me write in the garden the last few weeks." I hope she won't mind.

"You write?" She visibly stiffens.

I glance at Dom, wondering if he only told Quinton that I write. I hope this isn't a blind pitch, that they know I'm here tonight to meet them, but also to discuss my film project.

"I do . . ."

"What are you writing?" She grabs a head of broccolini and a wooden cutting board. She starts chopping away at it, throwing the pieces into a hot pan over the stove that sizzles with every toss.

I lick my lips, letting her question sink in while my heart pounds in my ears. *This is going to be a blind pitch.* They have no idea I'm here to discuss my script.

"Funny enough, I've just finished a film script, actually." I fight the urge to close my eyes and hide. I feel sick as the words leave my mouth, saying a silent prayer that she lights up and begs to hear more.

Selma stops chopping. The long knife hovers over the cutting board for a mere four seconds before she resumes. Hitting the board loudly with each chop. Then she flings a handful of broccolini into the wok from across the counter. Half of the bundle misses the pan and tumbles onto the counter beside it.

"Ah, well, we're not here to talk shop, tonight, are we Quinton?" She says this almost to no one, and certainly not to Quinton, who is too busy across the room, discussing the next whiskey bottle with Dom to hear her. "Can you put that in the pan, please?" She gestures to the pile of broccolini that landed on the counter.

"Right." I force a smile. *What the hell?* My nervous energy starts to drain out of me, slowly replaced with a sinking feeling of disappointment.

"We're on vacation." Selma raises her brows at me. She grabs a head of cabbage and starts shredding it with the same butcher knife. "I love cooking, don't you? We're too busy back home, but, when we're on *vacation*, I have all the time in the world to get my hands dirty in the kitchen." My mouth goes dry as cabbage flies around the cutting board. "It relaxes me." She pauses to take a long sip of her wine until the glass is empty. She sure doesn't look relaxed. "Pour me more?" She's looking directly at me, holding out her glass. "Please?"

I try not to widen my eyeballs too much. The bottle is sitting right next to her, easily within reach. Why would she want me to pour it for her?

She holds up her hands and laughs like she's embarrassed. "My hands are a little dirty. If you wouldn't mind."

Her hands look perfectly clean to me.

"Of course." I grab the wine bottle off the counter. Then I fill her glass and hand it back to her very clean hand.

"So, do you cook?" The charming Selma who hugged me at the door has disappeared. I'm left with this very impatient version of Selma who is all but tapping her foot at me.

"You know, I'm more of a takeout girl myself." I grab a long red pepper from the stack of produce that I assume she's going to chop her way through. "But I know my way around the kitchen, thanks to my mom and dad insisting we never ate out growing up. Would you like help chopping these up?"

"Yes, please," she says. "The knives are there, and there's another cutting board under this shelf." She pulls a cupboard open next to her with her big toe. "Dom!" she calls out across the room. "Dom, can you put on some music? Jazz, perhaps. Pick something with pep. And Quinton, pull open those doors over there, if you could. I'd like the firepits on to start warming the air outside, to get a cross-breeze going. We're chopping onions next."

Selma sets two yellow onions and a bundle of scallions in front of me, watching me get to work chopping them without a word. Every couple of chops, she leans over to grab the veggies off my cutting board, adding them to the enormous wok over the stove. She's drained her wine glass by the time we're done.

"More?" she asks, wiping her hands on the spare towel she's slung over her shoulder like I saw Dom do on our first night here. Then she eyes the bottle that's clearly within her own reach and holds out her empty glass to me.

"Oh, yes, of course," I mumble. Then, even though her hands are wiped clean, and I've just finished all the chopping for her, I reach across the counter to fill her glass up.

CHAPTER 57

As the night wears on, it becomes clear to me why Dom has gotten a stilted look on his face every time his brother's name comes up.

Quinton's kind of an ass, and his wife is no better.

Once I finish chopping the vegetables, she promptly starts orchestrating how I can prepare the sauté seasoning to go with the seared ahi Dom is making on the big hibachi grill out back.

"There's sesame oil in the pantry," Selma instructs. "You'll know how to make an easy Asian stir fry to go with Dom's seared ahi, won't you? I just need to give my feet a rest after being on that jet all of yesterday."

"Of course." I smile at her — although I'm not so sure what would make her exhausted after spending a few hours on their private luxury jet. Dom told me they own two private jets, and utilize the larger or smaller one depending on the length of the flight. Since the trip to Hawaii from Los Angeles is around six hours, they chose the larger of the two, which I'm sure has a full bedroom to sleep in if they want.

After giving me orders on how to mix the sauce, she leaves the kitchen to sit with Quinton on the patio, overlooking a sunset over the water. His crystal tumbler is filled halfway with nearly straight whiskey. I saw him add a splash of soda and a twist of orange peel that Dom shaved for him at the bar, but otherwise it's been straight liquor all night.

After I've finished mixing the sauce for the sauté, I knit my brows and make eye contact with Dom, who smiles stiffly from his place at the hibachi. Then he comes inside to join me at the stove.

"Do they dress all your guests in aprons and hand them a spatula?" I grin — I know this can't be easy for him either.

"What guests? I never invite women over when Quinton's in town." He grabs my hip and pulls me in for a kiss. I don't like cooking, but I do like the idea of dressing up in an apron, with Dom manning the grill.

"Do they have *any* clue that I'll be talking to Quinton about my script?" I ask him.

I study his face, searching for anything useful in his eyes.

"Bringing it up organically will give you the best clout here." He averts his eyes and snatches a long chunk of pepper from the pan. He tosses it into his mouth while I watch him, unsure of what to say. "Quinton is . . . eccentric. High mainte-nance." He glances outside to make sure they aren't listening. "He fancies himself to be a bit of a genius — honestly because he *is* one. And geniuses don't like to be handed their next work of art. No matter who's suggesting it."

"I already mentioned to Selma that I write film scripts." I search his eyes for guidance. "Did I ruin the organic element of surprise?" My lips twist into a lopsided smile, trying to make light of all this. But, inside, I feel the pressure to make this work. Speeding up my path into film production means I could leave my job at UBN faster, and stay right here with Dom instead of having to go back.

"Well, that explains her sudden attitude tonight, then. She hates when people ask Quinton to work on vacation."

"I can just enjoy tonight with them as your girlfriend and bring this up some other day." The helium I'd been floating on before starts to drain right out of me. Maybe this wasn't meant to be after all.

"Listen, I know my brother, and I know his wife. They both love me, but they hate when people try to get a leg up by knowing someone in the industry. If I'd told them why we're all here tonight — honestly, they never would have agreed to it."

I untie the apron and slip the neck strap over my head, setting it down on the counter beside Selma's long knife.

I feel like screaming. Like I've already ruined this opportunity before it's really gotten underway.

"You need to pitch him tonight," Dom insists. "I want you to. Don't let whatever history with Taryn detract from the opportunity you have right in front of you. Nothing worth wanting comes easy." His deep voice is drawn lower so they can't hear him. "Use your gut to make tonight everything it needs to be. Trust me. I don't have the power to push this through that man's head. My brother is as egotistical as he is brilliant."

"So pretty egotistical then?" I cross my arms, fighting my face to remain neutral.

"I grew up around this industry. I know it like the back of my hand." His eyes are glowing like he knows I can do this. "If you want to break into film, if you want to leave UBN faster and make a real go at this, then you have to play the game. And your game is starting right now. You're the only one who can make this happen."

I finally relent. "Okay." Challenge accepted. If we're going to play ball tonight, I better get my head in the game.

"Trust me when I say it's the only way to do this. I may be powerful in my own right, but Quinton practically *owns* the film industry. Even if I gave you money to find a producer, and director, and hire all the actors, and rent out a production house, you still wouldn't get the respect you deserve, because everyone in the industry would know. That kind of beginning can sink someone trying to get started in Hollywood."

253

He's right. I know he is. This has to happen on my own terms, and with my own grit. Not handed to me on a silver platter by anyone, not even Dom.

"You have to trust me," he says again.

"Of course I trust you. I just wish your brother wasn't so intimidating."

I glance outside to make sure they're still engrossed in their own conversation. Selma is draped across Quinton's lap, sipping his whiskey between kissing him. They are every bit the Hollywood royalty all the tabloids make them out to be. She, stunning from head to manicured toe, drenched in this golden hour of the sunset. He, lapping up the attention of his supermodel wife, with one of the most breathtaking views in the world at their feet.

I consider how the hell I'm supposed to pull this off if I'm standing at a stove instead of sitting at the table with them, pouring it on so he becomes interested in hearing about what I want to do for a living. Or, at least, what I hope to do.

The veggies sizzle louder, so I grab a silicon spatula and start tossing them around as Dom watches me closely.

"Trust me on this," he repeats firmly. "I know how to work the Quinton Rockwell system. I've been around it my whole life. I'll finish this up so you can get out there and start schmoozing." He gently takes the spatula and gives me a kiss. "I'm going to give you as much time alone with him tonight as I can. Just don't come on too strong," he adds. "Easy does it."

While Dom pushes peppers and carrots around the wok, I stalk Quinton from a safe distance away. His thick head of hair is wavy and curled, a too-white smile surrounded by laugh lines, acquired from years of high-octane social events and nights spent in luxurious locations around the world. He wears a thick gold pinky ring with some unknown chunk of amber gemstone fixed in the center, probably yellow topaz if I had to guess. Although, it could be a yellow diamond. He oozes power, with his willowy trophy wife sitting atop his lap, staring down at him so lovingly that it makes me a little envious. I can see a resemblance to Dom in the way his eyes sparkle in the sunlight, crinkling at the edges.

Since working over ten years in high-stakes news, I've schmoozed with powerful people most of my adult life. I *am* capable of doing this right.

I can convince Quinton Rockwell to take a chance on me, while making it seem like it was his idea all along.

"Here goes nothing." I grab my wine glass and whatever is left in the bottle, and march outside to stalk, kill, and sink my teeth into exactly what I want.

CHAPTER 58

Selma looks up first when I make my way out to the lanai.

"Veronica! Honey! Did you bring that wine bottle with you?" She eyes my hand with the white wine bottle, now nearly empty.

I hold up the bottle in my hand, smiling.

"It's Olivia." I force a laugh. "And of course I did! It's right here."

I saunter over and set the bottle down in front of her, purposefully not adding another drop to her glass.

Lay the ground rules, I tell myself. *You're one of them, not beneath them.*

I sit down in one of the chairs facing the happy couple. Quinton's eyes graze the bit of cleavage peeking out over the top of my blouse. He doesn't seem ashamed when I pointedly make eye contact with him, bringing his eyes back up to face-level. I'm not surprised. Hollywood isn't known for churning out a strict moral code. But this is Dom's *brother*.

"I don't know how you ever leave this place!" I look around with a huge smile. "It's absolutely breathtaking. How long have you two owned it?"

Selma pushes Quinton's chin toward her, bringing his attention away from me and back to her. "How long have we owned this place, Quinny? Two years now? Or is it three?"

"No, we got that place in Aspen three years ago. We picked this place up after we went on the sailing trip around the islands. Remember? The charter we did with Roberto and Minnie."

It takes everything in me not to gush. Roberto and Minnie are the current *it* couple in Hollywood right now. Apparently they vacation with the couple I'm drinking wine with.

Be cool, Olivia, I tell myself. *Don't fuck this up.*

"That's right! Minnie wanted to find something bigger. Something that didn't have all those memories of her and her ex. She gave us a steal of a deal on this place after we stopped here during her divorce." Selma nods at Quinton while she recounts the details of their real estate deal. "Thirty-four million for this place. Can you believe it? Bargain, right? Of course, we still need to update the pool. But it works for now."

"The pool?" I squeak out, then shoot myself another reminder to relax. "I love the pool. It's the most gorgeous thing I've ever seen in real life."

Selma smiles at me sweetly. "That's cute." Then she grins at Quinton like I'm just here to entertain them. "So, you and Dom must be spending time at our pool too, then?"

I nod, forcing a smile.

"Sounds like you've been working *all your angles* to make this introduction happen."

I try not to react, keeping the smile frozen to my face. Sometimes powerful people have a need to make others feel small. Especially when trying to put them in their place.

"Sometimes I forget how lucky we are, Quinny. What seems absolutely disgusting to us seems like God's gift to others."

Damn, Selma.

"Are the veggies done, Olive?" she asks. "Or should you maybe go in to check on them?"

I look to see Dom placing a lid on the wok, keeping them warm until the fish is ready.

"No, it looks like Dom has it all in hand." I don't bother to correct my name again. What's the point? She'll forget I exist by the time her head hits the pillow tonight. I turn my attention back to Quinton. He's the one holding the key to what I want.

"What are you planning to do with the pool?" I ask him. "You obviously have an eye for beauty and design. That last film you did about the orphan family from the Congo was incredible. I think I went through an entire box of tissues at the end."

Selma shifts off his lap, looking bored. She grabs the bottle and dumps the remaining inch of wine into her glass.

"Looks like I'm out." She looks directly at me.

When I don't move, Quinton pipes up. "I know Dom stocked the cellar with your favorites, honey. Why don't you go pick out your next bottle or three?" Quinton hands her the nearly empty wine glass to finish his point.

She glares at me but takes the glass from him as she rises from the table. Then she marches inside.

With Selma out of earshot, Quinton's smile slowly returns to his face. I can feel him watching me, so I force a grin. I came here to play ball, and in order to do that I need to be able to sit at the table with the big boys. He leans forward with his hands clasped in front of him.

Dom is watching us from inside. Purposefully hanging back a moment to give us this time alone.

"She hates talking about work on vacation," he tells me. "Selma has started to, um, age out of the industry, as they say. It puts her on edge to discuss my success right when hers has started to fade."

"Oh, I don't know how that can be," I mutter. I'm shocked he's telling me this about his wife. We barely know each other. But, besides that, I'd be horrified if my husband were to speak about me like that to another woman. "Sure,

258

she's not twenty-four anymore, like she was at the peak of her career, but she's every bit as stunning now."

"Some women age like fine wine. I knew that she would when I married her. But there's also nothing quite like plucking fruit, fresh from the vine, before it's had a chance to age."

I shift in my chair. The way he's looking at me is making me feel uncomfortable. But I manage to hold my ground, deciding I need to change the subject before Selma gets back if we're both going to make it out of here alive.

CHAPTER 59

The last thing I need is Selma overhearing her husband pick apart her career while hitting on me in the same breath.

"Speaking of fresh fruit, what's your next big project?" I ask. It's hardly subtle, but Selma will be done picking out wine within minutes. I get the feeling she's not going to let our conversation return to the subject of work once she returns.

"So you're a fan of my films?" A cocky smile tugs at the corner of his lips. "Which one is your favorite?"

I rewatched every one of Quinton's films recently, staying up way too late the last few weeks to memorize their plot structures. Twists and turns expertly worked into every sequence. Picking out the similarities in characters, and playing out how my film script might work its way into his treasured collection.

"*The French Notebook* was my absolute favorite," I tell him.

He slaps the table with this palm.

"Of course it was!" he says triumphantly. "Every woman tells me that was their favorite. I should have predicted that one would top your list."

I get the sense that he'd rather I chose a lesser-known film. Perhaps one he doesn't get the same accolades for, one that he loved making nonetheless.

"I also loved *Forget Me Evermore*." It was one of his first films to put him on the path toward success, but it didn't make the mainstream cut of turning into a cult classic, like most of his other films that followed.

I study his reaction carefully, to see if I've hit on some soft nerve that will take me from an everyday fan girl to perhaps something with more depth.

"You . . . you really liked *Forget Me Evermore*?" His eyes turn soft. He leans back in his chair, and, for the first time, all his bravado is gone. Replaced with the soul of him shining out of both eyes.

Bingo.

"Of course! I thought it was underrated. A treasure, no — a gift — that no one took the time to fully unwrap." I spell it out in measured tones for him, pouring my eyes into his as he soaks up the praise that he no doubt longs to hear. "Only a true genius could have turned the tables on Rita after Luca did that to her."

His eyes glisten in the final rays of the sun.

"And the ending?" he asks, as if hanging on my every word. Like a conductor pulling out the final notes of his own symphony.

The ending got destroyed by film critics, so I know what my answer could be based on those reviews alone. I'm curious if he saw the error of the ending post-production, after he was scalded by the backlash of those hoping for a happy ending that never came. I take a risk, hoping he maintains that his ending was right. That the critics got it wrong.

"The ending was . . ."

He's leaning into the table, watching me closely. I think he's scarcely breathing.

I take a deep breath and go for it. "Quinton, the ending was a work of art." He throws his hands in the air, as if I've just won the winner-takes-all round of Texas hold 'em. Relieved, I go on. "It was perfection. The critics got it all wrong. You were skewered for giving your audience the most humanistic ending you could, which went against the Hollywood fluff everyone usually wants. You gave us the most ugly side of being human, instead of the beauty we all have in us. It was bold. You were utterly destroyed by the critics for those last ten minutes, which put you on their radar. But I loved it. I hope you never second-guessed how that ending went for you."

He sits back in his chair, as if my words have both thrilled and exhausted him.

"You have an eye for the arts," he says appreciatively. "I knew I liked you when we first met."

Just then, Selma reappears with two bottles of wine. One chilled and white, one crimson red. I assume the white is to finish before we enjoy the other with the ahi Dom is carrying toward the grill to sear.

She holds a corkscrew out with an eyebrow raised. "Olive, can you open this for me?" I'm sure this woman could open a bottle of wine in her sleep. But why ruffle feathers when I've just made progress? I reach out to take the corkscrew and bottle, just as Quinton intercepts and takes it from her instead.

"I've got it, honey," he says to his wife.

Then he rips the foil from the top of the bottle — which I'm sure cost more than I make in a year — while he keeps talking.

"Sweetheart, you must have misheard her earlier during introductions. Her name isn't Olive or Veronica."

Selma crosses her arms, still standing beside him as he starts to work the cork out of the bottle. It pops open and he grabs my glass to fill first, leaving his wife burning a hole in the side of his temple with her eyes.

"Surely you can remember it now though. Our guest's name is Olivia."

CHAPTER 60

Selma is on her third bottle of wine by the time we've finished dinner. Quinton has had at least four bourbons. Dom is tipsy from trying to keep up with his brother. And I've been sneaking cans of ginger ale into my glass of white wine each time I go to the fridge for more water. The yellowed liquid mixed with chardonnay passes off as white wine quite well, especially to my liquored-up hosts who haven't noticed the difference. I know they'd likely feel awkward if they knew they were drinking each other under the table while I snuck nearly virgin drinks, so I keep it to myself.

Quinton has thoroughly warmed up to me after the discussion about the finale of *Forget Me Evermore*, which has made Selma pink with envy. However, I'm somewhat convinced that poor Selma deals with fangirls fawning all over her husband not infrequently — her jealousy quickly turned to boredom.

"I'm going to bed," she announces suddenly, after we've all had dessert.

It's only nine thirty, but I take it as my cue to head out as well.

"Goodnight, Selma." I'm half-panicking that I'll be leaving without pitching Quinton my script. I feel like I've made a high-powered friend in the industry, and, for tonight, that may need to be enough. "Thank you again for having me. It was so nice to meet you."

"Let me walk you back," Dom says to Selma. "I'll show you where I've been storing all the new towels and linens you had sent over." He winks at me subtly, then rises from the table.

He's giving me one last shot. His absence will give me the opening I need to pitch Quinton after all.

"Take your shot," he whispers to me in the kitchen, before disappearing down the hall with Selma.

I'm left standing in the kitchen with Quinton.

"Since you seem to have an eye for beautiful things, I'd like to show you my plans for the pool." Quinton's eyes shine at me like a kid waiting for his friend's approval.

"Oh, um, you're not . . ." I point my thumb toward Selma and his bedroom. I thought he might follow her to bed after saying a quick goodnight to me.

"No. She'll be snoring by the time her head hits the pillow. You'd never imagine a woman like that snores like a freight train, but with a couple of drinks in her, she's frightful to try and sleep next to."

I hold up my phone. "I was actually just requesting a ride." My plan was to head back to the rental again tonight, giving Quinton and Selma space. "But I'll cancel it. For now."

"Yes, cancel it. I want your opinion on some plans." He wraps one arm around my shoulders and starts walking me toward the lanai, leading down to the garden.

"What about Dom? Have you gotten his opinion yet? He's done a beautiful job on the garden and—"

"Ah, yes, Dom the gardener. Come on, let me show you."

Dom was right about Quinton's ego if he can refer to his immensely successful brother as *the gardener*. The tiny pit in my stomach grows to a crater.

We cross the threshold into the dark, lit only by the collection of firepits and solar lights leading toward the pool.

Something about this doesn't feel right.

I stop in my tracks.

"Let's bring Dom with us," I say. "I'd love to hear what he thinks too."

Quinton's breath tickles the inside of my ear as he leans down to whisper. It smells of sour whiskey and the chocolate from dessert. "I thought you wanted a moment alone to discuss something with me. Selma mentioned you wrote a script? But if you don't actually want to . . ."

He waits for me to either walk with him or turn around and go home.

I look behind us, hoping to see Dom reappear in the kitchen, ready to join my solitary walk with his brother down to the pool. But no such luck. He's giving me that space he promised to play the game with Quinton.

"Come on, I won't bite. It'll give us some time to talk about your little project."

Of course I'm not going to turn down the opportunity to have Quinton Rockwell listen to my pitch at his estate. Every opportunity comes with some type of price. Sometimes, the price is just taking a little risk. I'm not about to turn around and walk away from my lifelong dream potentially coming true.

"Show me the pool," I tell him.

CHAPTER 61

I look behind us again as we continue down the dimly lit path leading to the pool, hoping to see Dom coming down after me. I don't mind pitching Quinton in front of Dom, but I'd rather not troop off into the garden alone with a drunk man I hardly know.

"I hear you've been spending a lot of time here in my garden." Quinton lowers his arm from my shoulder to my waist. I stoop to pick up a plumeria from the path, taking it as an opportunity to gracefully wriggle out of his reach. "It must be a great spot to write if you're here so often." His eyes travel down my body as we're stopped on the path. "And swim." He gently takes my elbow, leading me further from the house.

I seize the opportunity now that he's mentioned my writing.

I muster up every bit of confidence I have left in me. "I've finished a full-length film script." *This is it.* "I'd like to tell you more about it."

I picture him spinning around, telling me he'd love to, but he doesn't even falter. His feet keep moving us toward the clearing where the pool is, as if he hasn't heard me at all.

"It's just through here." He pushes back the same palm branches Dom shoved aside on our first trip to the pool. A crippling sting of regret whips through me. I should have insisted more strongly that Dom come with us.

What am I doing? Forging through the garden in the dark with a very drunk, very powerful man. His status in Hollywood blinded me to the fact that I really have no idea who he is as a person. No idea of what he's capable of. And my stupidity has left me completely at his mercy out here, where no one else can hear us.

My heart starts thumping a warning sign when I register how far we are from the house. Dom won't know whether I left with Quinton or took a ride back home. He'll probably assume Quinton went to bed if I've left. I spin around, looking behind us again as we bounce down the path together, willing Dom's silhouette to appear along the gravel inlay behind us.

But the path is empty.

Quinton walks a bit faster. "Just a little farther." He seems to be sobering up as we close the space between us and the pool.

CHAPTER 62

We reach the pool in what feels like record time. When I came through the brush with Dom that first time, the view took my breath away. Now, arriving with Quinton, it looks beautiful as ever, but my impression of our surroundings has dampened. The aquarium light glowing behind the bar looks more gaudy, the setup overdone.

Quinton beelines for the bar, pulling a new glass from behind the thick stone wall of cupboards.

"Hello, old friend," he says to a new bottle of bourbon before kissing the crystal tumbler and placing it on the counter. I wrinkle my nose while I watch. He has a distinct charm that I imagine has taken him far in Hollywood, but it seems out of place here on the island. The scene on Oahu is too earthy for someone like him. Like he's made of plastic, and everything else is organic and raw.

He pulls a second tumbler out and, without asking, pours a heavy shot of bourbon into both glasses. Then he makes his way over to me and hands me the second glass.

We clink the crystal together — I force a smile as we both take a sip.

"Let me just tell you about the pool design, then I'd love to hear more about that script."

My heart skips a beat. "Sure." Maybe he really did come to show me the pool and listen to my pitch. "I'd love to hear your plans for this space. Although, I've got to be honest, I love the classic lines you have going on here. The bamboo baja shelf, the crisp white furniture. It's timeless."

"Or old school and boring," he says, "depending on how you look at it."

I mask a sigh. "What do you have in mind?"

"First, have you seen the hot tub?" He whisks me toward the hidden grotto.

I stop my feet from moving any further. "I have. I've seen the hot tub, yes." I fail to hide the annoyance in my voice.

"Let's go for a swim," he says. "I haven't swum here in months. Maybe a year. I keep the water at exactly body temperature, or I suppose Dom does." He eyeballs the path, and I turn, hoping to see Dom emerging from the greenery.

"Quinton, I've had a wonderful time tonight, but I don't think I'm going to go for a swim."

Either Quinton is going to listen to my pitch, or I'm going to head home. I don't feel right being tucked away in a makeshift jungle cove with Dom's very drunk brother, who seems to have plans for me tonight. I hope he can hear the deeper meaning of my words. *I won't be stripping down with you tonight, or ever.*

"Sit with me then." He takes a seat on one of the lounge chairs, patting the cushion right next to him. Instead of sitting on his chair, I sit on the lounge next to his, raising my brows.

"I'm not going to bite." He pats the spot next to him again.

I ignore his persistence. "So, what is it that you want to do with this pool?" I didn't come here to have sex with him. Even if it costs me my dream of having him produce my film. I can find another director who's interested in making it. If this isn't meant to be, then it's not meant to be.

"I thought you wanted to hear what I thought of your script?"

269

"I thought you wanted to tell me about your pool plans," I shoot back, hoping he finds the challenge in my voice to be charming, not abrasive.

He laughs, then lies back on his chair, resting his hands behind his head and staring up at the stars. "My brother likes you, you know."

I look at him, then back at the path that led us here, hoping Dom will appear any moment. *Why did I agree to come down here with him in the first place?* "I really like him too." *It's now or never.* "He insisted I come here tonight to tell you about the script I wrote. I've worked in television for years, but my heart is in film. I'd like you to read it and tell me what you think."

He sets his tumbler down on the ceramic side bar next to his chair, then turns his head toward me. His eyes eat into mine. I want to look away. Everything in me wants to turn away from his steely gaze, but I force myself to return the stare. He can't know he has the upper hand and makes me nervous, or he won't respect me. To him, I'll just be another budding writer, trying to do anything I can to get his attention. I won't allow it. He needs to think of me as an equal, a professional. Not just another woman willing to let him do whatever he wants with the promise of making me a star.

Finally, he speaks. "So, give it to me." He cocks his head to one side.

I recoil in disgust. "Give you what?"

He laughs, throwing his head back against the chaise.

"The pitch, Olivia. Give me your elevator pitch. The thing you practiced in your mirror over and over before meeting me tonight. Give it to me."

My heart is pounding out of my chest. I want to hate him, and yet there's this glimmer of relentless charm that goes into everything he says. He's annoyingly charismatic, while walking the line of being just plain annoying.

"You want my elevator pitch?" I set my glass down next to his, hoping he doesn't notice my hand is shaking.

"Isn't that why you followed me down here? To get me alone so you could pitch me your script?"

I feel myself turning red.

"I didn't get where I am today by being daft, dear." His smile is warmer than I would like it to be. It makes me feel like I can trust him, when just a moment ago I felt anything but trust toward him. "Come on then, let's hear it."

CHAPTER 63

It all comes tumbling out. The most perfect pitch I can muster. Quinton was right about me practicing in front of a mirror, but instead of twenty times, I probably shot this pitch out of my mouth a thousand times before saying it right now to his face.

All that practice was worth it — it comes flowing out, smooth as butter. Exactly how I'd planned.

"... and in the end, he remembers his wife was waiting for him back at the flower shop, while the owner hands Claire the note he'd left for her six years prior. The two of them run down the sidewalk, while the audience already has a hint at what's to come."

I sit back, my ribs flaring like I've just finished the most stunning vault routine at the Olympics. "End scene." I smile at him, unable to contain my excitement that I've just officially pitched Quinton Rockwell the film I've worked on for years, which I completed here in the last six weeks, while sitting in his very own garden.

He leans into his chaise lounge, then takes a small sip of his drink, setting it back down on the table without looking over. My heart is pounding so loudly I literally wonder if he can hear it over the sound of the waves crashing in the distance. The ocean sounds so feisty tonight.

I shuffle my feet, unable to contain the immense amount of adrenaline flowing through me. I want to stand up and scream, "*Well?*" Just to get him to say something. Anything. It's been too long. I was expecting him to at least give me his initial reaction. Something other than stone-cold silence.

My eyes widen, then close, and I exhale quietly. He's not even looking at me. He must hate it. I picture myself coming home tonight and, instead of popping champagne at midnight, I'm falling asleep crying into my pillow before having to leave tomorrow.

A full minute goes by where Quinton is just staring up at the stars. He picks up his glass and swirls it around a bit, not taking another sip.

I try breathing out slowly, but it comes out louder than I hope, sounding like an exasperated sigh. He turns to look at me, swirling his glass, then closes his eyes again.

"Quinton?"

This time he holds my eye, but still doesn't say a word.

I look right and left, the awkwardness taking over my better judgment.

"Well?" It comes out high-pitched and squirrely. Exactly the opposite of how I saw this moment going. But geniuses need time to process, so I'll just let him take whatever time he needs. I settle back against my chair. Willing myself to wait patiently.

"Well . . ." He breathes out steadily. "Do you want the good news? Or the bad news?" My breath hitches, and I can't respond. I can't choose good or bad. The good news is, he still thinks I'm pretty? And the bad news is, I don't have a future in film?

He shifts to his side and sets his glass down.

Oh God.

He hates it. He fucking hates it. Okay. Well, he's not the only director in Hollywood, right? He's just the only one I've got the undivided attention of in this moment, and he's about to give me a solid rejection. I can feel it.

"Let's start with something easier than my assessment of that script. Why did you *really* come here tonight?"

273

CHAPTER 64

Not exactly the question I imagined, but it's also not a rejection.

Yet.

"I came here tonight to meet the family of a guy I'm falling for. And to pitch you my film. To hand you a copy of the script. And to—"

"And to ride happily into the sunset with a new business partnership with me?" Quinton interrupts. It feels like he's staring into my very soul.

"Well, yeah, I guess. When you put it like that it just sounds so—"

He interrupts again. "Contrived?"

Everything in me wants to run. Nothing about tonight is going how I pictured it.

"Listen, I came here this evening with the best intentions. If I leave with only your feedback on how to do better next time, and I've had the opportunity to meet an incredible filmmaker, I'll take it. I know I could have used more time to polish the pitch. Hell, I could have used more time to *finish* the script, but when Dom told me you'd be coming, he insisted."

"Are you using my brother to get to me?"

A total gut punch. "No, I really like your brother. You being Dom's brother has nothing to do with my feelings for him."

Quinton watches me intently before speaking. "I watch the world's best actors for a living. I watch every micro-move in their face. Their lips, their eyes, the speed at which they breathe, even the angle at which their head hangs above their neck. I need everything about them to be believable, to convey their fake emotions to my strictest standards."

I hold my breath, waiting for another gut punch to fly in.

"I've been watching you all night. But, Olivia, you do look like you're telling the truth about how you feel regarding Dom."

"Of course I'm telling the truth. How could you think I was using him? He's — he's everything."

"Frankly, it wouldn't have been the first time someone tried to use people who are close to me in order to get to me. It happens to my brother, my wife — hell, it even happens to my housekeeper, my dog walker . . ."

"Well, that's not me. I can see how someone might do that. I mean, you're Quinton Rockwell for God's sake. And your wife is Selma Hatfield. You two are . . . well, you're legends in Hollywood. But that's not who I am. I wouldn't use Dom to get to his famous family. He's incredible all on his own."

"The thing is, when you're *legends*, as you put it" — he cringes, seemingly more human than he was only a moment ago — and a lot more sober — "or you're filthy rich *and* related to *legends* like my brother is, it's hard to tell who's genuine. Who truly cares for you. And who's just looking for a handout."

I sigh. "I think Dom knows I'm genuine."

Is he for real? It makes me feel cheap. Like he thinks I'd sleep with his brother just to get a dinner meeting about a film script. I can see his point, but I'm not Taryn. That's just not who I am. "I really like Dom. I fell for him long before I found out who he was. And certainly before I knew who his brother was."

"I can tell Dom likes you too." He sits back again and smiles up at the sky. "You know, he rarely even tells people we're related."

He looks more relaxed now. Quinton's entire demeanor seems to have changed since I finished my pitch with him. He doesn't even appear to be drunk anymore. His latest glass of whiskey has hardly been touched, and he's laid off the creepy vibe too, thank goodness. I don't know which version is the real him, but I like this side of him much better.

He goes on. "I love my brother more than anything. I think sometimes Dom feels like I'm difficult. But, the truth is, I just want the very best for him. I want to share the happiness I've found *with* him. With everyone in the family. We both know it can be lonely at the top of your game. I have Selma, who, by the way, is much kinder than she let on tonight. Once she heard about your script and all . . . But Dom? He has no one. At least, when it comes to love. I think he hides behind his success a bit too much. While Selma and I choose to live in the spotlight, Dom chooses to hide in the shadows."

He glances in my direction, all bravado drained from his face. He just looks tired now.

"What do you mean?" I ask.

"Most people just want to be near this level of success. Close enough to touch it, and everything that goes with it." He looks over at me somewhat sheepishly. "Who to trust, and who to keep on the fringe. It's something we all struggle with. Selma and I have been burned by so many people we saw as friends. Even some of our family members, a time or two."

"I hope Dom doesn't question my feelings for him. Your brother is everything to me. He makes me feel whole again, especially after my last very public breakup, and all the mistakes I've made since. I came here to escape some embarrassing viral fame back home. Dom saw through all that. He saw—" Quinton raises an eyebrow at me when I pause. Unsure of how to finish. "Well, he saw *me*. More clearly than anyone I've ever met."

"Yes, I recognized you from that silly meme the moment I saw you. You proposed to your boyfriend on national television. He said no."

I sigh and lie back in my chair. That stupid meme will be printed on my gravestone, as my one and only claim to fame.

"That's me." I take a small sip of whiskey and wince as it burns down my throat.

"Did you book Dom's rental just to get to me?" he asks suddenly. "I've told him not to use his real name in the listing as the property manager. People are crazy smart these days. I knew somewhere along the line someone would book one of his places, knowing who we are."

"His listing agent's new assistant made that mistake." I sit up straighter and swing my legs back over the chair, looking him dead in the eye. I will put this little notion to rest for good.

"Quinton, listen to me. You may be one of the best directors in the world, and I may have just completely bombed that pitch, but I really, really like your brother. I had no idea Dom was related to you until he told me a few weeks ago. I didn't even know who he was until long after we started seeing each other. I'm definitely not smart enough to book a rental owned by the brother of a Hollywood director. Okay? Thank you for thinking I'm that accomplished in my online sleuthing skills, but, really, you don't have to worry about that. I booked his place because it was cheap. I didn't even know it was a shared townhouse, more or less owned by a guy related to *you*."

I pause to catch my breath.

He starts laughing, putting his hands up in front of him like I have a gun pointed in his direction. "Okay, okay! I believe you. You know, sometimes I just have to make sure. We have a long history of fame-chasers in this family."

As long as I'm on a roll here, I dig my teeth in even further.

CHAPTER 65

If Quinton already hated my pitch, I may as well go for broke. If Quinton was truly hitting on me, Dom needs to know.

"What was that whole *hitting-on-your-brother's-date* thing earlier anyway? I'm with Dom. You're with Selma. Why be the creepy heavy-hitting Hollywood director to the girl who just wants to spout off a pitch and go home?"

I stare at him, blind rage filling my eyes, but he just sighs and shrugs, looking slightly embarrassed.

"I just wanted to see if you were genuine. I would have never actually put any real moves on you. I would have stopped things before they got started. If it seemed like you were willing to take the bait, just to get your script read by me, I would have known for certain that Dom was in trouble."

"What?" I feel rancid whiskey threaten to spill back out.

"I was pretending to hit on you to protect him."

"That sounds beyond twisted." I set my glass back down.

"It's been years since we met anyone he liked. The last one Dom introduced us to, Taryn, turned out to be engaged to him for the wrong reasons. We only found out when she tried to seduce me for a film role. I figured if I flipped the tables on you and presented the opportunity right off the bat, we'd know pretty quick if that was all you were after."

"You were testing me?" I'm both relieved and horrified.

He shrugs. "I'm sorry if I made you feel uncomfortable, Olivia. Truly, I am. There's always a method to my madness, even for how eccentric Dom likes to say I am. There's always a reason behind what I do. Tonight, it was to test your loyalty to him. You passed, if you're at all curious." I scoff, but he goes on. "Go ahead and think I'm an ass for it, but, to me, what matters is that Dom seems to have found someone worthy of him."

It all makes sense now. Everything from Selma's sudden attitude change once I mentioned the script, to the way Quinton seemed to transform into a better person the moment the pitch was done.

"Well, thank you for dinner," I say curtly, "and for listening to that pitch." I stand up. "You could have just said you weren't interested in my work without dragging me down here in an attempt to make a fool out of me."

"I would never have gone through with any of it." He's still acting more calm than I feel. Though if they're so used to putting up with fake people, maybe this whole conversation doesn't faze him nearly as much as me.

"Goodnight, Quinton," I say as calmly as I can. Then I turn to walk toward the path that will lead me back to the house.

"I just have one more question for you, Olivia," he says quietly.

"What?" I spin around, feeling hot tears pooling behind my eyes.

"If you didn't book that Airbnb just to meet Dom, what are you doing in Hawaii for eight weeks completely by yourself? Why else would you be here?"

Even though I'm afraid my eyes are going to spill over, I let it all out. "You know that stupid proposal? The meme?"

"Of course," he says. "Unwanted attention is never easy. Selma and I have lived with fame our entire adult lives. Tabloids will pay millions for dirt on us. I get how hard that can be, but it still doesn't explain why you're here."

"Yeah, well, after my face became recognizable to most of New York, my boss at UBN allowed me to take a sabbatical. I found the cheapest place on Airbnb. Took out a credit card and burned through my savings to book it. Then, what do you know? I show up, and my ex, who humiliated me on television, turning my face into a world-famous meme, is living on the other side of the rental wall."

I pause to let that sink in. The dark humor of my last eight weeks.

"The guy you proposed to was renting the other half of Dom's townhouse?"

"Not *was* renting. *Is* renting. He *is* renting the other half. As in, currently living on the other side of my wall. With his beautiful new girlfriend."

"No shit." Quinton swings his legs off the chair and turns toward me, fully invested now. "Why didn't you just leave? Go back to New York?"

I scoff. "It should have been that easy, right?"

"Dom wouldn't let you out of it?"

"No. Even though I begged him at first."

He has the nerve to laugh at this. "He was falling for you already, wasn't he? Was that the reason? Of course, it had to be. Dom is worth more than Selma and I combined. He never would've been cruel like that, unless there was a reason."

"Yeah, well." I cross my arms over my chest. "Turns out you're all a little mad. Always a method behind your madness, you said? That must run in the family."

"It seems to have worked out for the best."

I crack a smile, my first since we got down here. "I suppose it did."

"So what happened after that?"

I don't know why I'm suddenly spilling my life to Quinton, but I am. It almost feels therapeutic to just let it all hang out like this. My imperfect situation that, if it weren't me living it, would be moderately entertaining.

"After Dom wouldn't let me out of the reservation, I guess he probably felt bad, because he started coming around to hang out. At first, it was to make my ex jealous. Dom thought I'd stick through to the end of my reservation if I was having fun with it. Then it quickly became more than that. He taught me to surf. Took me to Cliff's. I met all his friends. I really love them."

His smile grows. "I heard about your awesome rendition of 'Sweet Caroline.'" He chuckles.

I like this version of him. I don't know what type of air he was putting on for me earlier, that whole act of the stereotypical drunken film director taking the innocent doe-eyed scriptwriter down to the pool. *This* version of him seems decent.

"Why aren't you drunk anymore?" I ask him suddenly.

"Ah. Well, that was all part of my show! I wasn't drinking as heavily as I let on. Right before you showed up, Dom was telling us that you were renting his place for two months, and you'd quickly befriended him. Selma and I quietly guessed you were using him to get my attention. We didn't mention it to Dom, but it didn't sit very well with either of us. It seemed too contrived that you'd be renting from him for the eight weeks leading up to our vacation."

"So it was all an act." Part of me thinks everything about him is twisted, and the other part finds it somewhat endearing that Quinton would be so protective over Dom like this. To risk his own reputation just to save his brother some future heartache.

"Guilty," he confirms. "I do enjoy putting on a great show." Then he winks at me, his smile growing wider, and I finally feel myself relax. "You're living a very interesting life lately, aren't you?"

He's listened closely to every word I've said. "Interesting doesn't begin to describe what my life has been lately." I crack a smile. "Which brings us to today. Me pitching you. Something Dom insisted I do, against my better judgment, considering what happened with Taryn."

I wait with bated breath, hoping that he's going to tell me he loves it, now that he knows I'm genuine.

"Olivia, I like you. I really do." I have a sinking feeling that this is starting out like the sweetest rejection letter I've ever gotten. "The pitch on your script was fine. I could give you some pointers on how to present it to the next director. Places to tighten it up here and there. Maybe an additional plot twist you could add in. However—"

He continues on, but I don't hear the rest of what he's saying.

After all the hell I've gone through to get here, what I'm getting right now is a very heartfelt rejection.

CHAPTER 66

It's close to midnight when I walk back into the townhouse. After crying as quietly as I could in the backseat of my ride — so the driver didn't feel the need to make small talk about my night — I didn't even bother checking my makeup before I got inside.

Dom and I didn't exactly end things well tonight.

He'd come outside to wait for the driver with me after I'd gotten nicely rejected by Quinton. Dom said he'd almost followed us out to the pool after dinner, but decided to give us the time alone so I could finally make my pitch to Quinton in private. But when he saw me coming back up to the house alone a half hour later, he knew from my face that Quinton had turned me down.

"Did he give you any feedback?" He'd hugged me while we waited on the front porch for the driver.

"Some." I'd shoved back a tear. "Though I hardly heard a word of his advice after he told me no. Basically, the script wasn't strong enough. Not fresh enough. He suggested I find a better plot twist, or start from scratch. These last few weeks, working like I did to get it to a place I was happy to pitch it, just seem like a waste when I could have just been spending all those hours with you."

"It wasn't all a waste. Just come back inside." He'd gently pulled my arm toward the house. "I'll tell the driver you changed your mind and don't need a ride anymore. Stay here with me tonight. You don't have to go back to the rental all upset. It's your last night here. Maybe we can all have breakfast in the morning and you can try again."

"I'm sorry." I'd crossed my arms. "I can't stay here in this house with them. Or wake up to them. I just need to think."

"Then let me come with you," he'd pleaded. "Or stay."

"I just feel like reality is crashing through me right now," I'd told him. "I'm about to fly back to New York tomorrow and face everything I ran from. Everything that nearly destroyed me. I'm about to go back to the station that made me a laughing stock. To a life I don't recognize myself in anymore. I thought that if tonight worked out with Quinton and this script, there was a chance I could stay. I hadn't really let myself think about what I'd do if it didn't work, and now it means that I don't have a backup plan. The only thing I can do while standing on my own two feet is to return to UBN. Which means turning back into the girl you won't even recognize anymore."

"Then stay," he'd pleaded. "I'll take care of you. You'll want for nothing. Why won't you let me do that for you?"

"Because I can't let you. I can't rely on you. Not yet. I was so blind in my last relationship that I proposed to a guy, in front of millions of people, who didn't even want to be with me. What if I can't trust my gut yet, even with you? What if everything about us falls apart without warning like my last relationship did? I won't have a career to fall back on if I walk away from it without another plan in place."

"But I'm not Rex." He'd lowered his voice. "I'd never do that to you."

"There was a time that he wouldn't have either. I just feel like I'm in a bit of a free-fall right now. The station won't give me any more time. I just need to think about what to do before I get on that plane."

Then he stepped back toward his door and watched me go.

"Please understand," I'd told him as I climbed into the car, feeling gutted. "I'll call you first thing in the morning. I need time to think."

He'd nodded, just once, his eyes like two raging storms, before closing the car door with me inside.

Now, walking into the rental again, the first thing I notice is the patio light on outside, and Rex sitting in a lounge chair with a book. Two glasses of red wine sit beside him, meaning Juju is probably somewhere around here, enjoying the balmy midnight air. A mostly empty bottle sits beside him on the deck.

Wonderful.

I walk over to shove the blinds closed, but he turns and jumps up from the chair, grabbing both glasses of red wine, like he's been waiting for me.

CHAPTER 67

Seeing Rex standing at the sliding door is the last thing I need right now.

"Quinton rejected it." I slide the door open with him on the other side. Better to start this conversation by getting it out in the open, so he doesn't have to pull it all out of me. I don't feel like retelling every single detail when the ending is all that matters. And I certainly don't want him to text me tomorrow morning, wanting to know more.

I start to slide the door closed again, but stop when he holds the full wine glass out to me.

"Shit," he says.

I guess our last goodbye earlier wasn't forever after all.

"This is for you." He holds the glass over the threshold, blocking the path of the sliding door.

I look across the lanai, then glance toward his side of the townhouse.

He reads my face. "She's not here."

"Oh." I'm suddenly so tired, it feels like gravity has hold of my brain, pulling me down to sleep.

"Juju and I broke up."

"What?" I wake right up. Wondering if I simply imagined him saying that.

He nods down at me, looking sad, and somewhat ashamed.

"When?"

"Earlier today. That's why I came over to talk. This is for you." He hands me the fuller glass of wine and I take a step back from him.

"What happened?" I ask.

"She figured out who you were. Who *we* were."

I close my eyes and sigh.

This night can't get any worse.

Rex shrugs, but my stomach drops like a rock. "You still hadn't filled her in?" I need to sit down.

"No. I was an idiot. I should have told her. I almost did so many times. I just liked the fresh start here. I liked not being the jerk that rejected the sweet, beloved news anchor on national television." He smiles weakly.

I just need to sit down. We slowly make our way over to the two lounge chairs that are set up facing the water.

"Fuck." I breathe out slowly, leaning back in the chair. "I can't believe she had to find out like that."

Rex settles into the chair next to mine, shaking his head like he can't believe it either.

"She said that friend she had over here from the shop showed her the video this morning. Right after meeting you."

I close my eyes again and shake my head. I'd been coming back up from a quick surf session earlier this morning when I passed Juju and a girl I'd never met before, sunbathing on their towels just off the back deck. Juju had introduced me as her boyfriend's neighbor, here for an extended stay in the townhouse next door. The girl had stared at me a beat too long, lowering her sunglasses to get a better look at my face. But she hadn't said a word about potentially recognizing me, so I let it go. I'd been so nervous about tonight, I'd forgotten to mention to Rex that Juju's friend might have recognized me. I guess she must have pulled up the video later to confirm it was me after all.

"Poor girl." My heart hurts for Juju. She shouldn't have had to find out like that.

"We'd kind of been living in this happy little bubble here. No one had recognized me yet, so I figured that whole thing might finally be behind us."

I take a big gulp of the wine, letting it all sink in.

Juju must hate me.

"I'm sorry. I really liked her. She deserved better. From both of us."

Rex drains his glass and reaches for the bottle, topping up with the last splash of red before setting the bottle down empty again. He must have been out here drinking alone while he waited for me.

"You're right, she definitely deserved better." He sets his glass down after draining it. "But so did you." Rex's profile hardens. "I fucked up, Liv." He turns toward me. "I fucked up with Juju. And I fucked up with you. If I could go back to that stupid news segment right before you popped the question, I would. I'd travel back in time and change everything. I—"

He pauses to take my hand, but I quickly shake it off.

"Olivia, I'm still in love with you."

CHAPTER 68

"You what?" I feel lightheaded.

I stare into his eyes, my face hardening. This can't be right.

"You heard me." He shifts his body onto the end of my chair — I cross my legs beneath me so we're not touching. He takes both my hands in his, his eyes pleading. "I never stopped loving you. That morning I found you locked out here, trying to disguise yourself in that stupid hat and sunglasses — the second I saw you again, I knew I wasn't over you." I stare at him, speechless. "I wasn't ready to get married when you asked. I was completely caught off guard. I panicked. But I feel ready now."

"What?" I sputter.

"Baby." Rex shifts down off the chair, onto one knee — *oh my God.* "You are everything I could ever want, and everything I could ever need. I am a better person because of you. Olivia Renee Hillcrest, I love you." He picks my hand back up. "Will you marry me?"

"Rex, I—" My heart is pounding out of my ears.

"Just say yes," Rex interrupts, his eyes shining.

But a long shadow falls over my chair, a tall figure lit from behind. I spin around to see Dom standing behind the glass wall of my rental, watching Rex propose.

Horrified, I see Dom shake his head at me, then turn and walk out my front door.

"Dom!" I yell after him, shaking Rex off, but he holds my hand harder, still hovering on one knee. I push past him. I need to go after Dom and tell him that I never intended to get back together with Rex, and that his proposal just blindsided me. I have no idea how much of that he heard, but it was enough for him to look furious.

Rex jumps to his feet, grabbing my arm. "Forget him. Say yes and we can leave here together. We can go back to New York—"

That hits another nerve.

I don't ever want to leave this place, especially with him.

I hear Dom's car scream out of the driveway and down the road. I've already missed him.

Rex finally releases my hand.

"I can't marry you." It's the same words he'd said to me just a few months ago, as cameras caught every word.

"Why? You're going to marry that loser?" He points a finger toward the spot where Dom was just standing.

"Maybe?" I smile at the thought. "I hope so."

Rex scoffs, standing up.

"He's just your rebound. You'll come crawling back to me when he breaks it off."

As if on cue, my phone pings next to me — I lunge at it, hoping it's a message from Dom.

But, it's a text from Juju.

It's Juju. I got your number from Rex's phone before we broke up. This is going to be hard for me to say, but I think you should know—

The text ends there.

A roll of nausea rushes through me, as if my gut knows what's coming before my mind can register it. I watch as the three little dots appear, letting me know that she's not done yet. She's about to drop a bomb into my life. I can feel it. I look up at Rex, about to ask him to explain, but my phone pings again.

After I found out about the video of you proposing to Rex, I looked up the date it happened. I had no idea Rex and you were together when we met online. We'd already been talking and seeing each other for about six months by the time you proposed to him on air. He'd already purchased his ticket to Hawaii to come be with me later that same week.

Blood runs cold in my veins as I finish reading the last line from Juju.

I look up at Rex. He looks pale.

"Who's it from?" He sounds nervous. Afraid that I might actually know the truth about him. About *us*. "Is it from Dom?"

I shake my head, watching cold fear run through him.

"Juju?" His voice cracks.

"Tell me when you two started dating."

He swallows, unable to speak.

"You were cheating on me for six months?" My voice is dripping with venom.

I want to wring his neck.

Right here, right now.

"Just let me explain." He steps toward me.

I hold up one finger to stop him, taking a bigger step back than the one he took forward. I don't want him touching me anymore tonight. Not now, not ever. My whole body starts shaking. I should have never agreed to talk to him.

"All this time, I knew something was off. I should have listened to my gut." I don't stop the wild-eyed grin creeping over my face. After everything that's happened tonight, I feel unhinged. "I don't think I ever truly wanted to marry you, Rex. Did I tell you it was all my producer's idea? That she was the one to tell me to ask you?"

Something in me breaks free, like a rope snapping from a pile of dead weight. I study his face as the last ounce of respect I have for him drains from me. Forever.

"You're not the man for me," I tell him coldly. "Not now, not ever again. But I think I know who is."

CHAPTER 69

I run to the front door, praying against all odds that I'll see Dom waiting for me on the driveway. But, just as I feared, the driveway is empty. There's no sign of his car anywhere.

He's gone.

I run back inside, grabbing my phone off the counter where I left it when I rushed out. No missed calls, no new messages.

I hit his name in my contacts list, my heart pounding, but the call goes straight to his voicemail.

I hit *Call* again, but his voicemail picks up without a single ring.

"I guess he wasn't the man for you after all," Rex mocks, bitterly. The back door is still slung open, and he's sitting on a lounge chair silently watching me. He looks like a villain, hiding out in the dark, and my heart pounds even harder knowing that he has a front row seat to all this.

I slam the door and pull the blinds across the glass so he can't see me. Then I type a quick text to Dom.

That wasn't what it looked like. I swear. Come back

Three little dots appear, then disappear.

"Fuck!" I ignore the urge to throw my phone, and I start typing again.

I saw you typing, so I know you have your phone in your hand. Please call me. Rex was out of line. I don't know how much of that you saw, but it wasn't what it looked like. Please come back.

I wait to see the three little typing dots appear again, but this time there's nothing.

I toss the phone onto the cushion next to me and slump down on the sofa, putting my head in my hands.

A few hours ago, I saw my whole life falling into place — only to have everything stripped away in one fell swoop. This entire trip I've pleaded, begged, and questioned my fate. But all I can say for certain, in this exact moment, is that fate, the universe, or whoever is pulling the strings of my life — none of it makes any sense.

* * *

After sleeping hardly a wink, I take the first available Uber to Dom's house the next morning. My redeye flight back to New York takes off at eight thirty tonight, but I'm not leaving this island until I've had a chance to set the record straight.

Abby is giving me a pep talk on the way over.

"Don't leave until Dom agrees to talk to you in person," she says.

"You've never dealt with people like Quinton and Selma," I tell her. "The way they are on-screen is nothing like who they are in real life. And after the way Dom left here last night, it'll be a miracle if I can get past them."

"First rule of negotiation," she coaches. "Don't let the conversation end on your side. Keep it going. As long as they're listening to you, there's still a chance."

"I can't believe this is happening," I whisper when we pull up to the driveway. "They've got to have cameras all over this place. I'm sure they already know I'm here and they're all just watching me from inside."

I feel like I might be sick.

"Just go up there, head high. You didn't do anything wrong and you're going to help them figure that out."

"Thanks, Abs," I say, wishing she was here.

"Call me after."

My heart sinks when Selma answers the door.

"Oh. You." She looks stripped of all patience. "Olivia, Dom isn't here this morning."

She starts to shut the door.

"So you do know my name!" I blurt out, holding the door open. It's a bold move to entice her into talking to me, so she'll tell me where he is, or at least not immediately slam the door in my face.

It seems to work — she rolls her eyes but doesn't shut the door quite yet. "Of course I know your actual name. Believe it or not, I was excited to meet you last night. *At first.* Congratulations on your engagement, by the way."

I try not to imagine how upset Dom must have been when he got back home. Selma and Quinton will probably blackball my name all over Hollywood after this.

"He needs to give me a chance to explain. I'm not engaged. Dom walked in on something he should never have seen last night. Something that shouldn't have happened at all. My ex was out of line."

"Quinton told me about you pitching him down by the pool after I went to bed." She raises a perfectly sculpted eyebrow at me. "If you weren't just using Dom to get to Quinton, then how do you explain that part?"

"Can you tell me where he is? Just give me a chance to explain."

"Sorry, honey." Just as the door is about to click shut, another hand curls around the edge to stop it.

When it swings back open, Dom is standing on the other side. His hair is mussed and his eyes look exhausted. He must have slept as poorly as I did.

"Oh, thank God," I say. "Talk to me. Please."

He looks over at Selma, who shrugs at him and walks away. "Was she acting like I wasn't here?"

"Honestly, I would probably do the same thing if I was her right now. But you have to let me explain."

Finally, he steps outside and shuts the door behind him. "I'd rather not walk you through the house right now. Quinton and Selma are nasty when they're pissed. Let's go around out back."

I shudder, imagining them both inside like chained guard dogs, waiting to shred me.

We silently walk around the garden, past the stone table where I've been writing, and out to the water's edge. It's a crystal-clear morning, with the waves lapping gently at the shore. We settle into the powdery white sand, and I take a deep breath, letting it all come out.

I tell him about the conversation I had with Rex when I got home. How he was waiting for me with a bottle of wine and two glasses. How he and Juju broke up, and how he used that to segway into a proposal.

When I get to the part about Rex getting down on one knee, he stops me. "I don't think I need to hear this part."

"Please just let me finish. You've had us both stuck in a moderate panic attack for the last six hours, when you should have just let me tell you what happened last night!"

He presses his palms into the sand, taking a deep breath like he's trying to calm down. "Go on, then."

"Juju broke up with him yesterday. She found out that Rex and I used to be together. Her friend showed her the video after recognizing me. Then Rex used that as an excuse to propose to me, but it was all wrong." I stop and speak more slowly, so he has no choice but to listen to this part extra close. "Dom, I stopped loving Rex a long time ago."

"You didn't run back to be with him as soon as your pitch to Quinton went sour?"

"I know exactly how this must feel. Especially since your old fiancée did something like that to you. Used your family, then devastated you. But I've done *nothing* to deserve that." My voice is firm. I know, deep down, I haven't done anything wrong.

He studies my face. "No? Then explain how you left here after completing your pitch to my brother, and immediately found yourself in the arms of your ex. Down on one knee, for Christ's sake. You two weren't secretly together this whole time, were you?"

"With me pretending to fall in love with you, just to get to Quinton? You can't be serious."

He stays quiet.

My voice cracks. "I found out that Rex was cheating on me with Juju last night. For six solid months before we broke up. She texted me that Rex was planning on leaving me the week I proposed to him. He already had his ticket purchased to come out here."

His jaw locks — his eyes burn into mine. Just seeing him this upset makes my eyes fill with tears.

"Dom, I would never do that to you."

"I fucking hate that guy," he growls.

His hand finally slides over mine, but the tiny grains of sand stuck to our skin feel like sandpaper between us.

"So that's right when I stormed out, leaving you to deal with that news all alone?" he asks, putting the pieces together.

I nod, my eyes filling with tears of relief that he's finally understanding what went wrong.

"Jesus Christ, Liv. I really had no idea. From my perspective, all I knew was that you left in a hurry after Quinton rejected your script. Then I walked in on the guy you swore was your ex proposing to you."

He brushes the sand off between our hands, so our skin feels soft and smooth pressed together. Then he scoots an inch closer to me.

"Selma and Quinton were acting so strangely last night. I kept letting them have it, every time you left the room to go to the bathroom or sneak more ginger ale—"

"How did you know I was sneaking ginger ale?" I crack a smile.

"Everyone in the room knew you were sneaking it." He leans into me with a smirk. He kisses me for the first time since I arrived. "I was trying to figure out why they were acting so weird. Selma's whole thing about calling you Veronica or Olive, and basically asking you to cook the meal like that. I was just trying to keep the peace and not call them out for it in front of you. I didn't want to embarrass you even more." He sighs. "After talking to them today, they really did have the best intentions at heart. Even if it was in an effort to protect me, they shouldn't have acted like that toward you."

I sigh. "I understand. I really do. Your brother cares a lot about you." Then I lean over to kiss him. It's a short kiss, and nothing to write home about, but he allows it. I scoot even closer to him, resting my head against his shoulder. "I'm so sorry you had to walk in on that with Rex. I should have never even gone out on the deck to talk to him. I shouldn't have made that mistake."

"I believe you." He gives me another kiss. This one feels more sincere. "And I'm sorry about leaving angry last night. I should have given you a chance to explain."

Then he pulls out his phone and clicks open his Airbnb app, scrolling through multiple screens until he comes to Rex's original reservation record. He reads the fine print, then lets out a shaky breath, holding it out to me so I can see what he's looking at. The app shows the date Rex's reservation was made, confirming it was done long before I proposed to him.

Juju was right.

I turn away from the screen and stare out at the water.

"I can't believe all that was going on behind my back. I somehow managed to propose to that asshat and throw my entire career into turmoil, while he was already making plans to leave me." I take a deep breath, reliving the rollercoaster of my last few months. Then I turn to Dom and climb onto his lap, straddling his hips in the sand, with our faces just inches apart. I cup his face between my hands. "But I would go through that a thousand more times if it meant that you'd be waiting for me at the end of it, like you are now."

CHAPTER 70

My plane is still leaving tonight. I have to be back at the UBN station in two days if I intend to keep my job.

Dom goes back to the rental with me to retrieve all of my things. When we walk in, it feels a world away from where my head was when I first walked in eight weeks ago. Like I'm seeing it clearly for the first time, with fresh eyes.

"I wasted so much energy keeping my mind in the past here," I say as we walk in, running my hands over the countertops, like I didn't give it enough of a shot when I first arrived.

I hear the familiar sound of Pru scooting her empty food dish across the floor. I bend down to refill it with the last of the cat food, then crouch down to pet her while she starts lapping it up.

"I don't want to leave you," I tell her, scratching behind her ears. Dom has agreed to keep her, falling in love with her just like I did, but I still feel gutted at the thought of it.

My flight leaves in ten hours. Which means in ten hours I'm supposed to board a plane and go back to everything that now feels so foreign.

I peek out the blinds to an empty deck, soaking in that view one more time. The streets of New York will feel excruciatingly hard and gray compared to what I feel when I look out there.

However, all that pales in comparison when I imagine having to leave the one part of this adventure that I can't fathom leaving behind. I rush over to give him a long hug, feeling a deep gratitude for all the ways he's helped me grow and open up over the last two months. Already looking forward to the trip he has planned to New York to see me next week.

We both startle at a bang on the other side of the wall, jumping in surprise.

"Rex must still be over there . . . I really hope we don't run into him."

"Oh, I had him kicked out of that place this morning after hearing what he did to you."

"You what?" I cover my mouth, trying not to smile.

"I had Phil tell him that if he wanted to stay on the island, he better find another place to stay by noon because it's not going to be in one of my units. And since I own about eighty-five percent of the private rentals on the island, plus a few of the hotel chains, that's going to make it pretty tough for him to stay."

"You what?" I glance over at the shared wall, imagining Rex angrily packing up his things on the other side. He came here to be with Juju, and in the process, he lost her, me, and now his reservation. Along with his potential to stay nearly anywhere on the island.

"I've had him blacklisted here for life." Then, grinning, he turns to me. "Now throw your stuff in your suitcase and come on back to my place. You're mine for the rest of the day."

"But your place is so far away . . ." I wrap my arms around his neck and start kissing his jawline, nibbling gently at his ear. I run my tongue down his neck, leaving little kisses, unbuttoning his shirt as slowly as I can. "Are you sure we can't make the most of this place one more time?"

He gives me a wicked grin. "You're not worried about the neighbors?"

"Not even a little." I smile back. "As long as you give me a reason to scream, I won't even try to hold it back."

He sets me back down and I slowly slip his board shorts down to his ankles, lowering to my knees to the floor in front of him. Keeping my eyes burning into his, I wrap my lips around his cock, flicking the tip with my tongue before taking the first half of him in my mouth, the skin like velvet. His eyes start to roll back as he pushes his hips toward me. I slip my mouth off, grabbing his balls in my hand while he groans and looks down at me, holding back my hair so he can see my eyes when I take him back in my mouth again.

But before I do, I add, "I promise I'll stay here all day, as long as you promise to be anything but quiet."

I hold his gaze and take him back in my mouth, sucking his shaft until he's nearly screaming my name.

Without warning, I release him and race into the bedroom, shrieking while he runs after me. Then we hold nothing back for the rest of the morning, free to be as loud as we please.

CHAPTER 71

"So the waiter brings the check over from Quinton's table," Selma says, nearly out of breath from laughing so hard. Turns out, her laughter is deliciously contagious, though I hadn't had the pleasure of hearing much of it the other night.

Tonight's early dinner is a complete one-eighty compared to last night. After hearing my side of the story, and having Dom verify the truth of it, Quinton and Selma welcomed me back into their home with open arms. Telling me that if Dom loves me (which he still hasn't said outright yet), then they will too.

Selma is telling us the story of when she first met Quinton, while Quinton pipes up with his memory of the meeting — I think it's to prove to us that sometimes love has a rocky start, and a relationship that begins with a bang can still last.

I'd bet Dom has heard this story a few times, but he's red in the face from laughing along with them. They're both fantastic storytellers, so much so that I can't help but be drawn into their world of memories, as if I was there myself.

"Well, I knew she'd actually have to look over at me if the waiter delivered my bill to her, so I slipped the guy a few bucks to do it," Quinton chimes in happily.

"I'd been avoiding his attention all night." Selma hits the table as she says it, leaning back in her chair, feigning anger, then cracking into a coy smile.

"I'd tried everything to get her to pay attention to me, but this beautiful woman was used to every man in the world being absolutely smitten with her." He grins, looking longingly at his wife of thirteen years. "Selma didn't care about some lowly film director trying to get her attention. She didn't need a damn thing from me. She already had it all. Still does."

He watches her smile appreciatively and kisses her hand. Everything he'd said about her aging out was all part of his *show* last night. They are absolutely smitten with each other still, and it shows.

The four of us are gathered at their table overlooking the ocean. A blazing pink and orange sunset is streaked across the sky, palm trees dancing peacefully in the breeze all around us.

A smile is glued to my face while I watch the love they share bouncing back and forth across the table as they tell their story. Now that their icy exteriors have melted, I can't help but adore them, exactly like I hoped I would. I watch the way they look at each other, and find myself hoping to have that kind of love one day as well.

I sneak a glance at Dom's face while Quinton continues, hardly able to believe I have to leave him soon.

"So by the time she had to get out of her chair and physically come talk to me about this erroneous bill that I insisted was hers to pay, well, she was good and mad."

"I wanted to wring his neck!" she howls. "But when I looked into Quinny's eyes . . ." Selma pauses and looks into Quinton's eyes like they're meeting again for the first time. I notice a few tears well up as she relives the memory, lost in the moment for a split second. "Well, that was it." She cracks into a smile, and turns to grin at us.

I'm officially transfixed by them. Charisma dripping from their every word, their every look — it all hits a tender spot in me. Reminds me of my own parents' relationship. I add Selma and Quinton to my mental list of things I'll never forget about from my time here on the island.

"Who knows," Selma continues, "maybe one day you'll be here at this exact table with a new guest — both of you thirteen years older and wiser — telling them about the unlikely circumstances that brought the two of you together."

I beam at Dom, imagining what Selma has said coming true one day.

"The story of how we met, how Dom and I got to today, is definitely pretty wild." I grin at him from ear to ear. Then I squeeze his hand and give him a kiss.

Quinton clears his throat.

"Olivia, your life, the one you've lived these last two months on this beautiful island, it is truly a once-in-a-lifetime kind of story." Quinton winks. "Unforgettable, really. One that I think you should not be afraid to tell. It's one that so many would love to hear."

My stomach does a little flip when I realize what he's saying.

"Sometimes life gives you exactly what you need, and you just need a little push to follow your gut. To grab what's right in front of you. The universe often takes the path less traveled — one you never saw coming — to end up in the spot where you were always meant to be."

Selma smiles softly at me, then grabs Quinton's hand just as Dom squeezes mine.

I'm suddenly feeling all warm and calm. "I think I know what you're telling me." I fight the urge to be filled with any kind of hope from his words, but I realize that's impossible.

"Then write it," Quinton says. "Write the story you were given to write."

So I do.

EPILOGUE

Three years later

"Olivia, slow down!" Dom is trailing behind me, but I can't slow down. We're on the way to film the first scene. "Quinton already said he wasn't going to start without you!"

"I know!" I shout behind me but I'm nearly breathless. Our driver got a flat tire on the way to the set. Of all the days, this can't be the one that I'm running behind.

"My love, they're not going to start without you." Dom grabs my hand, urging me to slow down.

We're running down the side of the highway. Dom is jogging behind me, insisting we can just grab another ride to the set, but we're only a mile off the exit we needed to take, and I don't mind running the rest of the way. I can't stand thinking of all those actors and actresses sitting on the set in the heat, waiting for me to start filming.

"I can't have Travis Simpson and Ashley Kent waiting for me while they burn up on the beach!" I call back to him.

My film, *The Best Wrong Move*, is officially starting production today. One silly little flat tire could never keep me away from that.

Just a few more minutes of sprinting and we'll be there.

After leaving Quinton, Selma, and Dom that night — almost exactly three years ago — I was filled with a desperate kind of craze, practically foregoing eating or sleeping in order to write the new script I was always meant to write.

The one the universe practically threw in my lap.

The story starts out with a girl proposing to a boy in front of the whole world, becoming famous after everything in her life failed. Ultimately, she runs away to fall in love with the man she was always meant to be with, working feverishly to start her life over somewhere beautiful.

The girl ends up leaving New York to follow her dream, draped in flowy kaftans while sitting in a beautiful emerald bay by the sea for the rest of her life. She lives with the man she loves, and eventually decides to marry him on their very own hill outside their home, underneath a hearty grove of mango trees.

They pick ripe fruit for their breakfast each morning, after passionately making love every night. And the girl eventually adds a little writing cottage nearby, surrounded by a breathtaking garden, with the money that she earned from selling her first full-length feature film to a famous director, the one who just so happens to be her new, eccentric brother-in-law.

It's the first of many stories I've got stored up in my head, now that I have all the time in the world to sit and write, while my husband tends to the beautiful garden growing around me.

But the biggest secret of all?

I've already let Quinton in on the next story I started writing a few weeks ago. It's the sequel to my first. And he's promised to help me surprise Dom with it when we arrive on the set today.

It's the story of a sweet little boy who grows up in the grove of fruit trees and gardens, overlooking the most beautiful view of the Pacific. He'll be as handsome as his daddy, and as strong-willed as his mama. And one day, after many, many years, he'll bring his own love story home. Then, while the sun sinks down behind a pale fuchsia sky, they'll all gather around their long, worn-in table, overlooking the ocean, retelling the story of how one day, when they least expected it, they met in the most peculiar way.

THE END

ACKNOWLEDGMENTS

First, topping the list, thank you to YOU, dear reader, for holding and reading this book. Thank you for picking up an author's debut title and for making it all the way to this page. You are actively making a little girl's dream come true. Right this very second. So, thank you.

To my two incredible author friends who encouraged me to attend a writers' conference in Las Vegas where we shared a smoky hotel room and dreamed about our futures. Where I had the fate-led fortune to run into my first editor and champion, the legendary Emma Grundy Haigh. Our serendipitous meet-cute at cocktail hour — followed by a second chance meeting as we both rushed to leave our hotel that last morning — has officially changed my life. Thank you, Emma and the rest of the team at Joffe, for believing in my work and signing me soon after. You all really do throw the best British garden parties, especially to a BBC-loving American like me, and I love you for making top-notch books.

To my editor, Becky Slorach, with the most brilliant mind and wallpaper that one has ever seen. Your endless encouragement has lit up both my Zoom screen and my heart more than you know. I've been blessed beyond measure for getting to work with an editor as talented and enthusiastic as you, and I felt it from the first moment we met. Thank you.

And a huge thanks to every person who has cheered me on along the way. To my oldest friend who encouraged me to write romance based on my ability to make up the best boy-crazy middle school fantasies. To my closest circle of friends who have helped shape my work and provided YouTube-worthy pep talks. To my kids, who will readily admit that having a mom who's a writer is both a blessing and a curse when it's time for homework. You each keep me humble and dreaming, always. And to my parents, for ensuring that libraries with stacks upon stacks of books were readily accessible; then continuing the tradition with Grandma's Traveling Library for all your book-obsessed grandchildren. We've all lived a thousand adventures because of you.

Last but not least, to my husband of nearly two decades. Thank you for showing me what swoon-worthy love is, and for letting me — simply and without hesitation — always be me. It really doesn't get any better than that.

THE CHOC LIT STORY

Established in 2009, Choc Lit is an independent, award-winning publisher dedicated to creating a delicious selection of quality women's fiction.

We have won 18 awards, including Publisher of the Year and the Romantic Novel of the Year, and have been shortlisted for countless others. In 2023, we were shortlisted for Publisher of the Year by the Romantic Novelists' Association.

All our novels are selected by genuine readers. We are proud to publish talented first-time authors, as well as established writers whose books we love introducing to a new generation of readers.

In 2023, we became a Joffe Books company. Best known for publishing a wide range of commercial fiction, Joffe Books has its roots in women's fiction. Today it is one of the largest independent publishers in the UK.

We love to hear from you, so please email us about absolutely anything bookish at choc-lit@joffebooks.com.

If you want to receive free books every Friday and hear about all our new releases, join our mailing list here: www.joffebooks.com/freebooks.

9 781781 898178